"You are supposed to kiss me."

"Make me."

His lips curved deliciously. "Don't worry, dear Jane. I will."

Towering over her like a beautiful dark angel, he stood close enough to overwhelm her without contact. Her throat tightened and her breasts rose and fell, silently begging him to touch them.

He held her head now, his thumbs caressing her cheekbones. "I don't know the limits of what I would do for you. You frighten me."

Not as much, surely, as he frightened her. "That's very good, Your Grace, very seductive," she replied mockingly.

A finger traced the rim of her mouth. "Say it."

"I will not."

"Why do you have to be so difficult?" A butterfly kiss landed on each eyelid. "Look at me and tell me what you want."

"Kiss me," she said.

At long last his lips met hers. The texture of his lips, his spicy taste spoiled her for any kiss, past or future. It was perfect and mind numbing and body awakening and utterly dangerous.

Romances by Miranda Neville

The Duke of Dark Desires
Lady Windermere's Lover
The Ruin of a Rogue
The Importance of Being Wicked
Confessions from an Arranged Marriage
The Amorous Education of Celia Seaton
The Dangerous Viscount
The Wild Marquis
Never Resist Temptation

From Avon Impulse

The Second Seduction of a Lady: A Novella

The Duke of Dark Desires

MIRANDA NEVILLE

AVON
An Imprint of HarperCollins*Publishers*

This is a work of fiction. Names, characters, places, and incidents are products of the author's imagination or are used fictitiously and are not to be construed as real. Any resemblance to actual events, locales, organizations, or persons, living or dead, is entirely coincidental.

AVON BOOKS
An Imprint of HarperCollins*Publishers*
195 Broadway
New York, New York 10007

ISBN 978-0-06-224334-8
www.avonromance.com

First Avon Books mass market printing: January 2015

Printed in the U.S.A.

10 9 8 7 6 5 4 3 2 1

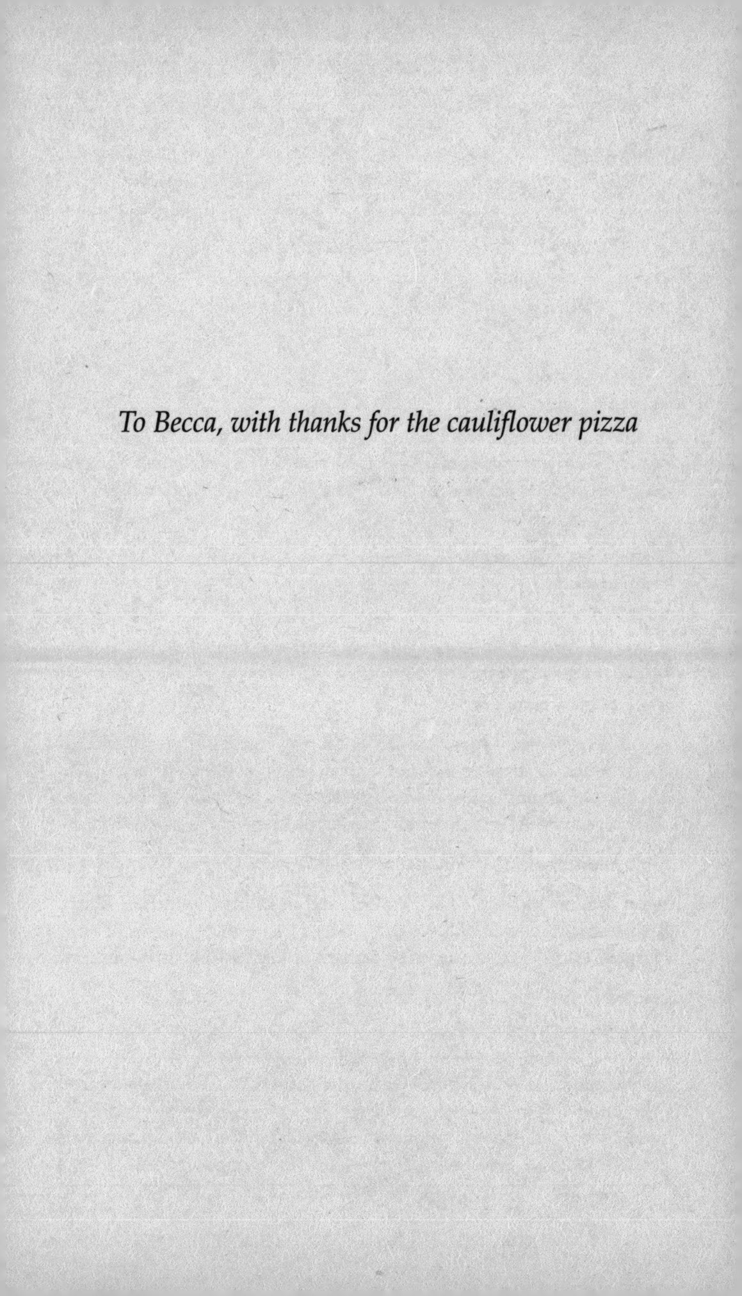

To Becca, with thanks for the cauliflower pizza

The Duke of Dark Desires

Chapter 1

London, 1802

Once she had been carefree, beloved of the gods and the world, marked by nature and birth for happiness and good fortune. Then everything was taken from her. Everything she possessed and everyone she loved. Everything except her life. She didn't know how she had survived, but she knew why. She had a destiny to fulfill, and the key to success lay within the solid brick walls of this house on the east side of Hanover Square.

Despite the variety of cramped apartments and near hovels she'd occupied in the last nine years, she still summoned a measure of scorn for the unassuming residences of the British nobility when compared to the glorious mansions of Paris. Imposing by London standards, Fortescue House with its neat brick façade and stone architraves couldn't hold a candle to the Hôtel Falleron.

Fortescue House.

The very name chilled her. She shivered in her

gray cloak at the name and because London was cold and dirty and inhabited by the race of Fortescues. She did not know the exact identity of the Englishman she'd heard of only as Mr. Fortescue. To discover his full name she had come to this house, home of the chief of all Fortescues, the Duke of Denford.

In the days she'd lingered in the square, the house had been busy. A youthful, worried gentleman came and went frequently. Also a tall man dressed always in black. She'd have taken him for a lawyer or other man of business except for something uncommon in his posture, something she couldn't define. She'd seen no one she could identify as a member of the ducal family.

How was she going to get into Fortescue House? An unknown woman of dubious antecedents was not readily given audience by a high-ranking nobleman.

But now a well-dressed lady descended from a carriage and mounted the steps to the front door. Was this the duchess come to town? Things were looking brighter. She could better inveigle her way into a house with a lady in residence.

When the house had taken her in and laid bare its secrets, she would find the Mr. Fortescue responsible for the death of her family.

And she would kill him.

Bad news always came in threes, while the miserly gods of good fortune meted out their gifts one at a time at long intervals. Though the first to admit that he didn't deserve much in the way of luck, Julian Fortescue, Duke of Denford, would have liked a little more time to savor his victory. A week maybe. Would that have been too much to ask? A week to enjoy the fact that two years after becoming a duke, he was now also a rich one?

Not that the arrival of his mother from Ireland was necessarily a bad thing. But he wondered what favor—or three—she was going to claim. Doubtless something vastly inconvenient.

She sailed into the faded grandeur of the first floor saloon at Fortescue House, trailing gauze scarves and a cloud of eau de cologne. "My darling boy! As handsome as ever. You haven't changed a bit."

He could say the same of her. Mrs. Osbourne, formerly Mrs. Fortescue, born Julia Hope Gore, had defied the passage of time. Her black hair contained barely a thread of gray and her pale skin, though the youthful glow had long faded, was a fine setting for blue eyes undulled by age. At almost fifty she still possessed the beauty and gaiety that used to provoke the Dublin gallants to poetry. Julian, her cynical son, attributed this eternal youth to always getting her own way and never worrying about anything.

"Neither have you, Mother." He took her hands and kissed her on both cheeks. "How are the girls?"

"They are well. But I've become an old lady in the years since you took the trouble to visit me," she said, tilting her head coquettishly. One corner of his brain registered that her bonnet, new and adorned with ostrich plumes, had not come cheap.

"I beg your pardon. My affairs kept me from making the journey to Ireland, and now there is no need. As for the rest of your speech, it is too absurd to answer. You know you look ravishing. What are you doing in London?"

"Are you not going to offer your poor mother a seat and a little something to fortify her after her voyage all the way across the Irish Sea?"

"I beg your pardon, my dear. Your toilette is perfection itself so it didn't occur to me that you were travel-soiled."

"As it happens I arrived yesterday. I came only from the Pulteney Hotel this morning."

"The arduous drive from Piccadilly must have worn you out."

As he led her to the sofa and fetched a glass of madeira, her favorite wine, from the tray on the console table, he wondered at this additional sign of prosperity; the hotel was one of the best in London. No doubt she would, in her own good time, reveal why she hadn't asked to stay with him at Fortescue House. Then again, given his home's meager comforts and inadequate staff, perhaps, now that he was rich, he should move into the Pulteney himself.

He raised his glass. "To you, Mother."

"To us," she responded. "And the pursuit of happiness." Julian felt a momentary pang at hearing the old toast again. His father had been impressed by the American Declaration of Independence, claiming to greatly admire a nation founded on such an admirable ambition. Osbourne, his mother's second husband, hadn't shared the sentiment.

Julia set aside her glass, arranged her modish green skirts about her, positioned her hands to display their fine-boned elegance, and looked about the room, the ends of her mouth upturned into a bewitching smile.

"It's a very grand house you have come into, Julian," she said with a satisfied air. "To be sure, it could use a fresh coat of paint and a skilled needlewoman." She poked at a hole in the French carpet with a dainty silk-slippered toe. "Whoever would have thought you'd end up as Denford? Look at you," she said, as he stood before the massive fireplace of Italian marble. "Monarch of all you survey. I always knew you were bound for greatness."

"I'd be flattered if I wasn't a clear case of a man who's had greatness thrust upon him."

It had taken the death of every male heir and a plague of female children to bring Julian, a distant cousin of the previous duke, into the title. Mothers, widows, aunts, and daughters of assorted deceased Fortescues had protested heartily at this manifest injustice, as had their non-Fortescue husbands and sons. There was nothing they could do about the laws of primogeniture when it came to the dukedom, but they could and did object to the despised and disreputable Julian making off with the family fortune. Lawyers had been engaged. Many, many lawyers.

"Do you have enough money to live here?"

"As of yesterday, I do. After interminable wrangling over one hundred years of trusts and entails, my quarrelsome cousins realized that there's plenty for everyone if they discharged the bloodsuckers. We came to a grand settlement. As well as this house and Denford Castle, I am now owner of twenty thousand acres of land and a nice sum in the funds to boot."

Julia arched her fine eyebrows and laughed. "Thank the Lord your father isn't alive. He'd have hated to be duke."

True. Fitzlyon Fortescue had possessed wit and charm in plenty but not an iota of greed and absolutely no sense of responsibility, the reason he had died leaving his young widow and son virtually penniless.

"Would you have enjoyed being a duchess?"

"Tush! What good would it do me to have the right to sit on a footstool in the presence of the King of France? The poor man is dead."

"I could be wrong, knowing little about the habits of dukes and nothing at all about their wives, but I believe that's only for French duchesses. Wouldn't you like to have been Your Grace? You're certainly dressed elegantly enough."

"Why, thank you. I do my poor best."

"It's less than a year since Mr. Osbourne died but you aren't in mourning."

"I never wore black for your father either. My dear Lyon would never have expected it."

"You also married Mr. Osbourne three months later."

"You know I had to," she said with a reproachful

look that would have chastened anyone less hardened to shame than Julian. "I couldn't let us starve."

Things hadn't been quite that bad. The Fortescues would have provided, grudgingly, for the widow of their black sheep, just as they later paid for Julian's education. At the age of eleven Julia's son had deeply resented her remarriage; the adult Julian could now concede that marriage to Frederick Osbourne had been a rational move for a young widow ill-suited to life without the support of a man. It wasn't her fault Osbourne and Julian loathed each other on sight. The pious Protestant Irish lawyer and his wild stepson had been oil and water.

"My father wouldn't have demanded mourning but I'm sure Osbourne expected it. I daresay he's trying the angels' patience complaining about that fine green gown." He couldn't disguise his lingering hostility toward a man who was, after all, quite dead and presumably in heaven. Julian thought heaven must be a devilish dull place, filled with disagreeable bores.

Unabashed, Julia nodded serenely and scanned her son from head to toe. "Why do *you* still wear nothing but black?"

"To frighten old ladies and small children."

"Really? Is that what you do?" she asked with a short laugh.

"No man is a sinister brooding presence to his mother," he said with the twisted smile that he was sure would terrify housemaids, if he had any. He'd test the theory as soon as he recruited some.

"I don't care for the style but I'll grant it suits

you. You're a fine black Irishman, just like *my* father. But are you happy? Something troubled you when last I saw you."

Julian paced over to the tall windows overlooking the square. On the off chance his mother had actually noticed something, he'd prefer to avoid her scrutiny. During that last visit to Dublin, the French business had still been fresh in his mind. Time had dulled the impact of horrors he could never entirely forget.

"I worry about you, Julian. A mother can always tell when something is wrong. I wish you would confide in me."

The pretense that she ever gave him more than a passing thought when he was out of sight annoyed him into a retort. "If I was unhappy during my last visit, you may look no further than the presence of your late husband. Since it is much, much wiser for us to avoid that topic, I have a convenient way to account for both my costume and my gloomy countenance. Let us say that I am in mourning for *all* your husbands."

"Not all." She spoke so softly he almost missed it.

"Don't tell me you've married again?" But of course she had. Julia Gore without a husband was as incomplete as a Rembrandt canvas without a frame. She defined herself by the devotion of a man. Demurely lowered eyes couldn't disguise their triumph. He was pleased for her—especially since it meant she wasn't coming to live with him—and hoped her newest spouse was a better specimen than the last. "Let me raise my glass to the new Mrs. . . . Or have I underestimated you. Are you a duchess after all, Mother? Did you at least catch a lord?"

"I am now Mrs. Elijah Lowell and very happy to be so. Captain Lowell is a better man than any lord I've encountered."

"With a name like that he must be a nonconformist."

"An American."

"Isn't that the same thing?"

Her lips curved. "I can assure you the captain is no Methodist."

"A naval man?"

"Let's say more in the private line."

"A lucrative profession, judging by the elegant bonnet and the Pulteney Hotel. Well done, Mother. May your pursuit of happiness be true and lasting. When do I meet this paragon?"

"He should be here in a few minutes. I wanted to speak with you first so I sent the hired carriage back to the hotel for him."

His attention flickered back to the window and his view of the square, where a delivery cart lumbered by, leaving horse droppings in its wake. A youthful crossing sweeper offered his services to a young woman standing next to the central garden, but she shook her head. The arrival of a well-appointed vehicle obscured his view of the pair and a man descended, a tall, fine figure of a man. Even through a thick beard Julian judged him to be a good decade younger than Julia. *Very well done, Mother.*

Then a girl stepped out onto the pavement, and another, and another.

His mother hadn't said that her children with the miserable Osbourne were in London. Her *three* children. He had a bad feeling about this.

"You didn't mention that your daughters are with you."

"I could hardly leave them alone in Ireland. May I remind you that my daughters are your sisters."

"Half sisters."

"It's not like you to lack generosity, Julian. Mr. Osbourne is dead and you should set aside your differences. Whatever your feelings for him, my poor dear girls are not to blame."

"I have no objection to entertaining them here, not that I can offer puppies or kittens or dolls, or whatever children need for amusement. I expect my kitchen can provide tea and cake since I suppose they are too young for madeira. Maria is what, twelve or thirteen now?"

"She's fifteen and bidding to be quite the beauty. You need to pay attention, seeing as I want you to be the children's guardian."

Julian's nose for danger never let him down. "Why not your new husband?"

"Because Captain Lowell and I sail for New York in a week and we can't take the girls into waters infested by the French, even in an American ship."

As usual she had thought only of herself. "I don't suppose it occurred to you to postpone the wedding until it was safe for all to travel. Or to remain with your daughters in Ireland."

"I couldn't do that, Julian. A woman's place is with her husband. So I'm leaving the girls with you. It shouldn't be for more than a year or two."

He ought to know better than to be amazed by her boundless effrontery. "Absolutely not," he said when he recovered his breath. "The house is barely furnished and I have very few servants. Even if I could accommodate three children in comfort, I am much too busy to look after them."

"Nurse Bride will do that."

"Good God, is Bridey still alive?" She had been Julian's nurse, and his mother's before that. "She must be a hundred years old."

"In the prime of life. The girls are no trouble at all, the little angels. Good as gold and excited as can be about staying with their big brother. Laura was a mere babe when you last visited us."

He saw what his mother was up to. Just as she had sent him off to school in England without a second thought when she acquired a new husband, now she meant to cast aside the fruits of *that* marriage. No, the Osbourne spawn were her responsibility and he was damned if he'd be landed with them. His plans for the enjoyment of his newfound wealth did not include the guardianship of a passel of sisters he barely knew and cared for even less.

"Let me make myself plain, Mother—"

He never got the chance. At that moment, Captain Lowell and the Misses Osbourne arrived and Julian lost control of events.

"Come in and greet His Grace, my loves," his

mother said. "Your brother's become a great man since you last saw him."

They stood in a row, looking nervous. Good. He'd see if he could turn alarm into fright.

"Ladies," he said, coming forward the better to loom over them, and staring down the considerable nose he'd inherited from his father.

Two of them, younger versions of their mother, curtseyed with reasonable poise. The middle sister, whom he'd last seen as a tiresome little girl—and tried to ignore—scowled at him. The image of the late, unlamented Osbourne, she appeared to have inherited her father's opinion of her half brother. Good. She might be an ally in foiling their mother's plans.

"It's a joy to see all my children together under one roof again," Julia said. She turned to her new husband with a winning smile. "Did you have the girls' luggage brought in, Elijah?"

"What—?"

"You'll tell your servants which rooms your sisters are to have, yes, Julian?"

"Mother! You can't leave us here," said the plain sister. What the devil was her name? Fiona? No, Fenella. "The duke doesn't want us and we don't want to stay."

"Quiet, Fenella." Julia turned to her son. "Will you tell your sisters that now you are a duke, you refuse to care for your own flesh and blood?" She sighed gustily. "It grieves me you should be an example to my poor girls of the terrible things that good fortune and high rank can do to a man."

Julian had forgotten his mother's ability to induce guilt like no one he had ever met. His resentment swelled even as his resolution weakened.

"Your father would be shocked to see you grown so proud," she said sorrowfully, and he knew he was a dead man.

A week after his mother's ruthless departure for another continent, Julian needed help. When he heard that his next-door neighbors had arrived in London, he lost no time knocking on the door of the Earl of Windermere's house. Shown to Lady Windermere's parlor, he found Damian, Lord Windermere, an excellent artist, working on a portrait of his wife, who posed on a sofa with a gray tabby cat on her lap.

"I need your help, Cynthia. I'm desperate."

Lady Windermere looked up and laughed. "I can it hear in your voice, Julian. Sit down and tell me what's got you so bothered." Her husband grumbled at the interruption but set aside his brush. Julian felt not an iota of compunction; Damian was going to enjoy hearing about his difficulties.

And he did, chuckling with irksome delight when he heard Julian had had three girls foisted on him. Cynthia was equally amused, though less irritating in her expression of mirth. "Of course you couldn't say no to such a request," she said.

In retrospect, Julian still wasn't quite sure how

his mother had managed it. He thought himself a master when it came to selfishness but he'd proved no match for her devious maneuvers. His defeat annoyed him no end.

"Anyway," he concluded, sitting next to the countess on the sofa and giving the sniggering Windermere a dirty look, "I need a governess, and soon. Those girls are running wild. They have no attendant but an old nurse who spends most of the time asleep, not surprising since she was already ancient when I was a boy. I found Fenella sitting on a bench in the Hanover Square garden, feeding bread and cheese to a crossing sweeper. My mother will kill me if she elopes with a lad whose sole means of support is shoveling . . . dirt."

Cynthia set aside her cat, smoothed her lap, and gave him her full attention. "Which one is Fenella? How old is she?"

"The middle one. She's about fourteen, I believe."

"Poor child. She has a kind heart. Those crossing boys are out in all weather and never have enough to eat."

"I leave care for the poor to you, Cynthia. I have enough trouble on my hands. The eldest is worried about my immortal soul."

"Already? What did you do?"

"Apparently it's not personal; Maria worries about everyone's, and damn tedious it is too."

"And the third?"

"She's nine. That's nuisance enough."

"They are your sisters, Julian," Cynthia said

with disapproval. "And what you need is a wife to look after them."

"Since you're not available, I'd rather not." He done his very best for almost a year to seduce her, and she'd ended up reconciled with her husband. Not content with breaking his heart, now she wanted to marry him off.

He exaggerated. His heart wasn't broken, though it would have been if he possessed one in the poetic sense. He'd wanted Cynthia very badly, and he was still fond of her. They were comfortable together, like former lovers but without the inevitable bitterness that followed a spoiled love affair.

While she relapsed into wedded bliss and motherhood, he'd moved on to another liaison. He was between women now, but trawling the theatrical greenrooms and the salons of the demimonde for a mistress held little appeal. He used to take satisfaction from charming a lady out of the arms of wealthier men. Now he could have anyone he wanted merely by offering money and jewelry. Where was the challenge in that? It was perhaps his empty bed and lack of an object for his pursuit that made him restless. That and having to share a house with three infernally tiresome females.

"I do not need a wife, but a governess, and I don't know a damn thing about them. I have come here to beg you to find one for me."

Cynthia's little red mouth, which he'd always found desperately enticing, twitched. "You are the most incompetent supplicant I've ever encountered. You could try kneeling. Or at least not sound like you're giving an order."

Windermere, who had so far confined his observations to unseemly mirth, watched from his stance by the mantelpiece. Successively friends and enemies in the past, he and Julian were now on cordial terms. Still, Julian knew Damian hadn't forgotten that Lady Windermere had been the object of Julian's designs. "If you had your own wife you wouldn't need mine to perform these tasks," he said. "Or get yourself a secretary."

Julian groaned. "Don't even mention that word. One of the minor provisions of my settlement with the family was to hire Fortescue Blackett, some kind of distant cousin. He's scarcely old enough to shave and jumps at every shadow."

"Patronage is the duty of the head of the family," Damian replied, not without a hint of malice. "Now that you're a rich duke you have to behave like one."

"I think I preferred being a poor, ne'er-do-well relation. If not for the cursed dukedom and my large house, my mother would have had to do something else with her daughters."

Cynthia's frown marred her pretty face. "You are fortunate to have your family with you. And they need you. Imagine how those girls must feel, with their mother traveling far away, so soon after losing their father."

"Anyone would be better off without a father like Frederick Osbourne."

"What was so terrible about him?"

Julian didn't answer. He didn't want to talk about his problems with his stepfather, and he had no reason to believe Osbourne had mistreated his daughters as he had his stepson. He hoped not. Little as he cared for family ties, he was vehemently opposed to beating females of any age.

"You have been offered a wonderful opportunity to know your sisters."

"You are right," he said, exploiting Cynthia's penchant for sentimental twaddle. "I shall have months, years even, to cultivate the fraternal relationship. My first job as a responsible guardian and brother is to see to their education. I know you will pick the ideal governess for them."

"We leave for France the day after tomorrow." Damian was gloating, no question. "I've been invited to join the delegation witnessing the signing of the treaty at Amiens, and then we're going to Paris."

"Will you leave me to interview a queue of plain, poorly dressed, charmless, middle-aged spinsters?"

"They aren't all like that," Cynthia said. "I once nearly became a governess myself. I will admit that I was poorly dressed."

"I'd hire you. Why don't you allow Windermere to perform his diplomatic duties without distraction and move into Fortescue House?"

Cynthia laughed and blew her husband a kiss. "Surely you don't begrudge me the opportunity to buy the latest French fashions?"

Julian bowed to the inevitable. "I recognize the

futility of trying to come between a woman and a Parisian dressmaker. If you tell me what to look for in a governess, I'll see to the matter myself, and soon. With peace on the way, I also plan to go abroad."

"Shall we see you in Paris?"

"I'm going to Belgium to collect certain property of mine."

Windermere stopped ogling his wife and looked interested. "The Falleron collection?"

"I think it's time I retrieved it." The famous art collection had been hidden in Belgium for almost ten years. The Windermeres had been intimately involved in an attempt to force Julian to hand over the paintings to an extortionist. They suspected a Foreign Office official called Sir Richard Radcliffe, but hadn't been able to prove it.

"Do you still insist on cloaking the business in a shroud of mystery?"

Julian hesitated. He'd kept his counsel about his dealings with the Marquis de Falleron for so long that discretion was second nature. He half closed his eyes and returned to the time he'd been a callow twenty-year-old who thought life was a wonderful game and himself too clever by half. "I was sworn to secrecy by one John Smith, an operative of the British foreign secretary." But that oath wasn't the reason he'd never told a soul, even his closest friends, about his foray into covert diplomacy.

"Though you hinted at it in the past, I find it hard to fathom that you acted on behalf of the government."

"That was my first mistake." His first in a series of events that culminated in tragedy.

"Things don't always turn out well, even when one's motives are pure," Damian said.

They had been friends long before they became enemies and, despite all their differences, Julian trusted Damian. More practically, as a diplomat Windermere might be in a position to help. He didn't have to confess the worst.

"You remember I returned to Paris alone in the autumn of 1793," he began.

"You never told us why, and it was a rash thing to do with things becoming dangerous."

"John Smith approached me in London."

"I never heard of anyone in the Foreign Office by that name," Damian said dryly.

"His real name was doubtless Bartholomew Snodgrass, or something similarly memorable."

"What did he want with you?"

"He offered me a bargain." A devil's bargain designed to appeal to a young picture dealer with more ambition than sense. "He needed a wellborn Englishman with a reputation as a purchaser of works of art to act as liaison between the Marquis de Falleron and a high-standing member of the Committee of Public Safety. The marquis was about to be denounced to the committee and needed to escape from France. Smith and I would take the art collection out of Paris. The committee member, who didn't wish his love of aristocratic art and susceptibility to bribery to be known, would issue safe conduct to the marquis and his family and would divide the spoils with me."

Damian frowned. "Everything to do with this collection seems to be ridiculously complicated."

"No question. Now that I am old and cynical, I would have turned down such an improbably convenient offer. Or perhaps not. I was ambitious enough, and to obtain even half of the Falleron collection would have been a coup of the first order for me. At the age of twenty I'd possess pictures that would have every collector in England beating down my doors. No, I would still take the bargain, but I'd ask a few more questions."

"Why you? Or is that another mystery?"

"The marquis was a stiff-necked, old-style aristocrat who didn't trust the common people. Not without charm, but narrow in his opinions. He trusted me, poor fool, because I was related to a duke. He believed in the honor of his kind." Julian found it painful to think about the marquis, whom he had liked for his genuine love of art. He'd said he felt better about relinquishing his precious pictures to a man like Julian who would take care of them.

"I assume things didn't go as planned."

"Before the planned escape, we delivered the passports to Monsieur le Marquis. The pictures had been taken down from the walls and packed in quilts. We loaded them into two carts in the middle of the night. Everything went smooth as silk. Our secret partner was as powerful as promised, and we got out of Paris and through northern

France without incident. But when we reached the rendezvous, where we were supposed to meet the official and divide the spoils, we were ambushed."

"The French authorities?"

"Maybe, but I'm not sure. Smith said we had been betrayed, and I had the impression he believed someone at the Foreign Office responsible. He died in the exchange of fire before he could explain."

"How did you get away?"

"In addition to the French carters, we had hired a Fleming to guide us over the border with my half of the booty, avoiding official interference. Jan turned out to be a wily old bird and an excellent shot, hitting two of the three men who ambushed us. The carters fled at the first hint of trouble, but Jan helped Smith and me fight off our attackers. When Smith fell, Jan and I took a cart each and escaped with all the pictures. I owe him my life. I'm sure I was supposed to die too."

Damian nodded. "I understand now why you are so sure that someone in the Foreign Office was involved, and Sir Richard Radcliffe seems the best candidate. I assume you found a new hiding place for them after Radcliffe's attempt to locate them last year."

"I couldn't get the pictures out of Belgium because of the war, but we moved them. Jan won't hand them over to anyone but me. If they kill me, they'll never find them."

"Why didn't you bring them to England straightaway, after you removed them from France?"

"I went back to Paris."

Cynthia gasped. "How could you, Julian? Why would you do anything so dangerous?"

"Because I was a young fool who thought he was immortal." And for the reason he would not speak of, even to his friends. He had wanted to make sure the marquis and his family had escaped from France.

Are you sure, Monsieur Fortescue? Do you give me your assurances that my family will be safe?

I promise. I swear on my honor.

Those final words to the marquis, before he left the Hôtel Falleron with the pictures, had haunted Julian for nearly nine years.

He could hide his guilt, but not the result of it. Damian knew what had happened. "As I recall, the Marquis and Marquise de Falleron and their daughters were arrested, tried, and sent to the guillotine."

"That wasn't Julian's fault," Cynthia said. "He did everything he was asked. He didn't know he would be betrayed."

Julian hadn't known but he'd suspected, based on the attitude and certain remarks of his French official contact. The risk had seemed worthwhile to him and he'd never thought about whether he had the right to make that decision for an entire family. He clenched his jaw. There was nothing to do about it now.

"Of course I didn't know," he said. "And now I have the Falleron collection without having to share it with a corrupt French official."

Cynthia, the little saint, quibbled, "Is it really yours? Is there not an heir?"

"I obtained the pictures from the marquis in good faith in return for a service. They are mine." Nothing he did would bring back the Fallerons, so why let himself be bothered by scruples? There had been times in the last nine years when he'd considered forgetting about the pictures, but they weren't doing anyone any good buried in a dark cellar, and he had plans for them.

"Did he have any sons?" she asked.

"Just the three daughters."

"And they all died. How old were they?"

"I don't know exactly. Children, young women perhaps," he lied, fighting to keep his face blank. He knew their ages and their names too.

"How tragic and barbaric and dreadfully sad."

He'd missed the execution of the parents, but he made himself go to the Place de la Révolution to witness the next day's batch of victims going under the blade. Only the two eldest girls had ridden in the tumbrel to meet their gruesome fates. The names had been called out, imprinted on his memory: Jeanne-Louise de Falleron and Marie-Thérèse de Falleron. Only two. The youngest, Antoinette, wasn't there. It was unlikely, however, that one had survived. She had most likely died in prison and cheated Madame Guillotine.

Julian fixed his eyes on Cynthia's pretty face to block the image of the blade slamming down on those fragile necks.

Chapter 2

It was a long time ago, almost nine years now, but Jeanne de Falleron had once been under the tutelage of a governess, so it stood to reason that she could be a governess herself. All she had to do was remember what the original Miss Grey had taught her, and how. She had long ago usurped Miss Jane Grey's name and identity. Stealing her occupation was a mere bagatelle. But to enter the employment of Duke of Denford, first she had to get past an interview.

Jane hadn't been back to Hanover Square since she saw the advertisement, for every hour had been spent preparing. Fortunately she'd worked hard during three months in London to improve her rusty English.

She hesitated before the shallow flight of steps, white stone blackened by coal dust, leading to the front door, which was in need of a coat of paint. Swallowing her pride, she wended her way down to the servants' entrance. She *was* a servant. And she'd been Jane Grey so long she no longer even thought of herself as Jeanne, except in the secret corners of her soul. What did it matter which door she used, as long as she gained entry to Fortescue House?

The unfavorable impression conveyed by the less than pristine main entrance was reinforced by the wizened little man in a soiled leather apron who opened the lower door, and the tumult behind him.

"Watcherwant?" he said, brandishing a villainous-looking brush whose fearsome bristles were caked with soot. She shrank back. The English spoken by London menials was a trial to her, not helped by the high volume of shouting emerging from the depths of this basement level. "I am here about the governess position."

"Don't know about any governess."

"Who is in charge of the female servants? The housekeeper?"

The fellow scratched his head with filthy hands. "Don't know about any housekeeper."

In a way this was a good thing. A female servant would be loath to hire a young and pretty governess. Should she ask for the majordomo? Somehow such a grand individual didn't seem plausible in this strange ducal household. As she was about to suggest the butler, an unmistakably Gallic scream cut through the commotion. *"Jamais, jamais, jamais. Les anglais sont impossible."* A torrent of French drew nearer, excoriating the manners, morals, parenthood, and sexual abilities of every Englishman and promising to leave this accursed house *toute de suite*. By the time he reached the door, Jane had his measure. He was a French cook, and she was acquainted with the breed.

He took one look at her and stopped mid-tirade for perhaps two seconds, long enough for a Frenchman to manage a comprehensive ogle, then started again with less volume and considerably cleaner language. She gathered that the kitchen at Fortescue House, where he had just started to work, was filthy, as *impossible* as the English servants, who were incapable of understanding his very reasonable requirements. It was even worse than the household of the earl of *quelque chose* whose employ he'd quit in a fit of pique. She uttered a soothing sentence or two, to the effect that his situation was *affreux* but soon all would appreciate the sublime creations of his art.

Her little speech provoked another torrent, this time of rapture. Never in England had he heard his language spoken with such precision, such elegance. She spoke the true French of the *noblesse,* before those Jacobin villains destroyed La France. Almost he could imagine himself back in the hôtel of his master, the Duc de Fleurigny.

Jane could imagine the same thing, having frequently visited the Hôtel Fleurigny and been intimately acquainted with the family. Too intimately for her present safety. She thought rapidly. "It is plain to me," she said, "that your genius will never flourish in such a ménage. Return to your earl. I am sure he wants you back."

"He does. He says no one cooks a duck like Albert. But, mademoiselle, if you will be here . . ."

"I will not," she said firmly. "I will not stay in such a place."

"We will go together and tell Monsieur le Duc de Denford. Bah! Even English names are ugly."

"That would be extremely unwise. Go, Monsieur Albert. I have a small matter of business here and I will convey your disgust and resignation."

"What's goin' on?" The brush-yielding doorman unwisely entered the fray and stoked the embers of Albert's ire. Delivering himself of a final volley of insults, the presence of a lady once more forgotten, the cook swept out of the door, slamming it behind him.

"Noisy, that Frenchie. Good riddance. Wonder what he was saying."

Deeming it unnecessary to inform her companion that he had been damned as a disgusting pig with a penis the size of a bantam's drumstick, she returned to the main point. "Who exactly is in charge around here?"

"I suppose that'd be Mr. Blackett."

"Take me to him."

Before he could obey, a harassed young man sped down the back passage. "Has he gone? Did Albert leave?"

"If you mean the cook," she said, "yes. I wouldn't count on his return either. He said something about going back to the employ of an earl who appreciates his genius." She was fairly confident her own part in Albert's decision would never be discovered. She was sorry to miss his food, but she couldn't share a household with a man who might know someone who would recognize her. Émigré circles in London, both of aristocrats and of their former servants, were close-knit. She had taken care to avoid them.

The young man, who was dressed soberly but as a gentleman, looked at her in amazement. She was used to that, but in this case it was not her appearance that drew his avid stare. "You speak French?"

"Of course I do. I am a governess." *I am a governess,* she repeated silently. If she believed it, so would he.

"At this moment, I'd rather you were a cook."

She smiled at the fretful fellow. "Do I look like a cook?"

His face reddened. "Not at all. It's just that . . . well, we need to eat, and Albert is the second one we have lost in two days."

"He said the kitchen was filthy. Perhaps if it was clean . . ."

Blackett brightened up. "It's worth trying. Thank you. Now what can I do for you?"

She reached into her pocket and retrieved the advertisement torn from the *Morning Post*. "I am here about the governess position. Whom should I speak to? It says only that applicants should apply at the Duke of Denford's residence."

"I'll take you to His Grace at once."

"What about Her Grace?" she asked, following Blackett along a chilly passage into the bowels of the mansion.

"There is no duchess."

The duke must be a widower and the lady she had seen only a visitor. "And you, sir?"

"I am His Grace's secretary."

"Have you been here long?"

"Two weeks."

She wondered if the duke was a particularly difficult employer to suffer such staff turnover. She prepared to manage a crotchety old man, or perhaps an arrogant beast. She'd dealt with worse.

They ascended the stairs and emerged into a hall of suitably ducal proportions. While a double stairway curved gracefully, the banisters needed polish, and flakes of plaster from the ceiling were strewn on the worn carpet. Along the painted paneled walls were lighter rectangles where pictures had obviously once hung. The place gave the impression of having been looted. She smiled sourly. Even in England, where the nobility had kept their heads, apparently they hadn't always kept their money.

Still, she enjoyed the luxury of space, the generously large windows that made the place bright, even on a cloudy day. Lowering her eyelids, she let herself imagine that her years in pokey Paris apartments had never happened. But such reminiscences were dangerous. She couldn't afford to encounter her prospective employer with even a glint of tears to disturb the projection of calm authority she deemed the paramount quality of a governess. A quality much needed in this household, judging by the anxious step and apologetic shoulders of Mr. Blackett.

At the top of the first flight of stairs, a broad

landing offered a choice of three doors, one double and all massive, hewn from some dark polished wood with carved architraves that spoke of long-established substance. Fortescue House might lack the rococo extravagance of the Hôtel Falleron, but its superficial shabbiness did not disguise the importance of the family.

Without first knocking, Mr. Blackett opened the door on the left to reveal a library. She'd barely had time to admire the ranks of gilded leather spines when she noticed the room's sole occupant, at which point observation of architecture and furnishings ceased and she might as well have been in a field, a market square, or a monk's cell for all she noticed of her surroundings.

She'd seen him before, coming in and out of the house, but too far away to experience the full impact of his presence. He was young, much younger than she'd expected, only about thirty years old, if that. Examining a landscape painting over the fireplace, he presented a striking profile dominated by a slightly hooked nose. He wore his black hair long and tied with a black ribbon, a style that had gone out of fashion since the Revolution, whose citizen leaders favored unaristocratic crops. But there was nothing *ancien régime* about his attire. His tall, lithe figure was clad entirely in black, from his well-polished boots to an intricate neckcloth. Only the white collar of his shirt relieved the sartorial gloom.

At a cough and a "Your Grace" from Mr. Blackett, he turned around, and she was transfixed by a pair of startling sky blue eyes that seemed to pierce her through and through.

This was how a duke should look and so rarely did: a model of refinement, elegance, and authority. Her stomach lurched, and forbidden tears threatened again.

"This lady is here about the governess position."

"Her name, Blackett?" The deep voice stroked her spine like chords from a viola da gamba.

Blackett appeared nonplussed, his favorite expression. "I forgot to ask."

The duke's finely wrought lips twisted into a semblance of a smile. "Well?" he said. "Since you have reduced Blackett to incoherence, not any great achievement, we'd better introduce ourselves. I am Denford."

For a mad moment she considered telling the truth, sweeping a magnificent curtsey and introducing herself as Mademoiselle Jeanne-Louise Marie-Adorée de Falleron, eldest daughter of the Marquis de Falleron and a worthy mate for any nobleman, even a duke. Especially a duke.

But she'd put all that behind her and behind her it must stay if she was to fulfill her goal. Nothing else mattered. He wasn't merely a duke, but also a Fortescue, the most detestable of names. He was her path to the discovery of the man who had killed her family and destroyed her life.

She made her curtsey restrained and obsequious as befitted her supposed station. "Miss Grey, Your Grace," she said. "Miss Jane Grey."

"Come in, Miss Jane Grey. You may go, Blackett." As the secretary scurried out, the duke crossed the room, his movements sleek and economical to match his figure. From a distance of perhaps four or five feet he looked at her, his blue gaze making her dizzy. Never in her life had she set eyes on a man and instantly desired him. How frustrating that this was a man she'd be unwise to encourage, let alone seduce.

Ignoring the bloom of heat in her blood, she pulled herself together and looked him in the eye. She would not bed him, neither would she let herself be intimidated. Since he was the duke and she was being interviewed, she waited for him to speak first. She sensed a controlled strength behind his complete stillness and found it hard not to fidget beneath a gaze whose intensity burned through her and a silence that seemed to spin out endlessly.

"Jane Grey," he said at last. "Like the queen."

She'd borne the name for so long she thought of it as her own, though she had a faint recollection of the true Miss Grey mentioning her namesake. She knew the kings of France inside out, but despite a recent review of the subject, she still got her English monarchs confused. Perhaps this other Jane was one of the wives of that terrible Henry.

She lifted her chin and stood her ground. "As far as I am concerned there is only one Jane Grey."

"Forgotten your history, have you? Never mind. She only lasted nine days before they cut off her head so she hardly counts."

Jane suppressed a wince at the reference to beheading. It was not a topic she could consider with any degree of insouciance. "Your daughters must be too small to learn history," she said firmly. The daughters of so young a man had be little more than infants. It wouldn't stretch her abilities to teach them what they needed to know.

"I am thankful to say I have no daughters, nor any other progeny to the best of my knowledge. I am also blissfully unwed. You mean my half sisters."

Not so good. "How old are my charges?"

"I'm not entirely sure. They'll tell you, if you take the job. And yes, Miss Grey, I am a most unnatural brother for not knowing such details, but my half sisters, whom I barely know, have only recently been deposited in my care by our mutual mother. I believe they are old enough to study history and any number of other useful topics."

"More useful than history. Languages, deportment . . ."

The duke interrupted the recitation of her major assets as a governess, luckily since it was about to come to a rapid halt for lack of material. "Before we discuss your doubtless unimpeachable qualifications, tell me about yourself. There is something in your voice, an intonation more than an accent, that is not quite English."

Jane expected the question and had an explanation for her slightly less than flawless English. "I come from Saint Lucia in the West Indies. The island has been passed between the English and the French so often that we are a mixture of both nations."

"I see. And which nation owns it now?"

Experience had taught Jane when in a tight spot to tell the truth whenever possible but always to have a story ready and to lie with conviction.

"France." She crossed her fingers behind her back, not sure about the current ownership of an obscure island she'd never visited, only read about in the *Gazette Nationale*. It had seemed ideal for her purposes and she gambled that Denford was equally ignorant of Saint Lucia's present status. "I was employed as governess by an English official and decided to leave with the family when they were called back to London. But now Mr. Johnson has been posted to America and I preferred to remain here. I have a letter of recommendation written by Mrs. Johnson."

He took the paper, a product of her own pen and imagination, glanced at it for perhaps two seconds, and set it on a table. "Come," he said. He turned his back on her, offering her an admirable view of his figure from behind. His well-tailored coat showed off shoulders broader than she'd first noticed, narrow hips, shapely calves, and a grace of movement that made her mouth water. There was no reason to believe that the controlled energy he displayed was any promise of bedroom skills and stamina, but Jane was sure the Duke of Denford would make a superior lover. A wave of the hand told her to follow him, and at that moment she'd have let him lead her to perdition and beyond.

This was not why she was here. She clenched her teeth and remembered that the man was a

Fortescue, even if he wasn't the man she sought, who hadn't possessed a title.

"Show me your island," the duke said.

She hurried past him to a corner occupied by a large globe in an elaborately carved, gilt-chased stand. If this was her only test she would pass easily. Study of geography had been one of her favorite lessons with the real Miss Grey. She spread out her hands and hovered over the North American continent, admiring the quality of the engraving and colors. "This is a very fine globe, a Vaugondy product if I am not mistaken."

He stood behind her, so close that the deep rumble of his words had an almost physical effect on her skin. "Nothing but the best for the Fortescues. They always lived well." It was an odd thing to say, as though he were not the head Fortescue, and as though the state of his house didn't contradict the statement. She adjusted the position of the globe, noting the solidity of the orb, skillfully mounted so that when she found the place she wanted, it stopped moving on her slightest command. The one in the schoolroom at the Hôtel Falleron—a smaller Vaugondy model—was too loose and took only a little push to spin wildly, sending one off to the wrong part of the world. She blinked away an incipient tear, glad the disturbing duke was behind her and couldn't see. Returning to aristocratic life, even in another country, affected her more than she had expected.

"Here," she said, finding a tiny island not far from South America.

She felt the duke's chest warm her back, his

breath on her neck. "This one?" Her ear buzzed. A black-clad arm snaked around her waist and a long finger touched the little blob of Saint Lucia, brushing her hand.

Enough. Catching her breath, she stepped sideways out of the lee of Denford's tall figure and retreated so that the globe lay between them. She had a position to win and a task to complete.

Julian had decided within a minute of Miss Grey's entrance; the position was hers. As his mistress. Such a delightful creature was wasted on his sisters when she could be in his bed. It was quite possible she could serve in both capacities but he supposed he'd better find out if she was qualified for the schoolroom. Of her suitability for the bedroom he had no doubt.

"Let us sit down," he said.

She ignored the divan against the far wall, which he'd planned to share with her, and lowered herself into a sensible chair next to the central library table, moving with innate grace and quiet deliberation. Her posture was flawless, yet the straight back and demurely folded hands didn't make her appear anything like a prickly spinster.

She had managed to snub his advance very neatly and his admiration grew, as did his determination to win her. This was no straitlaced virgin beneath a sensible gray cloak and plain bonnet. At first glance she was nothing extraordinary, pretty but not a beauty, with agreeable features and slightly rounded cheeks. From what he could detect, her figure was neatly proportioned. But after a minute in her company Julian had detected the indefinable appeal of the siren. Something in her eye and the way she carried herself sent a message straight to his groin.

She might be gray by name and in her dress, but there was nothing dull about this governess. She wore her drab attire with an air of confidence and style that reminded him of Paris. Neither for a second did he believe her a virgin. He tamped down his growing interest in her sensual experience and tried to consider the duties of a governess.

"You must have questions for me," she said, wresting his attention from a lust-blurred perusal of her pink mouth.

"How old are you?" he asked, taking the chair next to her so that his knee was only a tantalizing foot away from hers.

"Twenty-seven."

"You look younger." She had the dewy skin of youth, yet there was nothing innocent about her eyes. "How long have you been a governess?"

"Eight years." He wondered if she told the truth, but when it came down to it he didn't much care. Perhaps this Johnson fellow, her late employer, had been her lover too. That would make a useful precedent.

"What age children?"

"I have taught young ladies of all ages."

"What about your experience with gentlemen?"

"Whatever do you mean?"

"Don't governesses teach young gentlemen too?"

"I understand," she said firmly, "that there are no boys at Fortescue House." She knew what he was about and would be no easy conquest. Excellent.

Meanwhile, he must pretend to take the interview seriously. Mentally he consulted the list of qualifications Cynthia had enumerated. "Do you teach music?"

"But of course," she said, tilting her chin provocatively and meeting his eye with a mixture of severity and amusement. "What kind of governess does not? Do you wish me to demonstrate?"

"There is a music room next to the drawing room but I will take your word for it for now."

"Perhaps you should not," she said. "To tell the truth my skills at the piano and harp are only rudimentary, but I sing very well."

"Do you want this position?"

"Of course. But I don't want to promise more than I can deliver. I can oversee the musical education of young ladies of average aspirations. What level have your sisters reached?"

"I haven't the faintest idea. If they have progressed beyond your abilities we can hire a music teacher to come in. Do you draw and paint?"

"Indifferently."

"Never mind. I know a young artist named Oliver Bream who is always in need of a guinea or two. You mentioned languages?"

"French, *bien sûr.*" She switched to that language. "In Saint Lucia we speak French as well as we do English." She displayed a purity of accent and grammar he'd heard among the French nobility before the Revolution.

"Italian?"

"Only a little," she replied, in French.

"Never mind. I'll hire someone." He'd hire someone to tie her shoes if she wasn't up to it, just as long as she stayed. Come to think of it, he'd take care of any dressing and undressing problems himself.

"I have many excellent and more important skills," she said.

"I'm sure you do."

"I can teach dancing, table manners, and prepare your sisters for presentation at court."

"You learned court customs in your West Indian island?"

"The English governor's wife had an exaggerated notion of her own importance. She held drawing rooms like the queen for all the notables of Saint Lucia society."

He raised an eyebrow. "Really?"

"All the young ladies on the island had to attend her *en grande tenue* and exit backwards after making their curtseys."

"I always thought that sounded like nonsense." Julian Fortescue had never been important enough to attend court, and since he'd become duke he hadn't bothered. "It's not necessary. I doubt the girls will need to come out before my mother returns. What I need is someone to keep them busy and out of mischief. The things my mother would do if she hadn't gallivanted off across the Atlantic. Can you do that?"

"Certainly I can."

"Very well. Blackett will settle with you about salary and find you somewhere to sleep."

Cynthia would find it reprehensible that he hired a governess more for her suitability as his mistress than for her skills as a preceptress. Too bad. She'd had a chance to find someone better. Besides, no one expected Julian to behave properly, least of all himself.

Chapter 3

Returning to Fortescue House the next day to take up the position of governess, Jane thought of the day her family left the Hôtel Falleron for the last time and she became Jane Grey.

Most of the servants had long since left, consumed by revolutionary fervor. The governess had resigned her post a month before. Although her parents took care not to alarm the children, fifteen-year-old Jeanne knew that France was no longer safe for the nobility and they would be fortunate to escape. Everything in the house that could be easily moved had been sent away for safekeeping and what was left draped in dust sheets. Maman had woken them, not their nurse, and told them to dress in their plainest gowns, and hurry. Creeping through the silent house, Jeanne had known in her heart that it was good-bye forever. So she'd slipped into the gallery for one last look, even though the walls had been stripped bare of the magnificent art collection.

"Where are the pictures?" she had asked Maman.

"Don't concern yourself," the marquise replied. "They are safe. We are going on a journey and I want you all to listen carefully." She produced a sheaf of papers from a leather pouch. "You, Jeanne, are to carry Miss Grey's papers. If anyone asks who you are, say that you are Jane Grey, a governess. It's fortunate your command of English is excellent. You will have no trouble."

"But why, Maman?"

"Hush, and do as you are told." She turned to Marie-Thérèse. "You will be Jeanne-Louise, and Antoinette will pretend to be Marie-Thérèse. Think of it as a game, *mes enfants*."

"And who will be me?" Antoinette asked. A good question that was never answered.

The reason for the ruse that saved her life had died with her parents. There was a pleasing justice in using her identity as Jane Grey to breach the stronghold of the Fortescues in search of *the one* Mr. Fortescue.

She had done it! After all these years, retribution was so close she could taste it.

The fact that she was to be in charge of three girls struck her as a darker irony. At least *they* weren't Fortescues.

Once again she followed Mr. Blackett up the great staircase, this time trailed by a footman bearing her modest trunk, to a bedchamber on the second floor.

"Where do my charges sleep?" she asked.

"The young ladies are on the floor above with Nurse Bride."

"I would expect to be housed near them."

"The nursery quarters are a bit spartan. His Grace thought you would be more comfortable here."

His Grace was right about the comfort. The furnishings might be old-fashioned, but the spacious chamber was appointed with every luxury: a pair of tall windows overlooking the back garden hung with silk brocade curtains; a carpet to keep her feet warm, French-made if she wasn't mistaken; a charming writing desk; a chaise longue at the foot of the bed. A large tester bed.

Jane's eyes narrowed. She hadn't failed to notice the gleam in the duke's eye when he regarded her, and she had a very good idea why the governess had been given one of the best rooms in the house. At the time she'd gratefully accepted his admiration since it won her the position with an absurdly easy interview.

"The dressing room is that way," Blackett said. Jane peered through the open door and was somewhat reassured by the presence of a housemaid with a duster. "And this is Meg. She'll be assisting you as you need. I'll leave you to settle in. His Grace will see you in half an hour in the nursery. Meg will show you the way."

"I have hot water, miss," the maid said once they were alone. "Would you like me to unpack for you?"

"I'll do it myself, thank you." She didn't want

Meg gossiping about the contents of her luggage. "Perhaps you would be good enough to put away my cloak and bonnet while I wash."

Though her journey had been a short one, Jane appreciated the chance to tidy herself. The dressing room was too prosaic a name for a charming boudoir, as well appointed as the chamber, right down to a handsome copper bathtub in one corner, next to a door paneled and painted in the same style as the walls. "What is through there?" she asked.

"His Grace's rooms."

"Do these rooms customarily belong to the duchess?" Jane asked, every suspicion confirmed.

"I wouldn't rightly know, miss. I'm newly hired. Most of us are, except for His Grace's man."

The door was locked, with no sign of a key, which reassured Jane not a bit.

Long practice had made her deft in coaxing her wavy brown hair into the Grecian style. Henri Dupont, her lover for five years, liked everything about her to be à la mode since it lent him consequence to have his mistress smartly turned out. He believed she was English and this had been a slight embarrassment to him, but since her French was impeccable, he generally managed to forget the fact.

It amused her considerably when she discovered that English ladies had adopted the French style. Ladies of fashion, not governesses. She did wonder if an English governess could get away with looking like the fashionable *chère amie* of a

French official of the Consulat. During her months of reconnaissance in London, waiting for the opportunity to insinuate herself into the bosom of the Fortescues, she learned that governesses were almost without exception plain of dress and dowdy to boot. That was why she would be wearing her older, less costly garments, the ones she'd acquired from Mathieu Picard, her first and less wealthy lover. She regretted the necessity, not only because the gowns lacked style, but also because they reminded her of Mathieu. She never thought about Mathieu if she could help it.

She scowled at her face in the mirror and hoped her gown of olive green wool was governessy enough to dispel any ideas the duke had developed.

Yet he hadn't seemed the kind of man to force his attentions on an employee, or any other woman. Why would he need to when he was attractive enough to seduce anyone he wanted without much trouble? The surest guard against her unwelcome desire for the Duke of Denford was if he decided she wasn't worth the trouble. She removed the emerald green ribbon tied rakishly around the high neck of her gown and practiced an expression that was both humble and forbidding.

"I'm ready," she said finally, and followed Meg up yet another flight of stairs to the children's quarters. Her nerves fluttered as she entered a large schoolroom, unnecessarily as it happened. The only occupants were an elderly woman, stertorously sleeping by the fire, and two girls. It was easy to see that they were Denford's sisters.

They shared his luxuriant black hair and brows and bright blue eyes but had managed to avoid his prominent nose, giving them promise of great beauty in the future.

The elder rose from her seat by the central table where she had been writing. "You must be Miss Grey," she said in a soft voice with a trace of a lilt that wasn't quite English. She curtseyed politely, and Jane saw that she was already developing womanly curves. Another year and a new gown or two and she'd have young men at her feet.

Jane curtseyed back. "And you must be Miss Osbourne."

"I am Maria and this is my youngest sister. Get up, Laura, and greet Miss Grey."

The little girl put down her pencil and followed her sister's example. "Good morning, Miss Grey." Her accent was even more pronounced. Irish, Jane supposed. The duke had told her the young ladies were lately come from Dublin.

"Laura, is it? And how old are you?"

"I'm nine. How old are you?"

"Laura!" said her horrified sister.

"Never mind, Maria. I am . . . twenty-seven." She almost forgot the lie she'd told the duke and gave her real age of twenty-four. "Mind you, it's not a question that's thought polite to ask grown-ups."

"Why?"

"That's a good question. I suppose it's because some people, especially ladies, like to pretend to be younger than they are."

"That's silly. Maria wants to be older than fifteen. She can't wait to put her hair up and wear proper stays."

Maria blushed, the color in her cheeks increasing her loveliness.

"But you don't want people to think you are younger than you are, do you, Miss Grey?"

"I do not." If they only knew. "Another thing, Laura. Don't talk about undergarments."

"Even with my sisters? We help each other dress."

"With your sisters it is permissible."

"And with Bridey." She pointed at the sleeping woman. "Nurse Bride is her real name but we always call her Bridey," she said in an exaggerated whisper, little softer than her usual voice. The old woman slept on undisturbed.

"And with your nurse."

"And with you?"

Jane gave the matter some thought. "Since I am your governess, I believe it would be proper for you to consult me in matters of correct attire. But do not discuss such matters in company. Are there not three of you? Where is your other sister?"

Laura put her hands behind the back and shook her head with an air of innocence that had to be spurious. Maria pinched her lips and said nothing. Sisterly loyalty was a good thing and Jane would have to deal with the absent girl soon enough. The duke had mentioned she had a penchant for unsuitable company. "Chatting with riffraff" was how he phrased it. Clearly the middle girl was the difficult one. "I expect she is busy and will attend me when she is ready. Meanwhile, let us talk about your lessons. What have you been working on?"

"I'm writing about the history of Christianity at the court of King Arthur." Maria handed Jane her sheet, covered in beautiful, even penmanship. It didn't take long to see that the girl had an excellent grasp of language and aspects of the legend Jane had never heard of. Keeping up with her was going to be a challenge. After all, at fifteen, Maria's age, Jane's formal education had come to an end when she was offered the choice of bedding Captain Mathieu Picard or losing her head.

"Very good, Maria. I never thought of religion and King Arthur, only of noble knights and ladies."

The girl seemed pleased. "Papa said we must always look for God in the old stories. He never let us read about the pagans."

"No Greek or Roman stories? But they are so amusing. What can be the harm?"

"Maria likes to go to church *a lot*," Laura said.

"Very commendable, I am sure. It would be more of a challenge if you wrote in French."

"My French isn't very good."

Thank goodness! "Mine is. I shall help you. What about you, Laura?"

"I'm doing sums. I like adding and taking away and multiplying, but division is hard. How can I divide four hundred and sixteen by thirty-two? It's impossible." She stuck out her lower lip, reminding Jane that despite her resemblance to her older brother and sister, she was definitely a child.

"Luckily I am also very good at arithmetic." She'd practiced by keeping the household accounts, first for Mathieu and then for Henri. "Let us sit down and see what the trouble is. You, Maria, start translating your essay into French."

I can do this, she thought, as she managed to explain the mysteries of long division against the background of Maria's scratching pen and the nurse's snores.

"Thirteen!" Laura cried in triumph. "That's Fenella's age. I did it, Miss Grey."

"Do you think you can do the next one by yourself?"

"I'll try." The little girl's earnest enthusiasm was enough like Antoinette's to make Jane want to weep, or to catch her up in a hug. She had to remind herself that Laura was not her little sister. Her sisters were dead and she was only the governess.

Half an hour passed peacefully before a voice was heard from the passage. Instinctively Jane's hands went to her neck, before she remembered she had no ribbon to adjust. There was no reason to make herself look attractive for the duke, even though his unmistakable basso tones had every inch of her skin tingling. Quite the opposite, in fact. When he came through the door she rose and curtseyed, keeping her eyes low so they wouldn't be seduced by his dark magnificence.

"I've brought you your other pupil, Miss Grey," he said without preamble, exasperation cutting through the ironic detachment he'd displayed during their interview. "I found her by chance in the mews, chatting to the grooms and coachmen and upsetting the horses."

The girl who'd accompanied him, dragging her feet, began to protest. "I was not—"

"I don't care," the duke said. "Make your curtsey to your new governess, Fenella. It's Miss Grey's job now to check your starts. I happily wash my hands of you."

Fenella flinched at his biting tone but stood her ground, regarding him with the defiance of an Amazon. It was hard to believe she came from the same nest as her brother and sisters. Instead of being a black-haired beauty, she was as plain as a mouse. Even the family blue eyes seemed dull beneath lank brown hair that badly needed brushing. Her pugnacious expression did nothing to enhance her moderate attractions.

"I don't care either," she said. "There's nothing to do here. I wish we'd never come to London to live with you."

"That's because we haven't been here long," Maria said, acting the peacemaking eldest. "Our brother has promised to take us to see a play."

"Do you think you deserve it when you can't behave yourselves?"

"That's not fair!" Laura said. "Maria and I haven't done anything."

"It's up to you to control your sister. And now it's up to Miss Grey. I have an appointment."

Without another word, he turned on his heels and strode out, leaving Jane and the children in paralyzed silence. *What an ogre,* Jane thought, looking at the stricken young faces around her. But before she could say a word, the ogre reappeared in the doorway.

"Oh, Miss Grey," he said with perfect self-possession, as though the ugly little scene hadn't just happened. "I would like you to regularly attend me in the library after dinner, whenever I am not dining out, to report on the progress of the young ladies. Shall we say nine o'clock?"

"Certainly, Your Grace." She barely refrained from snapping at his retreating back. She'd give him progress. In fact she'd give him a piece of her mind, treating his sisters like that. Clearly the poor things were having a miserable time with their father dead, their mother remarried and gone away, and a brother they barely knew who didn't want them. Their only attendant was an elderly woman who had managed to sleep undisturbed through the whole altercation and exercised no control over her nurslings. They needed a governess very badly, someone to give them the loving attention and solid education she and *her* sisters had received from their mother and the real Miss Jane Grey.

Maria, peacemaking forgotten, was berating her middle sister. "You always spoil it for us. You always made Papa angry and now Julian won't take us anywhere and it's your fault. Why can't you be good?"

"I hate you!" Fenella cried. "You're mean and detestable and think you're so wonderful just because you're pretty and the eldest. But our brother doesn't care any more for you than he does for me, or Laura either, even if everyone else thinks she's so sweet and adorable."

Maria put a protective arm about Laura, who had started to cry. "You're just jealous, Fenella Osbourne. Don't you make faces at me because the wind will change and you'll be stuck like that forever and never get a husband."

"I don't want a husband. When I grow up I'm going to run away and then you'll be sorry."

"Oh certainly," Maria jeered. "I'll surely die of misery at never seeing you again."

"When you are dead, I will laugh."

No stranger to sisterly squabbles, Jane stepped into the melee before the hair pulling began. "Stop it at once, girls. If His Grace won't take you about town, I will. But not unless you behave like proper young ladies. The sun is out and I thought we'd all like to walk in the park and look at the fine ladies and gentlemen in their carriages."

The quarreling stopped like magic, with fervent thank-yous from the eldest and youngest.

"Maria and Laura, please go and put on your bonnets while I speak to your sister."

The more biddable sisters obeyed, leaving Jane with Fenella, who stood before her sniffing, her hair a mess, mud around her hem, and her shoe ribbons untied. Her mood had softened from rage to defiant sulkiness, and it didn't suit her pallid complexion. She was at war with the world, and winning her over wouldn't be easy.

There wasn't any real reason why Jane should

take the trouble. She wasn't a true governess and she wasn't going to be here for long. Only as long as it took to find out which member of the Fortescue family she sought. And yet there was something about the Osbourne girls that tugged at her heart, even the difficult middle girl. Jane remembered what it had been like to be thirteen, uncomfortable in her own skin. At that age she had had every advantage, although her later experience made the Osbournes seem darlings of Fortune by contrast. Still, Fenella was an unhappy girl and doubtless with reason.

Jane didn't make the mistake of tackling her grievances and misdemeanors head-on. "Does Nurse Bride sleep through everything?" she asked instead in a conversational tone. "I find it incredible that the row Laura was making didn't wake her up."

"I daresay she's been at the whiskey. I know she brought a bottle or two with her from Ireland."

"I don't drink whiskey, so you may find it harder to escape now I am here."

"You think so?" Fenella asked with a shrug and a gleam in her eye. Jane admired her spirit.

"Since I'm new, I beg you won't test me on my first day. We'll walk in the park together, but you can't go out looking like that or you truly will upset the horses." Fenella didn't laugh, but Jane thought she wanted to. "Show me your room and I'll help you tidy your hair."

Each girl had her own bedroom, decently furnished and heated but lacking in charm or the warmth that came from personal touches. In fact the entire nursery quarters were a little grim. A small and untidily shelved collection of books was the only evidence of scholarship and there was nothing to amuse: no toys or games or even pictures on the walls.

Annoyed as she was at the duke, it was good that she had an appointment with him this evening. She had a feeling that his aim was dalliance while her own goal was to interrogate him about which of his relations could have been in Paris in 1793. Neither wish was going to be satisfied. Instead the duke was going to hear about the need for improvements in the nursery and ways in which he could be a better brother. She didn't think he was going to enjoy it.

Chapter 4

A year and a half ago, engaging in a legal death match with various relations, Julian had won the dubious right to inhabit the family's London house. Dubious because despite its size and excellent address, the Hanover Square mansion was drafty, underfurnished, and lacking in creature comforts. Now that he could afford to hire a staff large enough for the place, it seemed less like a barracks. It would be better yet refurbished and modernized, if he decided to hold on to the house instead of moving to more convenient quarters. It wasn't as though he had any attachment to family tradition. It was just a house. What did he need with ten bedchambers and a series of rooms designed for grand entertainments?

But now he had his half sisters occupying an entire floor and a governess in the duchess's suite. The latter was why he'd excused himself after dinner with Isaac Bridges and a pair of art collectors, instead of attending a literary salon or entertainment of a less elevated kind.

The library was his favorite room, perhaps the only one he liked, and the only one that he would leave as it was. Unlike the rest of the house, it hadn't been looted during the years when the invalid fifth duke lived in retirement at Denford Castle while greedy relations made use of the London house and helped themselves to valuable souvenirs. The Fortescues were not, apparently, literary in their tastes. The shabbiness of the walls and carpet suited the gleaming gilt on the leather spines of the books. The paintings hung above the bookcases were quite good, the globe superior (Miss Grey had been right about Vaugondy and he wondered how she knew), the desk and library table solid, unpretentious old English pieces.

Amid this scholarly sobriety, set in an alcove of bookcases opposite the fireplace, was the oddity that appealed to Julian's sense of the ridiculous: a luxurious divan, upholstered in gold brocade. Unlike the closer, albeit female, relations of the former duke, he knew nothing of Fortescue history and traditions. Son of a black sheep, he'd never been welcomed into the family or visited the place before he inherited it. Thus, he liked to speculate about how the incongruous piece was introduced and for what purpose. Had the almost incoherent fifth duke enjoyed reclining while he read? Perhaps he, or one of his predecessors, used the cushioned magnificence to satisfy earthier desires. Or maybe—Julian particularly enjoyed this fantasy—a Duchess of Denford took private pleasure while feigning studious enlightenment. She would summon a footman, or perhaps her husband's secretary, and await him with her hooped skirt raised to reveal pretty legs in clocked silk stockings.

He'd never indulged himself on the couch. It was the scene of his failed seduction of Cynthia and he hadn't made the attempt with any other woman. Until now.

He poured himself a drink and took down a volume of prints to study while he awaited the appointed hour with keen anticipation. He hoped the governess wouldn't succumb too easily. The longer and harder the siege, the more satisfying the surrender.

"Your Grace?"

Miss Grey stood in the open doorway with that indefinable allure that belied her plain attire. If he couldn't have hoops, there was something equally beguiling about excavating the beauty muted by the spinsterish but full-skirted gown. One of the things he particularly noticed about Miss Grey was her skirts. The new, narrower skirts that went with the high waists from revolutionary France apparently hadn't reached that distant island of hers, for which he was profoundly grateful.

"Come in, Miss Grey." She stepped forward perhaps a yard or two, regarding him steadily, her displeasure evident. "Sit down, please." He indicated the divan, on which she perched with her hands folded gracefully in her lap, her back straight. His mind's eye envisioned her sprawled wantonly there, voluminous skirts raised for his exploration.

Knowing the power of silence to disconcert, he let her sit for a pause. He wasn't expecting an accommodating interview, knowing that he had ground to make up after his performance in the nursery. He'd been harsh with Fenella, too harsh, but the girl irritated him. Her superficial resemblance to his stepfather Osbourne was part of it, but that wasn't her fault. Beneath her rebellious exterior he detected a yearning for approval. He'd felt that way once and despised the emotion. At school and in society he'd cultivated an air of arrogance to combat indifference and scorn until the pretense became reality. Now he was a duke and could be as arrogant as he wanted, merited or not.

He stood in front of the governess with his arms folded, hoping to intimidate her with his large nose, his height, and his high rank. He couldn't congratulate himself on the outcome. She remained serene, finally giving him a quizzical look and a twitch of a smile. He had a feeling she was on to his game.

Going over to the drinks tray, he gestured with the decanter. "Will you join me in a glass of brandy?" he asked, expecting her to refuse. Even in Saint Lucia surely governesses didn't drink with their employers.

"Thank you, I would like that." She took the glass and sipped appreciatively at the excellent old spirit that has somehow escaped the Fortescue depredations. "You'd like to hear about your sisters?"

"Later," he said, pulling up a chair and leaning back, legs outstretched so their knees almost, but not quite, touched. "First tell me if there's anything you need. If they're anything like the rest of the house, the children's quarters are inadequately furnished and I'm sure there are things you need for teaching. Books and so forth. You may use the library, and order anything else you need."

"Thank you," she said, obviously gratified and surprised. "I will make a list."

"Speak to Blackett. He'll see to things. I've also arranged for drawing lessons. Bream will be here tomorrow morning after breakfast. Are they any good?"

"I don't know yet. We've mostly been getting to know each other today."

Julian listened while she talked about compositions and arithmetic and French. Considering how little weight he'd given to her qualifications when he hired her, he'd managed to provide his sisters with a surprisingly competent teacher. If she could instill them with even a tenth of her poise and charm, they might turn out quite well. Even Fenella.

"There's one area of study for the young ladies I cannot manage without your help," she said.

And there was only one area in which he wanted to help, and the young ladies would not be involved.

"They know nothing about the Fortescue family."

"There is no reason why they should. They aren't related to the Fortescues in any way."

"You are their brother and therefore they are part of the family. It is fitting that they should know about your relations. When they come out in society your connections will be theirs."

"I don't see the need. I am not on speaking terms with anyone on the Fortescue side—except for Blackett. He has to talk to me because I pay him."

"You don't speak to your family?" Now he'd shocked her. Her sherry brown eyes looked huge and her red mouth formed an appalled oval. Clearly he and Miss Grey had vastly different experiences of family life. "You have a position and a duty. You owe them your assistance and in return they give you respect and support. That is what it means to be a duke."

"Is that what it means? I had no idea. Perhaps you don't know, Miss Grey, but I was never intended to be duke. I came into this position only through a series of misfortunes. Fortescue males in the last twenty years have been plagued by early death and the inability to produce sons. When I, son of a disreputable and despised distant cousin, turned out to be the next in line, they were universally appalled. They did their best to make the title a hollow one, laying claim to most of the family fortune." He sipped his brandy, letting the mellow spirit soothe his bitterness. "You'll agree, I'm sure, that even a dukedom is worthless without an estate. They managed to get away with a sizable portion, and I consider they have received assistance enough."

The tale seemed to cause Miss Grey some concern. She frowned and appeared to be in deep thought.

"Don't worry, Miss Grey. Even half the Denford fortune is splendid by most standards. I can afford to pay your salary. And if you insist on learning about the glories of the Fortescues, I recommend you apply to Blackett for information. He was something like great nephew to the fifth duke, much closer than I. It was just his misfortune that his branch is through the female line."

"I will do that," she said, recovering her serenity. "Now I would like to speak a little more about your sisters. They tell me they spend little time in your company."

"What do they need me for?"

"They lost their father and now their mother has gone away. You are their family now."

"Family again. You seem monstrously keen on family, Miss Grey. I do not share your sentiments."

"Perhaps you don't know what it is to lose everyone." Her voice dropped and the very flatness of her expression, usually so bright and fluid, told him that she spoke from the heart. Beneath her blithe exterior lurked a sad history that could no doubt be exploited with a show of interest and sympathy. But he disdained such tactics, just as he refused to talk about his own past. Women liked that, he knew. They liked to think they had a man's confidence, that he was opening up and revealing his heart. He would not do it. A love affair was supposed to be a happy thing (until it ended badly), and his past was ghastly enough to cast a damper over what should be joyful. If hers was equally dismal he'd rather not know. He would woo her with wit and wine and a web of sensuality, and his own native cunning. If he couldn't succeed that way, then he would have to fail.

Thankfully she didn't allow herself to remain downcast. "You have a mother and sisters, and my task is to care for the latter and prepare them for life as the sisters of a duke. I wish you would be kinder to them, especially Fenella."

"Fenella has been told half a dozen times that she must not go out without permission or company. London is not the same as the Irish countryside."

"As I explained to her. But she is bored and lonely. She feels different from her sisters because she looks different, and from you since you share their appearance. It is hard to be plain among such beauty."

"Doubtless you are right but there's nothing to be done. She will get on much better if she curbs her defiance and learns to accept what she has." He talked fustian; he had never tamed his defiance. The truth was he understood his middle sister very well. "The girl needs to learn that the gods show no justice in the distribution of gifts. There is no magic solution to a dearth of advantage, whether it be beauty, talent, or worldly position. We must harden our hearts against the slings and arrows of outrageous fortune and make the best of what we have. No one can do it for us."

"We are not all lucky enough to have help, but if assistance is at hand, there is no point refusing it."

"My dear Miss Grey. I take it you are offering my recalcitrant sister your help and I wish you all success. It's a greater task than I would be willing to take on."

She swirled the brown liquid around her glass, gazed into it, and raised it to her lips. "Very fine cognac," she murmured. Had she given up the argument so easily? In that case she was like no woman he'd ever encountered. "Will you take them to the theater, as you promised? At least Maria and Laura. It is unjust to punish them for Fenella's disobedience."

Of course she hadn't given up. But it gave him a chance to turn the subject to what interested him: getting to know Miss Grey better. Much better. "I'll take them if you will come too."

"I cannot leave Fenella. There's no telling what mischief she'll get into if I leave her with only that drunken nurse for company."

"You've discovered Bridey's little vice."

"You knew! And yet you left your sisters in her charge."

"That's why I engaged you. If I take all three girls, and you, to the play at Drury Lane, what will you do for me?"

She tilted her head and narrowed her eyes. "If the skill of the actors and the pleasure of your sisters' company is not enough, you may take satisfaction in doing your duty."

"We have already established that I'm not much for duty. But I am not beyond satisfaction. I'll do it for a kiss from you."

"I am in your employ, Your Grace," she said bluntly. "It is not suitable."

"*Suitable* is one of those words—like *duty*—that I prefer to ignore."

"Do I have a choice? Will I lose my position if I say no?"

"Will you leave rather than kiss me?"

"That doesn't answer the question."

She held his gaze without flinching; neither did she shrink away. He was the one to blink first. "The choice is yours. I want no unwilling woman, not even for a mere kiss. If you refuse to kiss me there will be no theater trip, but you will continue as my sisters' governess."

"And if I say yes, will that be an end to it? You will make no more such demands?"

"That rather depends on how much we enjoy the kiss," he drawled. "If it is good, and I would be very surprised if it were not, one kiss will be only a beginning. I will want more and so will you."

"You flatter yourself."

"Perhaps. We'll find out."

"Or not."

"Or not," he agreed.

She was wary, but intrigued too. The disapproving set of her mouth was contradicted by the way her cheeks flushed, her eyes shone, and her bosom rose beneath the gray cloth. His instincts hadn't led him astray about Miss Jane Grey.

Straightening from a near-sprawl, he leaned forward. Almost idly he let his knee brush against hers. His fingers itched to feel the softness of her skin, to trace the plump lines of her mouth, to investigate the shape of flesh and bones hidden beneath layers of cloth and undergarments. Close enough for him to sense the heat of her body, a hint of a tangy scent, she silently summoned him, begging him to take her, but he held back. It was his own desire calling, the irresistible lure of a woman and yellow brocade cushions. Besides, there was no hurry. He let his gaze burn into hers, knowing full well the devastation his Irish eyes could wreak.

Cynthia had always become adorably flustered when he exerted his wiles. Jane Grey was made of sterner stuff. She returned his stare gravely, tilting her head as though he were an interesting botanical specimen, then her lips curved into a smile.

"That's very good, Your Grace." Her intriguing, slightly foreign voice carried a note of amusement. "Do you find those blue eyes knock the ladies over like kittle-pins?"

"Sometimes. You remain distressingly upright."

"I don't know about that. You may have melted my bones. Let me find out." Rising to her feet, she pretended to test her balance, then stepped out of his reach and turned her back on him.

"I was ready to catch you," he said, likewise standing, "but it appears I'm losing my touch and have failed to render you weak-kneed."

"Not that either. I don't know how it comes about, but both my limbs and my resolution remain strong."

Moving behind her, he gave in to temptation

and put his hands about her waist, a light touch but enough to discover the shape of the slender span. She tensed. "Well, Miss Grey. Do we have a bargain? We kiss and we all go to the theater," he said softly, breathing in the scent that was a refined blend of flowers with a spicy hint of orange. Encouraged, he brushed his lips over the base of her neck and sensed her quiver. For a moment he thought he had her.

Instead she pulled away and spun around. "I'll think about it."

"You'll enjoy it."

"Things that we enjoy are not always right."

"That's a dreary philosophy. I hold to the view that if I enjoy something, it must be right."

"Do you, Your Grace? Do you really?" He found her brown eyes uncomfortably penetrating. "Is your life so simple and your conscience so clear?"

"Of course," he said. "I only do what I want, and without a care in the world." The latter part of the statement was a lie of immeasurable proportions.

"I don't believe you. No one over the age of fifteen is without regrets."

This surely wasn't a number selected at random. "Why fifteen? What happened to you?" At that age he'd been thrown out of Oxford and begun the happiest years of his life, roaming around Europe with Damian and his other friends.

Ruefully he acknowledged the perversity of his question, just minutes after dismissing any curiosity about the governess's sad past. He was surprised to discover that he had developed an interest in her, beyond his strong desire to bed her. A mild interest.

"Nothing," she said hastily.

He reached for her hand and wouldn't let her pull away. "You didn't answer my other question."

"I said I'd let you know."

"You may give me an answer tomorrow night. Same time, same place."

Unable to remember when he'd been so intrigued, he placed a small bet with himself. If he had her in bed—or rather on the divan—before he left for Belgium, he'd reward himself with the Fragonard pastel that Bridges, the old robber, was demanding a ridiculous sum for.

He had to have it.

For, he realized, the sweet-faced girl in the drawing looked very much like Jane Grey.

It took all the control Jane possessed to withdraw from the library with her dignity and calm intact. Her body trembled with longing to say yes, yes, yes. To surrender to the duke's kiss, and another and another. It had been a few months since she left her second lover, Henri Dupont, whom she had not loved but had chosen because she desired him and he was different from Mathieu. Only at night sometimes did she miss him. Now she doubted she would ever think of him again. The longing he'd inspired was nothing to what Denford could arouse in her with a flash of his eyes, a touch of a finger. When she felt his hot breath and wicked lips on her neck, her nails had dented her palms resisting the urge to surrender to him among the silken cushions of the golden divan.

Such a sinful article of furniture did not belong in a library. It would be better if their meetings were held somewhere entirely functional, like a coal cellar. But a cellar would be dark. Being alone in the dark with the Duke of Denford was not a good idea.

She reached her bedchamber, welcomed by a fire and the soft glow of a lamp on the dressing table. Her candle cast flickering shadows in the luxurious room and, by some trick, illuminated the velvet-draped bed. She needed to think and this setting was not conducive to the application of cool reason. Closing the door again, she proceeded to the floor above.

Learning that the duke's inheritance had been unexpected was a surprise. She'd made the assumption that he had come into the title in the usual way, through the direct line and having held some lesser title. Instead, she learned, he must once have been a mere Mr. Fortescue. Never once had it occurred to her that the Duke of Denford himself was a candidate for her family's betrayer. Sitting on a hard schoolroom chair, she put her elbows on the table, cupped her cheeks, and closed her eyes to summon a distant memory.

She'd never been presented to *the* Mr. Fortescue. During the tense months following the execution of the King Louis XVI, as France grew more dangerous, Jeanne knew of the peril, catching snatches of whispered conversation, even while her mother and Miss Grey continued to prepare her for presentation at court—as though there was still a court—and for the celebration of her betrothal, formalizing an arrangement made at birth. The lessons had come to an abrupt end when Queen Marie-Antoinette was tried and followed her husband to the guillotine. Miss Grey left around the same time that her father had started to receive furtive visits from strangers, one in particular. Papa, an affectionate family man who took pride in his children and liked to show them off to visitors, never summoned them when Mr. Fortescue called. All Jeanne could gather was that Papa was engaged in some kind of negotiation with the Englishman.

One day she'd found her sisters crying because one of the manservants, before he departed the marquis's service, had spat at the girls and called them crude names.

"I am frightened," Antoinette said. "He said soon all the ci-devant nobility would be dead."

"Papa won't let that happen," Jeanne said, praying she spoke the truth. "Perhaps he intends for us to leave soon. I shall ask him."

With the excuse that she needed to take out their puppy—poor Mou-Mou; she often wondered what happened to the little bichon—she slipped down the back stairs and encountered a strange man, leaving by a side door into the street, not the main entrance in the great courtyard of the mansion. *"Excusez-moi, mademoiselle,"* he muttered, and hurried out. Having been well taught by her English governess, she recognized the accent though she didn't see his face.

"All will be well," Papa said a few minutes later when she found him in his study. "You may tell your sisters not to worry. Keep this to yourself, Jeanne, but we have help from an Englishman *de bon famille,* Mr. Fortescue."

Mentally Jane compared the Duke of Denford to the man she'd glimpsed that day.

Mr. Fortescue had been tall.

Denford was tall.

And of a similar build, a powerful man. It could have been he, though she'd expect the younger Denford to have been more slender.

But he'd worn a hat and she couldn't tell if the man had possessed that distinctive black hair.

Dressed in a normal way, quite plain in fact, he hadn't struck Jeanne as a man of great distinction. A green coat a little worn at the elbows and a white cravat tied without a hint of finesse, as though he were a man of the people, not the nobility. He hadn't worn black, but perhaps Denford hadn't always either. Still, she found it hard to believe that Denford, even as a youth, would have failed to impress her, given the intensity of her reaction to him now.

The most powerful argument against the identification of Mr. Fortescue with Denford was age. Nine years ago the duke would have been only about twenty. The man she'd seen was not a young man, she was certain. And her father had later spoken of him with respect, as though he were a man of substance and maturity.

"Mr. Fortescue will not let us down," Papa had said the day before their departure. The house was in chaos in preparation for their flight, and even to her naïve eyes her parents had been very frightened. "He promised that we would receive our passports. He is a noble Englishman, descended from a duke, and a man of his word. He will be here soon."

Very noble. He'd been well paid to bribe the officials, so Papa said. Jeanne was almost certain that Maman's magnificent jewels had been used. She knew it had been something her parents treasured and had to sacrifice for their safety. The very noble Mr. Fortescue had delivered the passports as promised, then proceeded to betray the Fallerons to the revolutionary authorities. Poor Papa. He paid for his trust with his life, and that of his wife and two of his daughters.

Jane sat in the schoolroom at Fortescue House and pressed fists into her eyes to block her tears. She could never block the pain of that morning when the knock came at the door, the arrogant rat-a-tat of soldiery. Marie-Thérèse and Antoinette had clung to her, and she'd feigned a serene courage, as though she really was the English governess whose papers she carried. Wrenching back a sob, she refused to think of the bitter parting, the final sight of those she loved. Dwelling on the past had cost her oceans of fruitless tears. The future was what mattered.

She didn't understand why her identity had been changed to that of Jane Grey, so that she had survived. But in the depths of her soul she knew the reason for her fate: to avenge her family and destroy Mr. Fortescue.

She hoped he hadn't died. It would be too bad if he had gone peacefully, one of the various Mr. Fortescues who had got out of the way so that Julian Fortescue could become Duke of Denford. Because Mr. Fortescue must be killed, and by her hand.

A sound pulled her from her reverie and she blinked in the candlelight. For a moment she thought it was her own sobs, after all, but her eyes were dry. Tiptoeing down the hall, she heard crying from Laura's room. Of course that wretched nurse wouldn't wake up for anything short of an earthquake or artillery attack.

"What is it, *ma bichette*?" she whispered, using her mother's favorite endearment as she perched on the child's bed and stroked her face, finding it hot with tears. "Did you have a nightmare?"

Laura sat up and threw her arms around Jane's waist. "I'm frightened. I want to go home."

"There's no need for fear. I am here."

"Don't leave me alone." She clung harder.

"I won't." Muttering soothing words, she wiped the girl's eyes, settled her back in bed, and adjusted her blankets. Then she lay down beside her. "I will stay until you are asleep."

"I want my mother."

So do I, Jane thought in the darkness. *At least yours is coming back.*

Chapter 5

Oliver Bream walked from his unheated, rent-free lodgings on Conduit Street and, with mixed feelings, knocked on the door of Fortescue House. He was hungry and ready for breakfast. But after eating he would have to sing for his supper in the form of giving drawing lessons to three girls. He hated teaching, especially amateurs, and especially young ladies. In his experience they lacked both talent and application. Yet how could he say no to Julian, who not only fed him regularly, but was also paying for his services?

He'd be able to afford paints and canvas for the latest series of paintings that occupied his mind. Biblical themes, he had decided. They could be noble and thrilling and surely they would sell. The picture-buying public might eschew his serious historical works, but they all went to church. He was quite proud of having come up with a plan that combined artistic integrity with commercial appeal. He couldn't wait to tell his friends, who kept assuring him the money was in portraits of children and dogs. Already flush with cash in his imagination, he thought about proposing marriage to Peg, the new serving girl at the Red Lion Tavern, with whom he was madly in love.

The servants at Hanover Square, even the ones recently hired, knew his habits. Dropping his satchel and sketch pad in the hall, he went straight to the small dining room on the ground floor. So intent was he on bread and meat and hot tea that he failed to notice he had company. A gentle cough across the table alerted him to the presence of the most ravishing woman he'd ever seen. All thoughts of Peg forgotten, he felt a bolt of lightning electrify his breast and knew that he would love this delicious creature for the rest of his days.

"Good morning." She had the voice of an angel. "I think you must be Mr. Bream, yes?" She raised her eyebrows at the huge pile of food on his plate. He was used to that. No one could believe how much was needed to sustain his slender frame, but no one understood how much strength the pursuit of art required, how greedy a mistress was his muse.

"Call me Oliver," he replied, a forkful of cold beef halted on the way to his mouth. "I shall call you Beautiful." He couldn't wait to paint her. She would be his inspiration for his Esther perhaps, or his Judith. No, his Delilah. Her beauty was worthy of only the greatest temptress.

She smiled, revealing regular white teeth. "Do you say that to all the ladies?"

"No!" he denied fervently. "Only you. Until now there has been no other woman in the world."

"There must be something in the air of this house that makes gentlemen extraordinarily forward. Outside these walls I find it usually takes at least two meetings before a man declares his devotion."

Easy to talk to as well as lovely. Oliver forgot about breakfast and started thinking how he would pose Delilah cutting off Samson's hair.

"I think it would be a good idea to step back a little, yes? Let us talk about drawing lessons. I am Miss Grey, governess to the Misses Osbourne."

"So you'll be present during our classes. Splendid. You shall be our model."

She looked at him with suspicion. "Are you by any chance suggesting I remove my clothing?"

"Oh no," Oliver said, shocked at the very notion. "I would never propose such a thing. I rarely paint nudes." A vague notion that she might not immediately wish to be portrayed as a villainess made him cunning. "I am sure we can find a comfortable pose that will require nothing more than something draped over you. Your gown is a little plain."

"We shall see." She glanced at the mantelpiece clock. "You are early. The young ladies will be finishing their own breakfast upstairs. I came down hoping to speak to the duke, but Mr. Blackett tells me he is riding. Have you known His Grace long?"

"Julian? Quite a few years."

Jane found Oliver Bream thoroughly amusing. She couldn't take his declaration of passion seriously, and wondered how good an artist he was. The duke didn't strike her as a man who would accept inferior performance in anyone he hired. Then she thought of the way he'd engaged her as governess with the slimmest of qualifications. On second thought Bream might be a complete incompetent.

"Does the duke buy your pictures?" she asked.

"Oh no! Julian would never do that."

"What happened to the pictures in here?" She pointed at six dark rectangles in the paint where art had been removed. "There are similar marks all over the house."

"One of the dukes was a patron of Hogarth. If that's what hung there it is a tragedy. Julian's taste in painting is execrable."

"Maligning me again, Oliver?"

The sight of him in the doorway, color heightened by exercise and his black hair so disheveled she itched to sweep it off his forehead, made the slight, fair-haired artist fade from her consciousness. Denford grinned at Bream with an unveiled affection that presented a new facet of the dark duke, and a most appealing one. Not that she needed a new reason to find him attractive.

"Julian!" Bream said. "I've been making the acquaintance of Miss Grey. She is a goddess, an Aphrodite or Artemis." He showed no embarrassment at speaking in such extravagant terms, and the duke merely cast his eyes heavenward. Jane would have done the same but she didn't want to hurt Bream's feelings. He was quite harmless, she was sure, and she wasn't a woman to object to being addressed like this. She knew men, Denford included, found her beddable; she also knew that she wasn't a great beauty.

"What is your name, Miss Grey? I cannot think of you like that. It's such a barren name. I'm sure your Christian name reflects your matchless beauty."

"I am afraid it is Jane."

"Never mind. You need no adornment. From this day forth, Jane is the finest of names and shall belong only to you."

"There may be a few thousand ladies who will object." She stole a look at Denford to share her appreciation of the nonsense.

Their glance of amusement turned hot and dark. She wrenched her eyes away and sipped her cooling tea.

"Are you in love again, Oliver?" the duke said.

"I have never been in love before, never! Jane has made me forget every other woman."

"Doubtless true, until the next one comes along. I don't wish to make light of your charms, Miss Grey, but I think I should mention that Oliver finds a new object of his adoration on average once a week. If his passion for you lasts a month you can claim to have inspired an exceptional degree of devotion. Héloïse and Abélard, Romeo and Juliet, Beatrice and Dante, Oliver and Jane. You will join the list of the world's most celebrated lovers."

Jane couldn't help it. She started to laugh. Fortunately Bream seemed undisturbed, merely continuing to gaze at her as though moonstruck. "I am honored to have inspired you, Mr. Bream," she said, shooting a duke a warning look. "I shouldn't laugh but His Grace is quite droll in his way. Please believe that I do not mean to mock you."

"Don't worry, Jane. I'm quite used to Julian and never take the least notice of him."

"True enough," the duke said.

"Your Grace," Jane said. "I have a request if you can spare me a few minutes."

"I do hope it's one I'll enjoy fulfilling. If so, I'll agree to anything."

"I doubt this matter will affect your pleasure either way."

"You disappoint me again. Oliver, just this once do what I ask and leave. Go up to the Blue Saloon to prepare for your pupils. I need to speak to Miss Grey."

"My request is not a private one."

"You've made that perfectly clear, alas. Go, Oliver."

"You will be coming, Jane, won't you?"

"Of course, Mr. Bream. I won't be long. The young ladies will be down soon with their drawing materials."

She watched him go with some trepidation, leaving her alone with Denford. He took a place at the table and, as though he had all the time in the world, poured himself some coffee. She ought to be safe from her unruly desires at nine o'clock in the morning with the humdrum accouterments of breakfast spread on the table; nevertheless she averted her eyes from his lips on the rim of the china cup.

"Oliver doesn't always show such good taste,"

he remarked. "The array of women he has loved in the five or six years I've known him is positively dizzying. They have only one trait in common: that of being unattainable. Women always seem able to resist him."

"What makes you think I could? Mr. Bream is a very agreeable young man. For all you know he could be the kind of man I prefer."

"No, he isn't."

"What kind of man do you think I prefer?"

She peeked at him from lowered eyelids and found him staring at her with a wolfish smile. "The matter is still under investigation but I am making progress. You are flirting with me."

"I am not!" But she was, of course. Dalliance should be the last thing on her mind, especially with a member of the Fortescue family. She stiffened her spine and tried to think like a governess. "Last night," she began, "I was up late."

"Do go on. Your bedtime habits interest me greatly."

"I found Laura crying in bed."

"Oh."

"She was well, thank you for your concern, merely missing her mother. But had she been ill no one would have known. Miss Bride was, as usual, in a drunken stupor."

"Is this your request, that I dismiss Bridey? I won't do it. For your information, Miss Grey, Bridey suffers badly from rheumatism. If she were a fine lady maybe she'd dose herself with laudanum. It happens she prefers a nip of whiskey to make the aches and pains of age easier to bear at night."

"Not just at night, but that's not the point. I wouldn't presume to recommend you dismiss one of your servants. I was going to suggest, rather, that I sleep up in the nursery, where I can keep an eye on your sisters' well-being." She didn't mention that this morning she'd been woken on Laura's bed by the sound of Fenella trying to sneak out. She didn't want to get the girl in trouble again. "They need more attention than Nurse Bride can give them."

"You can give them attention when they aren't asleep."

His patent indifference raised her hackles. "They are your sisters," she said, striving for calm. "They would appreciate more attention from you too."

"I promised to take them to the theater, didn't I? Under certain circumstances."

"Your Grace," she said, as politely as she could. "I am asking you for permission to move to the nursery floor. It's more suitable than the room you gave me."

"You don't like your quarters?"

"Of course I like them. Who would not?"

"Then keep them. I'll hire a maid for the nursery to watch the girls at night. Better still, you choose someone. You'll have to work with her. Pick someone alert."

"The rooms you gave me should belong to your duchess, not to a governess."

"Since I have no duchess, it pleases me to have you use them."

"I'll be honest, Your Grace. I do not feel at ease in the rooms adjacent to yours. The door between the dressing rooms is locked, but I don't have the key. I presume you do."

"I thought I'd made myself clear last night," Denford said with a look that made her think it better not to arouse his enmity, "but apparently it bears repeating in daylight. You have nothing to fear from me. I am not interested in unwilling women and you may sleep in peace, knowing that I have no intention of using that door."

"Good," Jane said. There wasn't much more she could say or do, apart from speaking to herself very firmly about wishing the door to remain closed. "Now I must go. It's time for the lesson, and I shouldn't leave the young ladies alone with Mr. Bream."

"Heaven forbid," the duke said, pouring more coffee. "He's a danger to all womankind." She turned her back smartly, but he called to her when she was halfway to the door.

"One more thing, Jane. Should you decide to knock on my door, I will welcome you in."

What Julian should be doing today was planning his foray into Belgium to retrieve forty priceless masterpieces. Moving such bulky and precious cargo presented a logistical problem he hadn't been able to solve during the years of war. What he'd do with them, he wasn't sure. When he was offered a stake in a collection that included works by Raphael, Titian, and Veronese, his twenty-year-old mouth had watered with intense lust. He still wanted them. What lover of art would not?

Yet he found he was in no hurry. Another work of art, one made of delectable flesh and blood, held his attention. Right now he was consumed, to the exclusion of all else, by the ambition to possess Jane Grey, and he wasn't above using guile to achieve it. It was time to give her a little encouragement. After a leisurely breakfast and a consultation with Blackett about hiring a couple of nursery maids, he wandered up to the Blue Saloon where the drawing lesson was in progress with Jane as the model—for both teacher and students. If he'd had any worries about a potential romance between Oliver and Jane, they would have been set to rest by the quarrel he discovered in progress.

"I will not stand for it," Jane said. To be accurate, she was half reclining on a chaise longue and for some reason brandishing a knife. Not a very dangerous weapon—he recognized the pearl-handled fruit knife that Oliver must have filched from the breakfast table—and he couldn't tell if her fierce expression was part of the pose or exasperation with the artist.

"Please, Jane. Ten more minutes and I'll have the pose sketched."

"You are supposed to be teaching the young ladies to draw, not planning your own masterpiece." The dripping sarcasm in the last word told Julian all he needed to know about the progress of the conversation. He'd heard—and largely ignored—a hundred descriptions of dozens of Oliver's grandiose paintings, few of which ever came to canvas.

"And so I shall, but I know you won't want me to lose this. The look on your face is *perfect* now. Hold it there."

Judging by her scowl, she was posing for the role of a murderess. A very seductive one. Despite the nunlike gown, slate blue today, seeing Jane Grey leaning back against the cushions, her legs slightly parted and bosom thrust forward, made Julian think of her naked and in bed, not a new sensation. He stood in the doorway and watched for a while, trying to define what it was about her he found so fascinating. His reaction was akin to what he felt when he saw a great picture, an instant recognition of extraordinary quality. But while he'd often experienced that frisson in the presence of a painted masterpiece, he couldn't remember ever having such a feeling about a woman.

Oliver was the first to notice his presence, when he stopped drawing to scratch his nose. "Julian! The very man we need. Lie down with Jane and be Samson. You are perfect for the part."

Lying down with Jane was very much his plan, but not in public. She was as alluring as the biblical temptress; he trusted she wouldn't turn out to be equally treacherous. "I don't think you'll do much damage to my hair with that knife, Miss Grey."

"I doubt they had scissors in those days."

"Many of the masters, such as Rubens and Van

Dyck, have painted the scene and used the costumes of their own age and sometimes the tools as well. I recall a Guercino Delilah wielding a pair of scissors."

He strolled across the floor to stand next to her sofa. She looked up at him and, as if suddenly conscious of her wanton pose, snapped her knees together, even though he'd been careful not to be obvious about which of her attractions he was examining. Indeed, her pretty round face with the improbably knowing eyes was as appealing in its own way as the promise of her luscious body.

"Don't you think," he said softly, "that Delilah should be rather less covered? She and Samson are in bed when she betrays him."

"Caravaggio painted her fully dressed. I daresay it was cold at night." She sat upright and planted her feet firmly on the floor against Oliver's protest. "This is not proper conversation in front of your sisters."

A distinct giggle—or two—greeted this admonition. He hadn't given the girls a thought since he entered the room. They were seated on a row of chairs, oldest to youngest, each with a sketchbook and pencil, observing the byplay as though butter wouldn't melt in their mouths. Which had laughed? Was it intractable Fenella? Or had pretty, pious Maria shown a glimmer of humor? Not Laura, he thought. The youngest alone appeared rapt by her drawing and plied her pencil with unabated diligence.

"I'm not a proper man," Julian replied. "That's

why I hired a governess: to mitigate the dire consequences of time spent in my company."

"No danger of bad influence when they see so little of you."

She kept her voice low so the children wouldn't hear. Just to bait her he raised his. "I knew there was a reason I left them alone: my overdeveloped sense of responsibility."

"You are impossible, Your Grace."

"And you, Miss Grey"—he bent over to whisper in her ear—"are impertinent for an employee."

Watching her bite back her retort amused him, though he was sorry to miss the retort itself. He liked his governess just the way she was and she knew it too. He raised his voice again. "I have offered the Misses Osbourne my company at the theater." He cut off three girlish gasps of glee. "Under certain conditions. Miss Grey knows what they are and the matter is in her hands."

The governess narrowed her eyes in disgust and he smiled blandly.

A chorus of "Please, Miss Grey" arose from the schoolgirl ranks, but Oliver, insensitive as ever, balked him of the pleasure of learning how she'd deal with the fox he'd tossed into her dovecote. "Ten minutes, Jane. Sit down again for ten minutes."

A woman of uncommon intelligence, Jane had clearly already learned that Oliver, however much he might claim to adore her, was not easily gainsaid when it came to his work. With no more protest than a toss of the head, she resumed her inviting posture, threatening fruit knife, and expression of murderous fury worthy of Mrs. Siddons as Lady Macbeth. This time, surely, Julian was the object of her violent thoughts. Just as long as he eventually became the object of her passion.

"Won't you be Samson, Julian? Go to sleep against Jane's bosom and let her cut your hair."

"A tempting offer that I must, I fear, decline. In all the years we've known each other I've never sat for you," he said, "and I certainly won't break my rule for Samson. You need someone much beefier. Besides, if I won't permit a barber to cut my hair, I'm not going to risk it in the vicinity of a governess with a fruit knife."

"Why do you keep it long, Your Grace?" Maria ventured to ask. "I still see longer hair in Ireland where they aren't so fashionable. Everyone in London seems to wear a crop."

"Mere affectation." He dismissed her question with a flick of the wrist. "You are my sisters," he said brusquely. "You may as well call me Julian. Or Denford if you insist on formality." Then, because it would please Jane Grey and for no other reason, he decided to display a little interest in them. "Show me your drawing, if you like, but I warn you I'm a harsh critic. Oliver will be kinder, when he gets round to looking at your work."

Maria held up her drawing with an air of modest pride. She'd sketched Jane's body roughly and concentrated on the face.

"You have a certain facility and it's a passable likeness. But there's no life to the portrait. I don't recommend you set up as an artist."

"Well, of course I wouldn't do that," Maria said.

"I'm almost old enough to be married. Gentlemen admire a lady who is accomplished with a pencil or brush."

"I suppose some do." Personally Julian despised genteel lady painters, finding the banality of their production an insult to his senses. "What about you, Fenella? Do you aspire to catch a husband the same way?"

Fenella scowled. "Here," she said, thrusting her pad of paper at him. He choked back laughter. True to form, the troublesome middle sister hadn't made the slightest effort to sketch the designated model. Instead she'd drawn a tall male figure with dark clothing and long hair and endowed him with a beard, horns, and a tail. What she lacked in skill she made up in raw emotion, so lacking in her sister's bloodless effort. He turned his attention to the fledgling caricaturist, who met his gaze with a kind of fearful scorn.

His mouth twitched with amusement. "That's very . . . interesting, Fenella. I look forward to hearing Oliver's judgment. I'm sure he'll be able to give you some hints to help you improve." He would not have expected one of Frederick Osbourne's spawn capable of such originality in her defiance. "Tell me," he asked, despite his resolution never to speak to them of the pompous hypocrite who'd ejected him from the family, "what did your father think of your drawing?"

Fenella pinched her lips tightly, to the detriment of her already indifferent beauty, and said nothing.

"I believe he would have enjoyed this effort of

yours. It seems you and he held the same opinion of me."

"I never thought the same as Papa about anything. And I never will think the same as you either."

"Too late," Julian said. "We already have something in common."

"What?" she asked suspiciously.

"I also never agreed with your father."

Fenella chewed her lower lip while she digested this statement. "Is that why you never came to visit us?"

"I was busy," he said shortly, having no intention of going into the cruelty inflicted on him by a stepfather who resented any attention paid him by his beautiful mother and made it very clear he wasn't welcome in their home, with their new family. He'd locked the door on that part of his life, and Osbourne's death meant he could throw away the key. Withdrawing from the group, he stared out of the window with his back to the room. He emptied his mind, taking himself out of the company, even that of the delectable Miss Grey. The early spring garden in the middle of Hanover Square, a prosaic collection of trees and shrubs bearing their first leaves like a misty green veil, held no interest for him, and he let his mind drift to the limpid skies and blue hills found in paintings of the Italian Renaissance. No wonder England rarely produced decent artists. They might have the skill but they lacked the inspiration.

A tug on his sleeve recalled him to the present.

"Julian? Brother?" It was Laura. "Will you look at my picture?"

"Are you any better than your sisters?"

Laura wafted him a sly grin that made him rethink his assessment of Maria as the beauty of the family. The youngest had also inherited her mother's looks, but she had a saucy charm that he hoped she wouldn't lose as she grew up. Not with Jane Grey as example, possessor of her own saucy appeal. "I don't know. I didn't draw the same thing. I wanted to do something different."

"I see." Had this little black-haired cherub also depicted her brother as Mephistopheles? Probably not. After this morning he wouldn't make the mistake of regarding his sisters as indistinguishable. They were still a confounded nuisance, but a slightly interesting one.

"I didn't want to draw Miss Grey," she said. "I drew a cat instead."

He supposed it was a cat. It had whiskers. And a tail. And those must be ears. "It's terrible," he said.

She giggled. "I know. Can I have a real one instead? Papa never let us have a cat. Or a dog."

"Certainly not," he said, disguising his amusement at the blatant manipulation. No question that this one was related to him. "Or perhaps," he said softly, "I might change my mind if Miss Grey thinks it's a good idea. You should speak to her about it. Make sure you discuss it with her in great detail."

Chapter 6

Jane spent the rest of the day being badgered by her charges about the theater and a cat and a dog, all of which she was supposed to speak to the duke about. The wretched man had managed to get his sisters to unwittingly plead his cause for him.

She looked forward keenly to giving him a piece of her mind about his behavior when they met after dinner. Then perhaps, maybe, she would negotiate. A kiss wouldn't be so terrible, and the girls didn't need to know what means she'd used to obtain their theater excursion. However, there would be only a kiss. She did not like to imagine what he might demand for a cat or dog, but she was determined there would be no pets. For the moment.

Half an hour before nine o'clock, she descended to her unsuitably ornate chamber to get ready. She had pretty gowns hidden in the back of the wardrobe, including an evening gown that had been the latest mode in Paris last year. Henri had given it to her to celebrate his most recent promotion, along with an offer of marriage.

Henri had courted her while Mathieu was away in Italy with the army. When news arrived of the latter's death, she hadn't hesitated to accept Henri's protection, relieved to be free of her seducer. As Henri's career advanced she'd been able to hide away some money, with the idea of eventually coming to England in search of revenge.

His unexpected proposal had forced her decision, finally, to make the break. She had wavered. In some ways it would have been easy to settle down as Madame Henri Dupont. But she couldn't forget that her family had died horribly while she lived in relative comfort; her nightmares came back; there could be no peace for her in France. While Henri professed to be heartbroken, she knew that he was also slightly relieved. He loved her but he was an ambitious man, and an English wife, even one who spoke French perfectly, was a small patch of rust on the shining patriotic shield of his reputation. She left him a week later, keeping the gown and other gifts. She didn't feel guilty. She'd used Henri for her own purposes, as he had her. She had been a good mistress but agreeing to be his wife would mean forgetting the past, turning her back on Jeanne de Falleron forever.

She fingered the fine material, picturing the appreciative gleam in Denford's eye should she present herself in the dark rose silk, cunningly designed to cling to her body. But a governess would never own such a luxurious thing. While she could claim it came from Saint Lucia, she wouldn't put it past Denford to recognize the fashion. Despite several years of war, the English were still able to find out what was worn in Paris and copy it.

Regretfully she closed the wardrobe door, washed her hands and face and tidied her hair. Her sole concession to the occasion was a crisp muslin fichu to lighten the unrelieved gray of her plain, round gown and a small gold cross and chain that had belonged to Mathieu's mother. Considering what Mathieu had done to her, she certainly deserved this small piece of jewelry.

She needn't have taken the trouble. A footman appeared at the door with a small package containing a key and a curt note.

I am dining out so we will not meet tonight. This is the key to the door between our chambers. You are welcome to use it at any time.

Denford

She grasped his game. He was toying with her, hoping to pique her with a show of indifference. Annoyingly, it worked, or would have done so had she not understood him so well.

Returning to the wardrobe, she opened the drawer at the bottom. Folded inside a gauze shawl, another item too fine for a governess, was the knife Mathieu had given her when he left for Italy. He'd shown her how to defend herself. Holding it up, she let the wicked blade catch the candlelight. She'd never had to wield it in defense but she knew how to use it to kill.

It was a good thing that the duke had canceled tonight's meeting because her attraction to him interfered with her purpose. Denford must mean nothing to her save as a source of information about his unidentified relation. As anything else he was a distraction from her main goal.

And she must never, would never, use the key.

Mr. Blackett, Jane had discovered, didn't live at Fortescue House. After breakfast, putting Maria in charge of making the girls study French verbs, she sought him out in his office on the ground floor. After half an hour discussing furnishings and the hiring of nursery maids, they were on the best of terms.

"How, precisely, are you related to His Grace?" she asked, settling in for what she hoped would be a revealing chat about the Fortescue family.

Blackett, who tended to be anxious, relaxed a little, resting his elbow on the desk and rubbing his forehead thoughtfully. There was no family resemblance between him and the duke that Jane could detect. "I'm not sure exactly what degree of cousinhood we share. I am the grandson of one of the daughters of the fourth Duke of Denford. He is descended from the third."

"Which number is he?"

"The seventh. The sixth duke was killed in a fall on the hunting field within months of inheriting."

"And there were no closer heirs than the current duke?"

"Several, but none alive." Blackett was warming to his subject. "It's remarkable how unfortunate the members of the family have been. The fourth duke had three sons and each of them had sons, yet none survived. The third duke had ten children in all. I can't remember offhand how many of them were sons. At least a couple of the lines died out. His Grace's great-grandfather was one of the younger ones. There were several potential heirs descended from the third duke but Julian Fortescue, as His Grace was then, was the first in line." Jane's head was awhirl. There were so many Fortescues who were dead, and the ones that remained were very distantly related to any recent dukes. "This must be very dull for you," Blackett said. "Not to mention bewildering."

"Oh no! Very interesting," she said. "But I am confused. Do you perhaps have a . . . chart . . . I could study?" She wasn't sure of the English term for an *arbre généalogique.*

Blackett poked at the papers on his desk, as though expecting to find such a thing there. "A family tree? There may be one here but I doubt it. The family archives are kept in the muniment room at Denford Castle."

"I would like to see it if you should come across such a thing. Did you know many of these unfortunates who died? You were close cousins to some, I think."

"Despite the duke's poor health, we were all welcome at Denford Castle and used to spend weeks there, especially in the summer."

"What were they like? All families have their eccentrics, yes? You must have some wonderful stories."

"My grandmother Lady Sophia Fortescue invented the powdered wig for ladies."

Jane found this totally improbable, but all families have their legends that exaggerate or invent history. Why, her own *grandmère* claimed to have been a secret granddaughter of Louis XIV. According to Jane's mother, this would only have been possible if the grandmother in question had bedded the aged *grand monarque* when she was ten years old. Personally Jane thought it much more amusing to have been responsible for a famous hairstyle. However, her quest did not require knowledge of the enterprising Lady Sophia. Blackett proved willing to ramble on, mostly about the less numerous and also less entertaining male Fortescues.

Occasionally she'd put in a question, hoping to steer him in a helpful direction. "Many Englishmen travel abroad, I think."

"They used to, before the French plunged Europe into war."

Jane seized the opening. "Ah, the dreadful Revolution. Was anyone in Paris at that time? It must have been terrible! All those poor aristocrats slaughtered by the mob."

"There was a John Fortescue who spent much of his time wandering around Europe." He coughed discreetly. "Very fond of the ladies, if you know what I mean."

"What kind of age man?"

"He was one of my mother's cousins. If he'd lived he'd be about forty-five or fifty now."

"What did he look like?" Jane held her breath, waiting to hear if this Mr. John Fortescue could have been the man she saw.

"On the tall side, otherwise quite ordinary-looking. He was stabbed to death by a jealous husband in Copenhagen in '94."

"Any others?"

"There's Charles. He's another descendant of the third duke. He's the current heir, until Denford marries and has a son. I've never met him but I remember my mother saying he spent a lot of time abroad." He coughed significantly. "A bit of a black sheep, you know. Of course we used to think that about Julian, but not now. Picture of respectability."

Mr. Blackett was, in her opinion, deluding himself on that count. Or merely displaying discretion and loyalty toward the new head of the family. Now she knew that Denford had not been born to his position, she understood his unorthodox approach to life. A man accustomed to occupying the highest levels of nobility, her father, for example, would never brook impertinence from a servant, even one he wanted to bed. Especially one he wanted to bed.

The Duke of Denford did not belong to the breed that exercised *droit du seigneur* on unwilling servants. Only willing ones. She pictured the key to his room, resting safely in the drawer of her writing desk.

But the current duke didn't concern her, not in the present context, anyway. He was too young to be *the* Mr. Fortescue. In John and Charles she had two promising candidates who merited investigation.

At nine o'clock Jane presented herself at the door of the library. He was there. To calm her anticipating heart, she applied logic and her knowledge of men to remind herself of the moves Denford was making on the chessboard of their relationship. Last night he'd missed their meeting to intrigue her. Avoiding her a second time would look like indifference, and the Duke of Denford was not indifferent to Jane Grey. He intended to have her and he would not cease to press her until he did. Her gambit was to resist for as long as she remained at Fortescue House. However difficult that might be, with the progress she'd made with Blackett, it shouldn't be too much longer.

The thought made her a little sad. She was becoming fond of the girls, not least because they brought back the family life she had lost. On the other hand, her vengeful task would be easier without the distraction of Denford's pursuit.

If only the sight of him, his lithe, black body pacing moodily about the room, didn't have such an effect. She swallowed convulsively and gathered her wits.

"Your Grace." She curtseyed demurely.

"Come in, Jane."

"You don't have my permission to call me Jane," she said, tilting her chin.

"As your employer and your superior I may call you whatever I want."

"No, Your Grace, you may not. I demand you address me with respect, as I address you."

His eyes gleamed as blue as the summer sea viewed from her father's Normandy château. "Aren't you afraid I'll dismiss you?"

"No."

He enjoyed that. "Why not?"

"Because you're hoping to seduce me."

"I'm so glad we understand each other. I see it as a promising step."

"I regret to inform you that I am not to be seduced."

"Then why are you flirting with me again?"

It was on the tip of her tongue to retort that a Frenchwoman always flirts with an attractive gentleman. She'd been taught to do so along with her lessons in music and deportment. Or she could tell him that she was twenty-four years old and healthy and accustomed to having a man in her life and her bed. But none of these true things could be confessed to her employer. "I am merely humoring you, Your Grace. By the way, I haven't thanked you for sending me the key to my room. It was thoughtful."

"It's the key to *my* room and I look forward to the day that you use it."

"That day will never come."

He turned aside, shaking his head in mock disgust. "In that case, why should I keep you on?"

"Because you need me to look after your sisters. And I amuse you."

"And because I live in hope." Again he settled the full power of his gaze on her and she could scarcely stand.

"Are we going to the theater?" His matter-of-fact tone belied the meaning of the question.

"I haven't decided yet."

"You'd better let me know soon. Boxes to see Mrs. Siddons aren't to be had without difficulty."

"I trust your ingenuity, Your Grace."

"For the love of God, Jane, stop Your Gracing me. Call me Julian."

"Certainly not. It would be most improper."

"How many times must I remind you that I'm an improper man." Beautiful as a leopard, he sauntered toward her. "And I have every hope that you are an improper woman. In fact I know you are. Underneath that drab exterior there's a siren waiting to come out."

She tilted her chin as high as it would go. "You will wait until the world ends to find out."

"I don't think so," he said, and she very much feared he was right. "However, clearly this evening we are not going to proceed straight to the activity I, for one, would prefer. Sit down, let me pour you some brandy, and tell me what you did today."

How funny. Those were the very words with which she would greet Henri when he came home from a hard day untangling red tape and conspiring to advance in the bureaucracy. After dinner, cooked by the maid Henri was proud to be able to afford, she'd seduce him and they'd go to bed. Denford would like that, but it wasn't going to happen. Too bad Jane desired the duke ten times more than she ever had her adoring French lover. And proving that she was in a very bad way, she was touched by the solicitous way he settled her in a comfortable chair beside the fire and brought her a drink. Across the room the golden divan mocked the scene of domesticity.

"So," he said, settling across the hearth from her and warming his glass of brandy between his well-shaped hands. "Did my sisters make vast strides in their acquisition of useless feminine accomplishments?"

"Not useless," she said, averting her eyes from the mouth emitting those basso profundo tones. "Today we worked on our French."

"Now that we are at peace with France once more, all the English will pour across the Channel to buy new clothes and inflict their execrable accents on the natives."

Jane bit back a comment that no foreigner would ever speak French well enough to satisfy the denizens of Paris. "Your French is quite good," she said instead.

"Not as good as yours. Clearly Saint Lucia is the place to go to acquire the accent of Tours."

"Just because I was on an island, it doesn't mean I wasn't well educated. You are lucky to have found such an excellent governess." She changed the subject before he could start nosing out her past. "I spoke to Mr. Blackett today about the furniture in the nursery. He was very helpful."

"He is ever obliging."

"He told me stories about the Fortescue family. Very amusing."

"Really? I had no idea. Clearly there's more to be had from Blackett apart from his competent, if lackluster, performance as a secretary. He has never amused me much."

"Ask about his grandmother and powdered wigs. We talked about France too. Or rather about Fortescues who enjoyed travel." She glanced over at the Vaugondy globe. "I wish I could see the great cities of Europe. I suppose you have visited them all."

He nodded. "Not all but many. I traveled a fair amount myself, in my distant youth."

"And now you are so old?"

"Old in experience."

"Did you go to Paris?"

"Several times. I even witnessed the fall of the Bastille. I was sixteen years old and thought it the greatest thing that ever happened in the history of the world. The heady wine of liberty."

"It started well, perhaps." She didn't want to talk about the progress of events in France, afraid that she would display emotions beyond a horror that might be felt by an Englishwoman living halfway around the world. But having established that Denford had been in Paris in 1789, she wanted to know about the period closer to her family's betrayal. "It is sad how many innocents lost their lives later. Did you see the Terror?"

"Why do you ask?" There was an odd note in his voice. Had she given herself away?

She tried to speak with nothing but indifferent

curiosity. "I was talking about it with Mr. Blackett and he thought one of your cousins might have been there. John or Charles Fortescue. I wondered if perhaps you had seen either of them in Paris."

Denford grimaced. "I don't know why you find my very dull relations of interest. Let me see. John is dead or else he'd be duke. I met him a few times. Come to think of it, I ran into him in Berlin once." He stood up and walked over to a flat glass-topped case. "Come here and see him for yourself. The fourth duke had miniatures done of all his grandchildren, including John. He didn't hire a very good painter or someone would have pilfered them from the house. They are a remarkably unprepossessing group."

Excitement rose in her gorge, then abated as fast. The young man in the gold-framed oval could be the man she'd glimpsed. It might equally well not be. The face meant nothing to her, and why should it? She'd never had a good look at Mr. Fortescue. "What about Charles?" she asked, as she pretended to peruse the other miniatures.

"I know Charles better, but he isn't here. Like me he was from a more distant branch of the Fortescues. He's ten years older than I but his grandfather was younger than mine. Otherwise *he* would be duke. The accidents of birth are quite remarkable."

"Where have you run into him? St. Petersburg? Vienna? Constantinople?"

"I've never been to Constantinople, so not there. Last I heard he was living in Naples, though with the arrival of the French he may have fled to Turkey for all I know. I did see him in Paris in 1793. He was picking up bargains from terrified aristocrats desperate for cash."

Her heart thudded and her throat was so tight she could hardly speak. "He remained in Paris?" It had been in November of that year that the Fallerons had been betrayed. Then her stomach turned over when she realized that Denford might have been there too. Was she wrong to have excluded him from the list of possibilities? If his knowledge of art had been as great then as it was now, he could have gained her father's respect and confidence despite his youth. There was nothing the late marquis preferred to talk about.

Denford said nothing, his face inscrutable. "I left France in May," he said. "Before things got out of hand."

"You never went back to France?" She had to ask.

"Only a fool or a madman would return to Paris later that year," he said.

"Is your cousin Charles a fool?"

"I never asked him how long he stayed. I didn't see him until a couple of years later, when he was back in London for a stretch."

Her excitement that she had most likely identified her villain was tempered by fear that he might be out of her reach. "You should know where your heir is," she said. "Suppose something happened to you."

"If something happened to me I would be dead and in no position to care. I'll let the Fortescues worry about it." He gave a brief crack of unamused laughter. "If there's anyone in the world they disapprove of more than me, it's Charles. I'd love to see him lay his hands on their precious dukedom. Unfortunately that's by definition an ambition I can never achieve."

Having been brought up by a man who took his position very seriously, Jane could not condone such levity. "You should feel responsible for the future of your estates."

"My dear, my very dear Jane. Surely you've seen enough of me to realize I have no sense of responsibility whatsoever. I am an entirely selfish man."

Chapter 7

Now that she had a name and some personal details, Jane resumed her search with fresh optimism.

Three months earlier, on her arrival in London, she had taken rooms in the City of London, an address she'd mistakenly believed to be fashionable, like the Ile de la Cité in Paris, site of the Hôtel Falleron. Soon after realizing that she'd need help finding one man in a city of over a million, she'd consulted Mr. Russell, a solicitor with an office near her lodging.

She had spun a tale about tracking down a Mr. Fortescue, a long-lost family friend. Mr. Russell swallowed the story whole, including the odd fact that she didn't know this man's Christian name. He was quite prepared to track down every Fortescue in England, and charge her a goodly sum for his pains. With some regret, Jane turned down the offer on the grounds of expense. Such a service would cost much of the money she had saved over the years and would need for her escape to America when her revenge was complete. More importantly, Russell very reasonably suggested that he should write to these Fortescues, inquiring if they had been acquainted with a clergyman named Grey and his family. She couldn't very well explain that far from wishing for a happy resumption of this invented friendship, she intended to kill the man.

The morning after her discovery, slipping away after breakfast, she returned to his office, where Mr. Russell promised to make discreet inquiries and tell her when he'd found Charles Fortescue.

"Please do not contact him for me," she said. "I want it to be a surprise."

Since her lack of progress finding Mr. Fortescue had weighed heavily on her conscience, she left the task in the hands of Russell and his hired investigator with a lighter heart. Now, for a week or two at least, she could forget her savage, sacred mission and concentrate on her duties as governess. She worried a little at having left the Misses Osbourne in the inebriated care of Nurse Bride that morning. Fenella had been less defiant with her, but she didn't fool herself that the girl was incapable of taking advantage of her governess's absence. As her hackney turned into St. George's Street her suspicion was confirmed in a surprising way. Beneath the massive Corinthian portico of St. George's Church, she detected the eldest Miss Osbourne in close conversation with a young man.

Bidding her driver stop, she raised the window flap. "Miss Osbourne," she called.

Maria jumped and turned, the picture of guilt,

gloved hands covering her mouth. The young man—not as young as he should be to consort with a fifteen-year-old—looked shifty. He was handsome enough and well dressed in a flashy way, but Jane's eyes narrowed as she detected poorly polished shoes with worn-down heels and loose threads in his stockings.

"Get into the carriage. I daresay it will rain any moment." Maria glanced at the unthreatening sky but appeared too cowed to quibble. Murmuring a hasty farewell to her swain, she joined Jane. Five minutes later they climbed the steps to the front door of Fortescue House. "Wait for me in my room," Jane said, sounding more governessy than she would have believed possible. "I must make sure all is well in the nursery, then we will talk."

When she had answered Denford's advertisement she'd thought only about fooling her way into the position. In her first days as a governess she'd done quite well. What she hadn't counted on was developing an affection for her charges and a desire to do her duty properly. Who was she to handle the delicate matter of a well-brought-up young lady's first love?

Standing in the center of Jane's lavish chamber, Maria presented a picture of youthful defiance on the verge of tears, and Jane wanted nothing more than to put her arms about her.

Instead she adopted a tone that was no-nonsense without being overbearing. "I was surprised to see you out without an escort. Did Nurse Bride give you permission?" She hardly needed an answer, neither did she receive one, beyond a slight hunching of the shoulders and a pouting lower lip. "Tell me about your acquaintance."

Maria eyed her warily. "Mr. Godfrey Norville."

"Is he a family friend?"

"Our family friends are all in Ireland. We met Mr. Norville when we were walking in the park with Bridey."

Jane affected an air of puzzlement. "I don't understand. Who introduced you?"

"No one. We were feeding the ducks in the lake and so was he. We started talking and I knew at once." She sighed. "He is so handsome."

Jane nodded. "Kindness to animals is always an appealing trait in a man. When I was about your age I had quite a tendre for a gentleman who could ride the wildest of horses. The sight of him taming a huge black stallion sent my heart aflutter. I imagine the sight of Mr. Norville throwing bread at the ducklings must have had the same effect."

Maria didn't ask for further details of this entirely fictitious affair. "He is easy to talk to, as well. It's dull in London having no one but Fenella and Laura. At least in Ireland we had neighbors."

"Did he call on your brother and ask permission to see you?"

"Julian wouldn't care."

"He cares about your safety. You're a sensible girl, not like your sisters. I think you know that it is wrong to sneak out to meet a man without the knowledge of your guardians."

Showing a lack of guile and invention that

would have got her killed in revolutionary Paris, Maria made no attempt to pretend they'd met by chance. "I *had* to see him," she said. "I'm sorry, Miss Grey, but when he sent a note by one of the maids, begging me to meet him at the church, I couldn't leave him to wait, could I?"

"Being incapable of penning a short note yourself."

"I wanted to see him. I think I love him."

"After two meetings?"

"Four." The girl wasn't canny enough to know that information was being extracted from her. "You are too old to understand."

Perhaps she was. Nine years' difference in age and nine decades in experience. At fifteen Jane had been a pampered and sheltered mademoiselle who would never have dreamed of going out to meet a man of dubious suitability. Until one day changed her life and she became the mistress of a proletarian, garlic-breathing soldier more than twice her age. She'd never had a first love, or surrendered to a stolen kiss. Maria's ridiculous and innocent love saddened her, and made her envious. There had been no one to save her from Mathieu Picard, but Maria was not going to fall into the clutches of an unscrupulous man. If no one else stopped her, Jane would.

"You are too young to be presented, let alone married."

"I'm almost sixteen. Why should I wait, just because Mama decided to go to America? It's not fair."

"Is Mr. Norville a gentleman of means?"

"He has a large estate in Wales and he has come to London to see to some business regarding the arrival of a ship. I think he must be very rich."

Jane wanted to roll her eyes. She might not be familiar with the nuances of English society, but she could spot a *flâneur* at ten meters. "My dear Maria, I doubt that men of property and wealth scrape up the acquaintance of young girls in public parks." She trod carefully, feeling her inexperience as both a governess and a Londoner and wishing there was someone she could consult. "If Mr. Norville is suitable—"

"He is!"

"If he is suitable, when you are old enough to come out, he may court you. In the meantime, with your brother's permission, he may call. But only with your brother's permission. You are the sister of a duke and must be especially careful of whom you consort with." Denford was abundantly capable of assessing the fellow. Surely he'd give short shrift to a man who battened on his sister.

"I told you, Julian doesn't care for us or what we do." Maria's face settled into a mulish determination, quite unlike her usual pleasant acquiescence. "We're only here because Mama's new husband didn't want us. She forced him to take us in."

"I'm sure that's not true."

"It is too. We hardly know him."

"He is much older than you, yes?" Jane did rapid calculations in her head. "But he wasn't grown up when you were born. Surely he must have still been at home."

"He went to school in England. I never saw him above three times in my life before we came to live with him."

"Didn't he visit his family?"

"He and Papa didn't like each other. I'm not sure, but I think when Papa married Mama he sent Julian away. Papa had a very bad temper and I daresay Julian provoked him."

"Even so, your mother must have missed her son."

Maria shook her head. "Now Mama has a new husband and he has sent *us* away. I think she cares more for husbands than for children."

"All the more reason why you and your brother should become close. You must tell him about this young man of yours, or I will."

"Please, Miss Grey! Don't tell him."

Jane hesitated. It was certainly her duty to inform Denford of the incident but was it the best course? The last thing she wanted was for the girls to be in more trouble with an indifferent brother. What they needed was distraction and more entertainment than was found at Fortescue House or Hyde Park.

"Please," Maria said. "He won't take us to the theater if he knows."

"I'm not sure he's going to take you to the theater anyway. I haven't been able to persuade him."

"But you will, Miss Grey. You can do anything."

Indeed. It looked as though Miss Grey was going to be kissing the Duke of Denford in the near future. She'd enjoy it, and doubtless regret it, but she couldn't resist the plea in Maria's big blue eyes, so like her brother's. She'd like to see Denford plead. He was far too confident. She'd like to have him on his knees, begging for her favors . . .

"I will do my best," she said. "And you must do something for me."

"What?"

"If Mr. Norville writes to you again—"

"He will."

"—you will reply that you cannot meet him alone but he may call at Fortescue House and ask for Miss Grey. I will decide if he is a suitable acquaintance for you."

"He is suitable, as you will see. Thank you, thank you!"

"And in return you will do something for me."

"Anything."

"You will work with me on deportment, manners, and clothing in preparation for your presentation. You are almost old enough to be out and there is much to learn."

The blue eyes gleamed with avarice. "New clothes?"

The Duke of Denford was about to discover an additional drain on his purse. That kiss was going to be very expensive.

Two years after becoming Duke of Denford, Julian found life as a high member of the nobility rather tedious. Now that the title came with a handsome income, he had to endure endless meetings with various men of affairs and stewards about the running of his estates. Necessary, of course, but not the kind of business he had been bred to. As for the House of Lords, the less said (or thought) about the practice of politics, the better.

He missed the cut and thrust of life as a dealer in pictures, a confluence of high art and low cunning that suited him. Since the dignity of the aristocracy merited no more than a curl of the lip, he would have happily continued to conduct his trade, but his former customers didn't see it that way. Nor was he having much luck with one of the few collectors who now outranked him. The Prince of Wales might be capable of exerting charm on his future subjects but Julian had seen no evidence of it.

Thoroughly irritated by an interview with the heir to the throne, he departed the overheated halls of Carlton House. A walk would clear his head, but in which direction? He could return to Hanover Square and make a surprise visit to the nursery. He'd enjoy baiting Jane Grey as she tried to decide if he was taking a genuine interest in his sisters, or pretending in order to ingratiate himself with their governess. As he contemplated the governess's confusion, a worm of unease gnawed his brain. Which was it? Perhaps a bit of both.

Not prepared to admit to a scintilla of fraternal affection, he set off at a brisk walk to Leicester Square and the lavish premises of London's leading picture dealer, Isaac Bridges. His old friend and rival was about the only man who treated the Duke of Denford exactly the same as he had Julian Fortescue.

Half an hour in the elegant gallery, especially

built with clerestory ceiling lights for the best viewing, left Julian calmed and inspired. The great works that Bridges had to offer also aroused his competitive urges. He consoled himself with the thought that soon he would have the Falleron collection and, in his last glorious action as a seller of art, blow anything Bridges had right out of the water.

"I don't trust that smile, Julian," Bridges said. "If you've seen enough, come and take a glass of wine with me. I want to hear what mischief you have in mind."

Tucking his walking stick under his arm, he followed Bridges to the private office that resembled the library of a man of substance and taste. The older man's origins were obscure, but during thirty years he'd taken advantage of wealthy Englishmen's passion for collecting foreign art. As a beginner, Julian had sold pictures to Bridges and bought from him, often begging for credit. Either way, Bridges drove a hard bargain. Today Julian was in the market for information.

While Bridges poured sherry from an engraved glass decanter, Julian pondered how much intelligence he would have to give to learn what he wanted.

"I've just come from Carlton House," he said.

Bridges responded to this promising gambit with nothing more than a twitch of his brow. "Is that a new walking stick?"

Of course it wasn't, as the man knew well. "I had an audience with His Highness."

"I imagine the Prince of Wales is always ready to receive a duke of the realm."

admiration. Bridges had acquired an exceptional group of Dutch masters from a marquess whose financial difficulties were a close-kept secret. "I see one problem," he said once he'd read the list carefully, twice. "The same one you just pointed out in my collection. Where is the masterwork?"

"Maddening, isn't it," Bridges replied. "Had I known of this opportunity I wouldn't have sold the Michelangelo tondo or the Van Eyck altarpiece."

"Seller's remorse is a hazard of the business."

"What we need is something big." Bridges stressed the *we*. "Something like, I don't know, a Raphael Madonna."

"That would indeed be perfect," Julian said. "I wish I had any idea where to acquire such a thing, but I can assure you I don't have one hidden away in my cellar."

He rose, having got what he'd come for, and more besides: the fact that Bridges knew about the Falleron collection. Or else it was a coincidence that he'd named a Raphael Madonna. Julian didn't believe in coincidence.

"Before I go," he said, "I've made up my mind about the Fragonard. I want it." To hell with waiting until he'd seduced Jane Grey. He wanted her likeness now.

"I'm glad," Bridges said. "Sir Richard Radcliffe wants it too, but I'd rather sell it to you." He opened a drawer of his print cabinet and extracted the delicate pastel.

Julian examined it hungrily. The subject, a girl on the cusp of womanhood, wasn't Jane. The shape of the face and the nose were similar, the mouth smaller. The resemblance lay in the spirit, the indefinable charm that came from an inner light. Julian frowned and closed his eyes, summoning the governess's features. Fragonard's lady lacked the strain of melancholy that sometimes disturbed Jane's spirits.

"I'll take it with me," he said. Radcliffe might appear at any time and make Bridges an offer he couldn't resist. The man had no scruples, and Bridges very few.

The package securely under his arm, he stepped into the square to find Sir Richard Radcliffe descending from his carriage.

"Denford." The exquisitely dressed elderly baronet always greeted him affably, as friendly as a viper.

Julian nodded curtly.

"I'm glad to meet you here."

"Why?"

"Do I need a reason?"

"Yes." Julian's quarrel with Radcliffe went back years, long before the business with Cynthia last year.

"I won't beat around the bush then. You have a pretty little Bosschaert still life. What is your price? I want it as a gift, you understand, not for myself."

If Radcliffe thought to soften Julian by this assurance, he failed. "It's not for sale. To you. I think you know why."

Radcliffe smiled, unabashed by the blunt refusal or by Julian's superior height, looming over the elegant old villain. "I know you and Windermere have a ridiculous notion that I had something to do with endangering Lady Windermere. Utter nonsense, of course. I have nothing but the greatest respect for the dear lady."

A respect that if genuine, which it certainly wasn't, was entirely unreciprocated. Cynthia Windermere had expressed herself frequently and at length on the subject of her loathing for Radcliffe and his wife, Lady Belinda.

Julian wondered why Radcliffe had even raised the subject.

"I would be interested in the Falleron pictures, of course." That was why.

"What pictures?" he asked.

"Don't let us be coy. I know you have them. What I don't know is where they are: in England, or still in Belgium, or perhaps you moved them to another country entirely."

That was all the admission Julian needed of Radcliffe's complicity. Otherwise there would be no way he knew the collection had been moved. "And yet you claim to have had nothing to do with the effort, last year, to force me to reveal their hiding place."

"My dear duke! I ask only for information. Should you be in possession of the collection, I would wish to know, that is all."

"You won't hear it from me."

"Never mind. News has a way of getting out, and long experience has taught me to keep several irons in the fire." He turned to the footman waiting silently next to his sumptuous town coach. "Come back in an hour. Good day, Denford. I'm sorry we can't come to terms. I trust my negotiation with Bridges will be a happier one."

Too late. It was a small satisfaction to deprive Radcliffe of the Fragonard, and a larger one not to have his malevolent pale eyes defiling Jane's likeness. The man got away with everything. He'd parlayed wealth and connections into an unassailable political and social position. He could only be beaten at his own game and Julian decided to learn how to play it.

With his new wealth he could afford to make the Prince of Wales a trifling loan. He'd send over a bank draft along with a gift. The Bosschaert was just the kind of picture the Prinny liked and well worth the sacrifice to have the heir to the ailing king doubly in his debt. Meanwhile, George III was alive and healthy so Julian needed to find a way to reach Lord Cazalet. Time to mend fences with his well-connected Fortescue relations and other members of the *ton.* He was a duke, for goodness' sake, and should begin to behave like one.

Jane had given him one of her little lectures on the subject. *That is what it means to be a duke,* she had said. He wondered how she knew.

Since he'd collected on his own bet in advance, tonight he'd summon her to the library for brandy and conversation and kisses. He was feeling exceptionally lucky.

Whistling happily, he walked home. Near the

corner of St. George's Street and Hanover Square, he noticed a man leaning against a railing. He'd seen the fellow before, in his mid-twenties and good-looking in a rather commonplace way. Shabby shoes. Nothing suspicious about that; he could be a resident of the square. But it was a chilly April afternoon, hardly good weather for loitering. And he was staring at Fortescue House.

Was he one of the irons in Radcliffe's fire?

"If you weren't living with your mother and sisters in Ireland, where were you?" Jane asked. "What were you doing?"

They were seated in a pair of armchairs on either side of the fire, like an old married couple or a pair of good friends. But the mood in the library was anything but cozy. The prospect of the kiss hung over their evening. Every word they spoke, every breath, every gesture either of them made heightened her anticipation. She couldn't know for certain that Denford was in the same state of elevated awareness but she didn't doubt it. She didn't imagine the heat in the unwavering blue eyes trained on her face, or the subtle caress of his voice. She cared about the words that were formed by those sensitive lips too. She enjoyed the duke's company far too much.

"I went to school in England, putting the Irish Sea between me and my stepfather, an arrangement that suited us both very well. I went up to Oxford, briefly, then I was on my own."

"Since you didn't expect to be a duke, what did you do?"

"I bought and sold pictures. I was very good at it."

"What a wonderful occupation! I love to look at pictures."

"I can't believe that your Saint Lucia possessed an abundance of good examples."

Unable to admit she had grown up among one of France's finest collections of masterpieces, she searched for a new lie. "We had prints," she said.

"The productions of the excellent Bartolozzi, I suppose. They are everywhere. Who is your favorite artist? You mentioned Caravaggio once."

"Raphael." Everyone loved Raphael. There was no reason to connect her with her family's famous Madonna.

"I am not surprised you have impeccable taste, Jane. Though Bartolozzi's prints give but a pallid flavor of the glories of the Italian masterpieces."

"What inspired you to make art your profession?"

"I matriculated at Oxford at Christ Church College, which happens to own some of the finest paintings and drawings in England. They changed my life. That such life and emotion could be expressed by a brush wielded by man astonished me."

"You speak with reverence," she said. Not just reverence but fervor. She wouldn't have guessed Denford could express himself without mockery.

"To me the great masters seem like gods in their ability to create flesh and blood, trees and rocks, castles and ruins, from the humble ingredients of canvas and pigment."

"Do you paint yourself?"

"I have no talent, but even if I had some ability, what would be the use? I could never rival the sublimity achieved by the least of Michelangelo's efforts. No one does these days."

"Yet you help Mr. Bream."

"Don't tell Oliver, but I think him talented. I do not, however, admire his work. I abhor the products of modern artists. Either sentimental hack work to please the masses or overblown historical scenes intended to express some important worldly point. Oliver's always got some theory about what his painting means—the decline of the nation or the corruption of the government—but I pay no attention. I feed him because I like *him*, not his work."

Never before had Jane been so frustrated by her disguise, by the suppression not only of her deep past but also her more recent life in Paris. If she could converse openly she would ask Denford if he'd seen the work of Monsieur David, a leading French painter and ardent revolutionary whose atelier she had visited with Henri. She had to content herself with a general question. "You do not think politics belong in art?"

"I don't think politics *belong* anywhere."

"Even the Garden of Eden had politics in the influence of the serpent. Perhaps the practitioners are always corrupt."

"If not all, most. I suppose some form of government is a necessary evil. I prefer to have as little to do with it as possible."

"You are cynical."

"Of course. And you are too, Jane. How did you learn to have such a jaded view of life on your tiny West Indian island?"

"I have seen regimes come and go, and most have both good and bad points."

She was talking about France, not Saint Lucia. In the years since the end of the Terror she had become philosophical about both the French Revolution and the abuses it replaced. She didn't even blame it for her family's disaster. The Revolution was a great, unstoppable wave, and you did not blame the ocean for being large and wet and likely to drown the unwary. You blamed the man who threw you overboard.

"Shall I tell you one thing I admire about France after the fall of the monarchy?" Denford said. "The Musée du Louvre. Opening the collection to the public is, in my opinion, the greatest achievement of the Revolution. I only went there once, but it was an inspiration. Only when the English have such an institution may we call ourselves a civilized nation."

Jane wanted to cry out her agreement. Her father had also approved this action of the government and they had all visited the Louvre galleries soon after the opening, despite the fact that it was timed to coincide with the anniversary of the demise of the monarchy. At least, she thought so. She vaguely remembered that it had been summer, but Denford had said he left Paris in May so it must have been earlier. In any case, it was some months before the Terror closed in on her family. During the visit to the museum her parents had still been optimistic about coming to terms with the new order in France. The marquis had even mentioned donating parts of the family collection to the nation, so that they could be enjoyed by all. Not knowing whether the marquis's efforts to hide his valuables had succeeded, she had no idea what had happened to his pictures. Perhaps they had been seized and ended up in the Louvre. Denford, as an art dealer, might have heard. But she dared not mention the name Falleron. There was absolutely no reason why an English governess from the West Indies would know it.

"I would like to visit such a place," she said.

"Exactly. If there was such a museum in London, an ordinary person would be able to see the glories that now are available only to the wealthy few."

"And this from a man who claims to be entirely selfish."

"Oh, I am. I have my own motives but it doesn't mean I can't also wish for the good of the nation. As long as it suits my interests as well."

"How would a public gallery suit your selfish needs?"

"I have accumulated a collection of pictures over the years that I have tried to sell to a single buyer. I was in negotiation with the King of Prussia at one point, but nothing came of it. This group of fine works would make an excellent core of the national collection. Unfortunately selling them to the king gets us into the realm of politics."

She smiled, enjoying the glimpse of Denford's history. "Now that you are a duke, and presumably rich, why don't you keep them? That would be the action of the self-interested connoisseur that you claim to be."

"I have asked myself that question. It used to pain me to let go of a particularly fine canvas. But now that I can afford to own them, I find I miss the thrill of the chase after a rare masterpiece and a rich collector. There's no joy in possession if all you do is throw money at it." The intensity of his gaze hinted at a deeper meaning.

"So you no longer buy pictures?"

"Sometimes a work holds a special appeal to me." He set aside his glass and walked over to the library table, returning with something extracted from a portfolio. "I bought this today. I paid too much but I didn't care. I wanted it."

It was an unframed colored drawing, set in a circular mat, of a young girl, no longer a child but not quite a woman. "Fragonard," she whispered.

"You have a fine eye as well as good taste, Jane. Yes, a rare pastel by the greatest French master. Do you know why I wanted it so much?"

The drawing transfixed her. It wasn't exactly the same as the one in her father's collection, but close. The same model in a different pose. This girl was peeping out from behind a hand mirror while her father's had been sitting with a book in her lap. Tears threatened as she remembered her father saying it reminded him of her. He would never have let the drawing go. She wondered if he'd carried it with him to his death.

"She's lovely, isn't she? I bought her because she reminds me of you."

Her hand stole to her chest. She'd never seen the resemblance but apparently her father had not been wrong. "No," she said, as she'd always told Papa. "I am not so pretty."

"Yes you are." Denford stood behind her, looking over the shoulder at the drawing. "And something more, something even better. Earlier I said that the great painters were gods because they breathed life into their creations." His breath was warm on her neck. "But not even Raphael himself invented anything as fine as you. I wish I had the skill of a genius with brush or pen to describe how you affect me."

"I think you do very well, Your Grace." Her voice wobbled. "You are the most accomplished seducer."

"Are you seduced?" As his lips brushed her ear she yearned to lean back into his embrace.

"No," she said, jerking forward, away from his lethal proximity. "I told you before I would not be."

"And I still think you are wrong."

She had come to this meeting with the intention of kissing him, and she still meant to. But the encounter must be on her terms, not his, at a time of her choosing. Not when her heart fluttered wildly at his nearness and her mind blossomed at the pleasure of his conversation. Not when it was spring and she yearned to be a girl in love instead of a woman out for blood. Not now, when she would be putty in his hands.

"I must speak to you about the children, Your Grace."

He responded with a lavish sigh and sat down opposite her, resting one elegant leg over the other knee. "Very well, Miss Grey. Let us speak of my tiresome sisters. I hope the conversation involves a visit to the theater but I have a feeling it's going to be far more expensive than a box at Drury Lane."

She laughed, trying to relax. "How did you guess? Maria needs new clothes."

"Only Maria?"

"They all do, but especially Maria. She's old enough now that the simple dresses of a young girl are no longer right for her. She needs to be refitted from head to toe."

"And underneath too?"

"I have been at pains to instruct your sisters that one does not discuss undergarments with gentlemen, even brothers."

"By all means, buy her some new stays. You see, Jane, I know all about ladies' intimate necessities." His hot gaze pierced her bosom. "Why do I wager that what you have on under that dreary gown is a good deal less practical?"

"You'll never find out."

His eyes gleamed brighter but he merely shook his head. "Fit them all out, and buy yourself a gown or two as well. I can stand the expense."

"That wouldn't be proper."

"You grow tedious on the subject. You know I do not believe either of us slaves to propriety."

How could she argue? For her, true propriety was a distant memory. Even if Denford couldn't be sure, he seemed to have detected her lack of virtue. "When I accompany you to the theater I expect you *all* to be dressed as befits a party of ladies escorted by a duke. Don't forget that I am a duke. A very important man."

"So you will take us to the theater?" she asked, taken aback and a little disappointed by his kiss-less capitulation.

"I have already reserved the box. I knew you'd give in."

"I haven't given in, you have."

His grin was positively devilish. "No theater, no new clothes. No kiss, no theater. Ergo, no kiss, no new clothes."

"You are an evil man."

"I believe you like me for it."

Adopting the pose of a martyr, she stood, arms at her side and chin raised. "Get on with it, then."

"You are supposed to kiss me."

"Make me."

His lips curved deliciously. "Don't worry, dear Jane. I will."

Towering over her like a beautiful dark angel, he stood close enough to overwhelm her without contact. Her throat tightened and her breasts rose and fell, silently begging him to touch them. She glanced up, then hastily lowered her eyes, refusing to reveal a desire that equaled, perhaps even exceeded, his own. When he raised his hands she closed her eyes tight to concentrate on suppressing a moan of longing. In the dark she felt fingers on her hair, soft as a gentle breeze.

"Why do you dress your hair like a Botticelli goddess?" The bass voice vibrated the strings of her heart. "Are you trying to drive me mad?"

"Why do you keep yours long?"

"Because it pleases me to flout the fashion."

"And it pleases me to follow it."

"I will cut mine if you wish it."

No! She didn't say it aloud, merely envisioned loosening the queue and threading her finger through the black tresses. "Don't do anything on my account."

He held her head now, his thumbs caressing her cheekbones. "I don't know the limits of what I would do for you. You frighten me."

Not as much, surely, as he frightened her. "That's very good, Your Grace, very seductive," she replied mockingly.

"Julian. Say it." A finger traced the rim of her mouth. "Say it."

"I will not."

"Why do you have to be so difficult?" A butterfly kiss landed on each eyelid. "Look at me and tell me what you want."

Instead she clenched her eyes shut and choked back a sob. Why didn't he get on and kiss her? Then she would flee the room before giving in to her devastating desire to sink into the golden cushions of the divan, raise her skirts, and beg him to fill her, hard and fast, to assuage the ache that burned inside her. "Kiss me," she said. *Take me*, she did not.

At long last his lips met hers, but in a sad, pathetic, meaningless brush of a kiss that did nothing but stoke her frustration.

"Damn you, kiss me," she cried.

"Damn you, *Julian*."

"Damn you, Your Grace. Kiss me. And put your arms about me too."

He allowed her one victory because she had rendered him a greater one. With a shudder of relief she was pulled against his chest and enclosed by an arm like an iron band, while his other hand raised her chin.

But he didn't kiss her. After a little while, during which their hearts thumped in counterpoint in the silent room, she gave in and looked at him. Oh, but she would drown in those magnificent eyes. Before she could talk herself out of it, she seized his head and pulled his mouth down onto her parted lips and knew that she had never been kissed before.

The texture of his lips, his spicy taste spoiled her for any kiss, past or future. It was perfect and mind numbing and body awakening and utterly dangerous. He possessed her and she owned him back in blazing mutual exploration. Her fingers clawed his scalp to tug him closer, as though she would consume him as she felt consumed, by heat and the drumbeat of surging desire.

In a second's pause for breath he murmured her name. *Jane Jane Jane*. His hand spread tingles along the sensitive skin of her neck and reached into the high but loose bodice of her gown. Ravished by joy, she clung harder to stay upright and demanded the return of his mouth.

Only when she felt her skirts shift upward did a modicum of reality penetrate the sensual fog that had invaded her brain. When she thrust aside his questing hand he withdrew from the kiss and his dark tones flooded her ears. "Let me, Jane. Please. Let me lay you on golden cushions and pleasure you until you scream." His hand on her bottom reaching between her legs gave her a taste of what he promised and she wanted desperately to accept.

With strength that almost slew her to summon, she stepped away and turned her back. Easier to say no away from his touch and the lure of his dark beauty. "You had your kiss, Your Grace."

"I want more." His words were ragged, his breathing rapid.

"You cannot have it. I will not let you ruin me."

"I think you were already *ruined*. I say that not as an insult but as a happy circumstance that means we can indulge ourselves without guilt. I am right in saying you are no innocent, am I not?"

"My past is none of your affair, Your Grace."

Not his business, but the reason she had come to his house, and she mustn't let herself forget it. Besides, to him she was just a servant whose convenient lack of virtue meant that he could seduce her without compunction and later discard her with impunity. If that wasn't enough, there was the uncomfortable fact that she had a large knife in her room with which she intended to murder his cousin and heir.

She smoothed her skirts and schooled her features to serenity. "Please speak to Mr. Blackett about the bills for your sisters' clothing. And send me a message with the date of our engagement at the theater."

Chapter 8

With an orgy of shopping in the week leading up to an evening at Drury Lane, excitement in the nursery floor of Fortescue House reached a fever pitch. A dressmaker had been found and bribed to deliver new gowns at impossible speed. Maria talked of nothing but silks and sarcenets and Brussels spot muslin and vandyked edges. Confident that the eldest Osbourne had, for the moment, put the ineligible Mr. Norville to the back of her mind, Jane entered into the selection of suitable garments for a fifteen-year-old with only an occasional unexpressed sigh of longing. She loved new clothes, and the London shops weren't to be sneezed at. This came as a surprise to her Parisian nose that expected to sneeze a good deal at the inferior merchandise of an inferior capital.

"You would look beautiful in that," Maria said when she saw her governess wistfully fingering a length of silver tissue threaded with gold at Bow's Silk Warehouse. "I daresay Julian wouldn't notice if we added a gown for you to the bill."

Julian would notice all right. Accepting his gift of new clothes would be tantamount to accepting his offer of other attentions.

"That would be dishonest," she said. "I have a perfectly good evening gown suitable to my station." It was a shabby thing, the first Henri had bought her, and thoroughly out of fashion.

"I'm sure you will look very pretty." Maria whirled about, hugging the bolt of white silk they'd selected for her. "Oh, Miss Grey, I am so happy I could die!"

Laura was happy too, because her governess was too busy to make her practice long division; Oliver Bream was happy because when he turned up for lessons his charges were out shopping and he got paid for doing nothing. The new nursery maid was happy because she had an undemanding job in a warm house. Nurse Bride slept happily through everything.

Whether the Duke of Denford was happy, Jane didn't know. She hadn't seen him since the night of the kiss. A message delivered via Mr. Blackett informed her that he had gone out of town for a few days.

Jane hadn't failed to notice that someone was distinctly unhappy. Fenella had chosen a gown for the theater, guided by Jane into a soft pink. The other two girls, with their black hair and flawless white skin, could carry off any shade; Fenella needed something that wouldn't fight her muted coloring.

The afternoon before the great day, all the

children bathed and washed their hair in the big tub next to the nursery fire. Jane and Maria were debating the merits of different hairstyles when an unmistakable sob came from Fenella's room. Jane found her lying on her bed dressed only in a wrapper, weeping piteously.

"What is it?"

Addressed to the pillow, the response was incomprehensible. Jane sat on the bed and pulled the girl into her arms. *"Ma chérie,"* she said, "what can be so dreadful when you have a new gown and tomorrow your brother is taking us to the theater? Are you unwell?"

"I don't want to go to the theater."

"But you've been looking forward to it! You will sit in a fine box in a new gown and see the most famous actress in England."

"I'm ugly!" Fenella wailed. "Everyone will look at me and think I'm so plain compared to the others. Maria and Laura are pretty like Mama, and Julian looks like her too. Everyone will be laughing at me because I'm the ugly sister. Why do I have to look like this?"

There was no use pointing out that few people in the theater would be terribly interested in a thirteen-year-old, even if her brother was a duke. "You will look lovely in your new gown. Besides, you won't be the only one left out. I'm very ordinary."

Fenella gave a choke of surprise. "You, Miss Grey? You are beautiful. Almost as beautiful as Mama."

"Put on your slippers and come with me. I have something to show you."

When they reached Jane's boudoir, she told Fenella to wait while she stripped to her shift and let down her hair. "Now," she said, sitting on the padded bench before her dressing table, "sit beside me and let us look in the mirror."

Even in the soft glass that Jane knew to be quite flattering, Fenella was an unprepossessing sight with her fine hair clinging to her scalp and an expression that had relaxed from pure misery to sulky skepticism. "I look horrid," she said, screwing up her mouth and nose.

"You do if you look like this." Jane imitated the monstrous pout. "Anyone would." She swept her hair back from her face and arranged her features in an approximation of Fenella's now less exaggerated scowl. "Do I look beautiful now?"

"No. You look quite ordinary."

"That is because I'm quite an ordinary-looking person. Now watch."

She picked up a comb and teased her hair so that it framed her face in a misty cloud. And she smiled. "What do you think?"

"Now you are quite pretty."

"I'll be prettier still when I dress." She took a fresh muslin fichu treaded with blue ribbon and arranged it over her shoulders. "I'm a governess so I do not have fine clothes, but that doesn't mean I can't look nice. You are the sister of a duke and your brother has given permission to buy whatever you need. You will look even better."

"I won't. I looked at myself in the long glass in my new gown and I appeared just like I always do."

"First let us arrange your hair more becomingly. Like mine, yours does not curl much so we must contrive."

When she was a gawky thirteen-year-old she'd had a loving mother to help smooth the awkward edges and build up confidence in her appearance. And she hadn't been cursed with beauties as sisters; the three Falleron girls had been peas in a pod. Combing volume into Fenella's hair and embellishing it with ribbons was a bittersweet experience. She couldn't help remembering the last time she'd done Marie-Thérèse's hair, the two girls sitting in their dressing room and pretending to be grown up. It was a happy memory and a terrible one. A short time afterward Marie-Thérèse was dead and she, Jeanne, was a whore.

"I am going to make you beautiful," she said fiercely.

The expression in Fenella's eyes battered at her heart. The girl was staring at her reflection with a desperate hope. Blinking back tears, Jane set to work.

"*Voilà*," she said, finally. "What do you think? Do you not look pretty?"

"I look better," Fenella said slowly, "but still not pretty."

"That's because you do not smile, *chérie*. Everyone looks pretty when they are happy." She gave her most dazzling smile, contrasting with her companion's mulish frown. "And everyone loves a smiling face. A happy person makes others feel happy."

Fenella pursed her lips. "Why should I smile when I don't want to? Why should I pretend to be happy, just to please others? They don't deserve it."

Because sometimes your life depends on it. Jane thought of Mathieu Picard and his message that "Jane Grey" had the choice between pleasing him, and being turned over to the Committee of Public Safety. Jane had been all smiles with Mathieu.

"Don't do it for them," she said. "Do it for yourself. If your company does not amuse you, think of something that does and smile at that."

"I don't understand."

"Quickly, think of something that makes you happy."

Fenella shut her eyes for a moment, then opened them, with a naughty grin that transformed her face from sulky plainness to a liveliness that made it possible to believe her a member of a very good-looking family.

"Perfect, my love! What are you thinking of?"

The grin turned into a sly little moue that made Jane reassess her opinion that this face would never break hearts. "It is for myself, not you."

"You are an abominable child to throw my words back at me," Jane complained, patting the top of Fenella's head.

"Careful of my hair!"

"Only if you tell me what you smile at."

Fenella's eyes narrowed. The child didn't trust easily. "Do I have to tell you?"

"I would like to know what you are thinking because I like you. I always want to know what my friends think, especially if it's something agreeable. But not unless you wish to tell me."

Fenella's face cleared. "So I don't have to explain what I'm smiling at when someone asks."

"No. In fact a mysterious smile can make people wild with curiosity to know what you are thinking. Let's practice thinking wonderful secret thoughts."

Side by side, they put their elbows on the dressing table, cupped their cheeks, and gazed into the mirror. Jane half lowered her eyelids and thought secret thoughts until she almost forgot her companion. Her mouth formed a half smile and her breath shortened. Tomorrow night she would see the Duke of Denford for the first time in a week. His absence had done nothing to dim the memory of their kiss, or make her less anxious for its repetition. While busy with the children she could put him out of her mind. But in bed at night, without distraction, the thought of him drove her wild.

Denford must surely return home today, and tonight he would want a report on the progress of his sisters. Or he would pretend to. Naturally it was to the benefit of her charges to make sure their brother knew what they were doing, whether he wanted to or not. He needed to hear what amiable girls they were and learn to appreciate them. Family was important, and in the absence of that neglectful mother, Denford and his sisters only had one another. Spending time with the duke was merely doing her duty. There was no reason for any kissing, none at all, unless . . .

"Ooh, Miss Grey! Whatever are you thinking? It must be lovely."

Jane emerged reluctantly from her trance. "It is, *chérie.* And what about you? You look very enigmatic. No one would ever guess what you were thinking."

"I know! It will drive my sisters mad." Fenella wriggled gleefully. "What *were* you thinking, Miss Grey?"

Jane smiled mysteriously. "That's my secret." It was quite impossible to tell Fenella she'd been thinking about doing dark deeds with the girl's brother.

Julian made no effort to find the schedule of the reopening packet boats across the Channel; he preferred to bring the Falleron collection from Belgium by less public means. He was acquainted with a sea captain based near Folkstone who had carried both his person and his goods before, in peacetime and in war.

Inclement spring weather kept him cooling his heels in a Folkstone inn for several days, awaiting the return of the captain and his sloop to port. They made arrangements according to the moon and tide tables, and haggled over the cost of a complicated run that involved waiting an unpredictable length of time off the coast of the Netherlands, and possible interference from

French soldiery, peace or no peace. As a result Julian swayed into Fortescue House in the early afternoon, saddle-sore and still bleary from a late night of sealing the deal with smuggled brandy.

"Send up hot water for a bath," he told the butler. "I'll be dining at home."

"I am aware, Your Grace. Before the theater."

He closed his eyes. That was today?

"He's here! He's here!"

God in heaven, why did girls have to have such piercing voices? Laura tore down the stairs and flung her arms around his waist. "I knew you'd come back in time, even if Fenella said you'd forgotten."

Fenella was no fool.

Looking down at the top of the little girl's head leaning against his midriff, he noted that her hair had been teased into ringlets and threaded with red satin ribbon. He patted her back awkwardly. But she was small and soft and sweet-smelling and pleased to see him, and he wasn't used to being greeted with enthusiasm coming home from a journey. His hand stilled and he felt her childish warmth.

She drew back and grinned up at him, a big, happy smile so like his mother's.

"You're looking very fine, Miss Laura," he said. "Are you going somewhere?"

"You know I am!"

"No, I didn't know. Tell me."

Her forehead creased. "The theater, remember?"

"You're going to the theater?"

"Your Grace, stop teasing." Jane Grey descended the stairs. How did she manage to look like a grand duchess, clad in her plain gown? Like Laura, she seemed pleased to see him. He hoped it was for reasons beyond relief that the theater expedition would not have to be canceled; he'd like to think she'd been anticipating his return for more personal reasons. The sight of her raised his spirits and dissipated his fatigue.

"Of course your brother hasn't forgotten, Laura, even if he is close to tardy. You will have to hurry, Your Grace, if you are to dress and dine and reach Drury Lane by seven o'clock."

"Does she speak to you like that?" he asked Laura.

She giggled. "Of course she does. She's our governess."

"I suppose she's my governess too. She's masterly enough."

"You're too old to need a governess," Laura said, vastly entertained.

"What a pity. Miss Grey, Laura says I don't need a governess. In that case I think you should greet me in the same delightful way that she did."

Jane had reached the bottom of the stairs and stood with her hands on her hips and an air of amused tolerance at his nonsense, a hint of warmth in her smile. This was not a woman disconcerted by the presence of the man with whom she had, the last time they met, exchanged a shattering kiss. Instead she looked stern. "And how was that?"

"I embraced him, Miss Grey," Laura said. "Do you think I should have, since he is a gentleman?"

"It is completely suitable for a sister to greet a brother with pleasure."

"I wasn't sure. My papa never embraced us, but perhaps it is different with brothers."

"It should be different with fathers too," Julian said. As he knew, Osbourne had believed in the proverb "Spare the rod, spoil the child." The idea of a cane to the back of this little creature rekindled the anger against his stepfather that these days mostly lay dormant. Laura looked alarmed at his angry tone, the last thing he wanted. He resumed his teasing voice. "I always enjoy it when ladies hug me," he said with a wink at Laura and a side glance at Jane that he hoped wasn't too smoldering considering the company.

"At what time shall we be ready for the carriage, Your Grace?" Jane asked pointedly.

The notion of postponing tonight's treat was abandoned. He wouldn't risk the displeasure of the governess, and surprisingly he didn't want to disappoint Laura either. "I will order it for six. Can you all be ready to dine with me at five?"

Laura gasped. "Dine with you? Downstairs? Like a grown-up?"

"I believe the occasion merits the dining room. See to it, please," he told the hovering butler. "Now I had better bathe or I won't be fit to be seen in such magnificent company."

They hadn't used the huge dining room in all the time he'd lived at Fortescue House. Leaving the practicalities of preparing the room for a meal in under two hours to his staff, he climbed into a tub and let hot water melt away his aches and dispel the fumes of overindulgence from his brain. The position of the tub gave him an excellent view of the door into the duchess's chamber.

Jane's chamber.

Why did he find Jane Grey so alluring? He'd like to bed her, of course, but that was not unusual. The depth of his fascination could not be ascribed to sensual desire alone, or even to a tendre for a charming and intelligent woman. An air of mystery was part of it. He didn't know much about her, and some of what she'd told him of her history seemed invented. He was curious about the facts of her past, yes. But he also wanted to understand *her.* Accustomed as he was to alarming people, he knew that Jane Grey, an employee, wasn't the least bit intimidated. He'd wager it had taken her less than five minutes to see through the affectations he'd cultivated as a young man and which had become second nature to him. She understood him thoroughly.

He suspected he'd never learn what went on behind the smiles and frowns unless she wanted him to. She struck him as a woman who exercised an unusual degree of control over herself and the world's perception of her. Breaking through that control and discovering the woman beneath would be an ambition worth achieving.

As he dressed for dinner he thought about varying his unrelieved black with something surprising, a red waistcoat perhaps. But Jane would merely smile her particular knowing smile to tell him she saw what he was up to and she was not surprised.

At the appointed hour he was ready in the hall. Maria led the procession down the curving staircase, followed shortly afterward by Fenella. Their new gowns in pale colors were appropriate to their age and station, as were their coiffures. As usual, Jane Grey had proven a worthy governess. Maria, the beauty, bore herself with the natural confidence of one who had never failed to please. But even Fenella looked pretty this evening with none of her habitual sulkiness. Laura brought up the rear, stepping carefully with a hand on the banister, her head held high and her eyes shining with excitement.

Julian bowed deeply. "Ladies. Your beauty renders me speechless."

Laura giggled; Maria greeted the compliment with a graceful curtsey and a murmured thank-you; Fenella merely tilted her head in exactly the way her governess did and smiled faintly.

"Where is Miss Grey?" he asked. "We must go up to dinner if we are not to be late."

"Why are we in the hall if we are eating upstairs in the dining room?" Laura asked.

"I knew your new gowns would show to advantage while you descended the stairs and I wanted to admire them, and you."

He'd sent a message to Jane to arrange the little procession. He might not understand everything that went on in the head of a certain governess but he was familiar with women. His sisters were women, small ones, and he understood *them*. But where the devil was Jane? With a twinge of anxiety he remembered her refusal to let him buy her a gown. Was she planning to recuse herself on the grounds of not being correctly dressed? The bargain had been that she would be a member of the theater party. He'd fetch her and carry her downstairs, in her nightgown if necessary.

Perhaps unfortunately, it wasn't necessary. He sensed a presence on the first floor landing and watched her make her own descent.

"Your Grace." Unlike her charges she wasn't trying to impress him. She wasn't a child but a grown woman of transcendent grace who held herself like a queen.

As she approached, the blur of sensual pleasure at her general appearance resolved into appreciation of the details. Her hair had been coaxed into a cluster of curls and confined by an ivory satin bandeau that matched her slippers. The headpiece was her only ornament, but she didn't need jewelry, any more than she needed a new gown, to look infinitely desirable. Jane Grey did indeed own an evening gown. For the first time he was treated to the sight of the bare skin of her neck and chest and the swell of breasts emerging from the confinement of a low bodice. The gown was old, or old in fashion, a simple affair of light blue material, a muslin or cambric, definitely not silk. A wide sash in a darker blue circled her natural waist, not the newer mode just below the bosom, matching a scattering of flowers embroidered around the hem. Best of all, the feature that sent blood rushing hot through his veins, was the fullness of the skirt. Yellow silk cushions intruded into his vision and his fingers itched to grasp those gathered ells of cloth and throw them over her head.

Behaving with indifference was a trial when Jane's first reaction on seeing Denford was to throw herself at him and resume the kiss where it had ended. Using all her skills, even down to the subtle application of eyelash blacking and rouge, was not sensible behavior for a governess, especially one who really shouldn't end up in the bed of her employer, but it had been months since she'd been anywhere just for pleasure. More than pleasure. She'd been sure before the evening began that a visit to the theater with the Duke of Denford and his sisters would beat dining in one of Paris's best restaurants with Henri and his political cronies.

Dinner presented a new challenge to her outward display of calm. The dining room turned out to be magnificent, plastered and gilded in the French style. Seated at the table, reduced to its smallest dimension, brought back meals in the beautiful *salle à manger* at her family's lost estate. In Paris the marquis and his wife dined with their children only on feast days; in the country they lived *en famille* every day. Jane couldn't help thinking of the three Falleron daughters seated with their parents, just as the Osbournes now sat with the Duke of Denford. And with her.

Not that Denford was anything like her father,

a kindly man and doting father who failed for too long to understand the magnitude of the cataclysm that had shaken his world. The Duke of Denford was much cleverer than the Marquis de Falleron; he wouldn't have been taken in by the scoundrel who, ironically, happened to be his heir. Papa was of course older than the man seated at the head of the table and he never abandoned the colorful silks and powdered hair of the French court. She, on the other hand, looked very like the marquise, although Maman wouldn't have been seen dead in a garment with fraying seams and a patch on the skirt. But she'd done many things that would have appalled her fastidious mother, things far worse than wearing an old gown.

Jane had given the girls instructions about dinner table conversation, but Maria seemed intimidated by the grandeur of her surroundings while Fenella, bless her, was practicing her mysterious smile. It was up to Laura, who had decided that her brother the duke was the best man in the entire world, to lead the way, commenting on the announcement in that morning's newspaper that the play for tonight's performance had been changed.

"I'm not too sorry that we shall not see *Henry VIII*. We read some of the play with Miss Grey and it was hard to understand."

"In that case," the duke said, "I will cease repining that Mrs. Siddons is ill."

"*The Rivals* sounds very amusing," Jane said. "Henry VIII does not seem to have been an amiable man and I am sure we will all enjoy a comedy instead."

"I know *Maria* will enjoy it," Laura said. "Mr. Bream told us during our drawing lesson that the play has *lovers* in it."

"You don't know what you are talking about," Maria said hastily, casting a guilty glance at her brother. Apparently Laura knew about her recent indiscretions, and if she didn't stop being indiscreet herself, Denford would too. "I'm sure I don't care about such things. I would have enjoyed the tragedy very much. Much as we may deplore King Henry's behavior toward Queen Catherine, we cannot regret the divorce since it was the cause of England breaking away from Rome."

Jane had been mildly surprised to learn that the Osbournes were not Catholic; apparently they had Protestants in Ireland too. In revolutionary Paris, religion had been anathema; even when it returned, Jane had no further truck with a God who would allow such horrors. Accompanying the girls to a service at St. George's, she'd been reassured to find the Church of England mercifully lacking in fervor.

Laura rolled her eyes at Maria's piety. "Who cares about *that*? Mr. Bream says there will be fighting with swords too. I hope no one will be killed."

"Don't be foolish," Maria said. "It's a play, not real."

"They might slip."

Before Jane could intervene, the duke rumbled into the melee. "You are quiet, Fenella, but I see you smile. Are you pleased about the change from tragedy to comedy or diverted by your sisters' squabble?"

Fenella said nothing, merely tilted her head at him and smiled some more. While applauding her efforts, Jane hadn't intended her to refuse to answer direct questions in polite company.

Denford looked amused. "A lady of mystery, I see. Very clever. Now we'll all wonder what pearls of wisdom you refuse to share."

"She's been doing that all day," Laura pointed out. "I think she looks stupid."

"It isn't polite to call your sister stupid," Jane said.

Maria narrowed her eyes at Fenella. "It isn't polite for Fenella to laugh at me. She *has* been doing it all day and I wish she would stop. Make her stop, Miss Grey."

"Why don't you ask her yourself, politely."

Maria took a deep breath. "Fenella," she enunciated carefully. "Please will you take that look off your face. I know you do it to annoy me."

"I never even think about you," Fenella said haughtily, and continued to eat her soup between smirks.

Wanting to laugh was not a governess's appropriate response. A quick glance at Denford was almost enough to set Jane off into peals, so she avoided his eye and took a sip of wine. "That is quite enough, young ladies. This is a fine burgundy, Your Grace. Do you know the vintage?"

"Wine is enjoyable to drink but boring to talk about," he said. "I'd rather discuss Fenella's smile. I am irresistibly drawn to a mystery."

"What kind of mystery do you think I am hiding?" Fenella asked.

"I have no idea, but I could doubtless discover if I set my mind to it."

"I can keep a secret."

"I've never met a woman who could, which is a pity. The unexplained is much more interesting than the obvious."

Jane felt his gaze pierce her as he spoke, as though probing *her* secrets.

"Don't you think Miss Grey looks beautiful, Julian?" Fenella asked. The girl was much too perceptive now that she was emerging from her self-pitying gloom.

"Miss Grey knows what I think."

Jane needed to control the conversation before the girls got the idea that something was going on between their brother and the governess. They might have lived quiet lives in Ireland but they weren't entirely naïve. They absolutely did not need to hear His Grace's thoughts on the subject. "Let us agree that we all look our best tonight, as is proper to honor His Grace for his immense kindness in taking us to Drury Lane."

"His Grace is most honored," he drawled.

"Do you think Julian looks his best too?" Fenella asked, still on the scent.

"I do," Laura piped up. "Even if he is always in black, like a parson."

"I don't think anyone has ever compared me to a parson."

"A crow then," Fenella said. "Why do you always wear black?"

"I'm in mourning for my lost youth."

"When did you lose it?" Laura asked.

"When I was twenty."

"What happened?"

"I should have said my twenty-first birthday, of course. That's when we all lose our youth."

"Is that when you started carrying your black walking stick?" Denford's cane was a favorite topic in the nursery.

"Exactly. As soon as I reached my majority I could no longer walk without help. Very sad."

The girls all giggled, even Maria.

"I'm not going to wear black when I'm twenty-one," Laura declared. "I'm going to have a red dress as soon as I'm old enough and don't have to wear pale colors because Miss Grey says they are correct for a *jeune fille*. Why do you sometimes speak in French, Miss Grey, and call me *chérie*?"

"Because I lived on a partly French island and because I am teaching you French."

"I don't like French," Laura muttered, not news to her governess.

"When I'm grown up I'm going to speak French and wear black gowns and live on an island with crocodiles and ostriches," Fenella said. "I'm going to be just like Julian and Miss Grey."

"I can assure you, Fenella, that *I* have never lived on an island with such exotic beasts. Neither have I ever worn a black gown," the duke said.

The quizzical look he gave her made Jane wonder a little about the stories she'd told about the flora and fauna of Saint Lucia. Did these creatures actually live there, or anywhere in the West Indies? And if not, would Denford know?

Chapter 9

Waiting for the curtain to rise, the three young ladies sat in the front of the box, awed by the magnificence of the theater. Exclamations of wonder at the decorations, the chandeliers, the huge audience punctuated the air. Jane sat behind them in the shadows. Unlike the Misses Osbourne she had attended the theater before, often; she was far more aware of Denford's dark presence occupying the plush chair next to hers than of the spectacle before them.

"What do you think of the Theatre Royal, Drury Lane, Miss Grey?" His deep voice lent the question a disproportionate significance. She felt the weight in her chest that was becoming familiar in his presence.

"It's very large."

"The largest in Europe, so it is said. Perhaps there is something larger in the Americas. On the island of Saint Lucia, for instance."

Unable to detect any motive in the remark, beyond a gentle teasing, Jane felt an unrestrained smile form. Denford had been delightful with his sisters at dinner. She *liked* him, as well as finding him desirable. "The theater there is not quite as large as this."

"Do you think it elegant?"

"It's well enough." She wondered if Denford had been to the theater in Paris.

"You're quite hard to impress. What do you think of the audience? Do you find our London notables fashionable enough for you?"

"Since my gown is years old, I am hardly in a position to decry their à la modality."

"You are more refined in your old gown than a roomful of London beauties. How do you manage that, Jane? How do you make other women look shabby?"

It was frightening how much the compliment pleased her. With the children absorbed by their surroundings, sitting next to Denford in the dim recesses of the box felt almost like being alone. "You talk nonsense, Your Grace."

"You also manage to make those two words sound like a cross between an insult and a caress."

Jane, who thought herself hardened beyond blushing, felt her cheeks warm. She hadn't been conscious of it, but that was exactly how she said *Your Grace*. "You have never seen me in company of ladies of the *ton*. I assure you, *sir*, I would look like nothing in comparison."

Denford shook his head, and her fingers itched to touch his thick hair. When he placed his hand on her shoulder, she almost jumped out of the box and flew over the heads of the girls into the crowded pit. "Look around you," he said, steering her attention back to the audience. "Especially at the second tier where the fashionables take their boxes. Tell me if you see a lady whose appearance meets your standards of elegance."

"They are too far away."

"So much the better. You may judge a lady's air of fashion without the unfortunate details like pockmarks and unskilled laundry."

"Later. The play is starting."

Jane would have enjoyed Sheridan's comedy more without the distracting presence of the duke, but not the evening. Half closing her eyes, she let herself imagine that all the horrors had never occurred and her life had proceeded as planned from childhood. She might very well be sitting in a theater with a duke, but the theater would be in Paris and the duke would be Monsieur le Duc to whom she had been betrothed as a child. She wondered what had happened to him; she never heard that Etienne de Fleurigny had lost his head. Very likely he had joined the stream of émigrés to Germany, Austria, or even England. She used to weave fancies about Etienne, creating a figure of romance out of a dull young man, very rich and of impeccable birth, but with a short, stout figure and undistinguished features. Doubtless they would have been content together, but would he ever have sent blood coursing through her veins and her heart beating a tattoo against her ribs the way Denford did?

The duke beside her this evening was not her

husband and never would be. Dukes did not wed governesses. Tonight was but a moment, a lovely byway from the grim path that had brought her to England. She must not allow herself to forget. She thought of Papa and Maman, Marie-Thérèse and Antoinette. She thought of the guillotine, that efficient killing machine, towering over the Place de la Révolution, as Place Louis XV had been renamed. And closed her eyes tight to dispel the painful visions that sometimes haunted her dreams and waking hours.

"Are you well?" Denford had been watching her. "Did something upset you?"

"Someone walked over my grave, that is all. Foolish when the play is so amusing."

"You look pale. Perhaps we are working you too hard."

"It's a hard life being a governess," she said with a wan smile. "I sleep in a duchess's bed, dine with a duke, and attend the theater in a box."

"We're almost at the end of the act. I shall fetch you a glass of wine."

When the curtain fell Denford rose. "Miss Grey is feeling faint," he said. "We shall leave her in peace for a spell, and I will show you the public foyer."

It made an incongruous sight as he escorted the girls from the box—the tall, lean nobleman like a great black bird of prey herding a small flock of ducks, but there was a rightness to it.

Not wanting again to succumb to the weakness of her emotions, she amused herself as Denford had suggested, appraising the clothing and appearance of the ladies in the opposite boxes.

Nothing she saw suggested that her countrywomen need fear for their long-held reputation as exemplars of fashion. It did her French soul good to criticize the English, who tended toward the opposing faults of dowdiness and excessive ornamentation. Really, that woman in red silk, gilt lace, a ruby necklace, and no fewer than three giant ostrich plumes in her black hair needed some lessons in restraint.

She was a handsome lady, even a beauty, in the prime of life rather than the first blush of youth. But her ensemble screamed that she was available for something more than morning calls and teacups. Perhaps she was a courtesan and the effect was intentional. Jane stood and moved to the front of the box to get a closer look at her, and at the two gentlemen in the woman's box. One was an elderly man, quietly but finely turned out. Husband or protector, depending on which side of respectability the lady in red resided. The other man caused Jane to stumble backward, collapse into her seat, and slide her chair as far back as it would go. She hardly dared look lest he notice and recognize her.

In an instant, everything she had assumed about being alone and without family changed. Her second cousin Louis was in London, seated only a few yards away.

She'd never learned what happened to him but he must have escaped. He could have been in London all this time. Peering across at the other box, she found him deep in conversation with the red lady. He was almost forty now but still the handsome man who had romanced half the members of the court, including the queen herself according to some rumors. Not that anyone had told Jane about *that*, but she had a way of seeing and hearing what went on in the house. That's how she knew about Mr. Fortescue and Papa's worries. And how she knew that Maman, who would never openly speak ill of a cousin, disliked and distrusted Louis de Falleron. Papa had his reservations, but he liked everyone, and Louis was close family and therefore to be loved and respected.

Her doubt about Louis's character wasn't the only reason she instinctively shrank from revealing her presence to him. In fact she was tempted to tear out of the box, find her cousin, and place her troubles and her future in his hands. Louis was the Marquis de Falleron now and it was his duty to avenge her family, her right as a Falleron to his protection. Yet she hesitated. Louis might not see things as she did, might even refuse to believe that Charles Fortescue was responsible and needed to pay. And she would have to confess to him that she'd surrendered her virtue in exchange for her life.

A footman entered the box bearing a glass of red wine with His Grace's compliments. Coming on top of her weakness in the face of her cousin's presence, the simple act of kindness almost undid her. For nine years she had lived under the care and protection of first Mathieu, then Henri, but she had essentially been alone. The innocent fifteen-year-old had to draw on strength and cunning for which her pampered upbringing had ill prepared her.

Fortescue House was not her home.

The Osbourne girls were not her sisters.

The Duke of Denford was not her love.

This was a small, happy respite, a reminder of a life she could never have back. And once her task had been accomplished her life of any kind might well be over.

Fenella led the party back into the box. Seeing the girl look pretty and happy shouldn't make her want to weep.

"Are you feeling better, Miss Grey?" she asked.

Jane wrenched her features into her brightest smile. "Much better, thank you, Fenella."

The girls clustered around her while Denford loomed in the doorway, back straight, one hand on the silver handle of his unnecessary cane. His blue eyes gleamed with neither mockery nor desire but genuine concern for her. "Do you wish to go home?"

"Certainly not. It was nothing but a moment's headache. The wine has revived me and I wouldn't dream of missing the rest of the play. I have been admiring the ladies' dress, as you recommended."

"You must tell me which you find most admirable."

The girls, newly awakened to the joys of dressing up, wanted to join the game. They examined the opposite tier of boxes, commenting on the gowns of the occupants and laughing a good deal. By the time they reached the red lady's box, Louis had left. Jane felt the tension drain out of her.

"That is the most extraordinary costume in the theater tonight," she said. "Better than anything on the stage. What do you think?"

Maria gasped. "She is wearing red gloves. Is that quite proper?"

Laura, nine-year-old magpie that she was, loved them.

"You wouldn't wear something like that, would you, Miss Grey?" Fenella asked.

"She is beautiful, I think," Jane said, "and it is a striking ensemble, but lacking in subtlety."

"If that garment were a weapon," Denford said, "it would be a club."

"Do you know her?" Jane asked, alerted by a trace of bitterness in his voice.

"We are acquainted though not, I am happy to say, intimately." Jane felt an irrational relief at the assertion. "Lady Belinda Radcliffe is a notable hostess with a very large house in Grosvenor Square."

"Lady . . ." Jane murmured.

"Did you think her a *putain*?" he asked. Jane was glad to see the girls look puzzled by the French word for *prostitute*. "You wouldn't be far wrong for all her high birth. I have it on good authority that her husband sometimes acts the pander."

"Is that him with her?"

"Yes, that's Sir Richard Radcliffe, one of the vilest men in England. If there was any justice he would be hanging from the gibbet."

"I am surprised to hear you speak so harshly. What has this Radcliffe done?"

"Nothing I can prove. He remains a pillar of the Foreign Office, but one day, I swear, he will pay."

Chapter 10

Julian had wanted to break through Jane Grey's controlled surface. He'd anticipated unleashing the passion he was convinced lay beneath the façade. The result would be a glorious end to his current bout of celibacy. When at Drury Lane, through no discernible action on his part, he'd seen the veil slip, her distress had affected him in a more emotional and less earthy manner. He didn't believe her truly unwell but he could tell she was profoundly upset. An urge to comfort and protect seized him, along with a desire to appoint himself her champion against any threat.

This unprecedented reaction unsettled him so much that after their return to Hanover Square he let her retire, instead of inviting her to the library for a thorough report on the state of her pupils, followed by brandy and a tumble of skirt and petticoats and golden silk cushions.

Three days later he returned from a long overdue visit to Denford Castle, dealing with estate affairs. More awaited him. As he removed his topcoat and hat, Blackett followed him through the front door. "I am glad to see you back, Your Grace. I have several urgent letters awaiting your signature."

"I hope this won't take long. Bring them to the library. No, I'll come to your office. It's closer."

"How was it at Denford?" Blackett asked.

"As usual," he said, not an entirely truthful answer. For the first time he had looked at the medieval pile as a residence rather than a drain on his purse. The possibilities of the Long Gallery particularly intrigued him and he had formed an inkling of a plan. First he had to make it to Belgium and back.

"We used to enjoy the summers there. There was always so much to do for all the cousins." Julian caught the wistfulness in Blackett's voice. The old duke had kept open house for the Fortescue family. Julian, however, had been a distant enough cousin to reside outside the charmed circle. He also had the impression his father had disgraced himself. Or perhaps no one had ever thought to tell him that he was welcome.

"You'll be there this year," he said carelessly. "We'll be going down in a couple of months." It was absurd to resent poor Blackett, who was as much a victim of capricious laws of inheritance as Julian was the unwitting beneficiary. He was also a competent secretary and, Julian had to admit, his knowledge of Fortescue history and tradition could be useful.

Blackett's obvious pleasure touched him. Was he going soft in his old age? Not so. Blackett held the key to cordial relations with the Fortescue family, that was all.

He signed the last letter with a flourish. "Those reports can wait," he said. He was too restless to concentrate. Why not step up to the nursery and tell his sisters that they would be spending the summer in Sussex? At Denford there were dogs and cats and horses, which would please the girls, though that wasn't the reason for his visit. Definitely not. When the girls were pleased, so was their governess. That was all.

The intensity of his disappointment when he entered the schoolroom warned him that he was in trouble. He found the girls hard at work and no sign of Jane.

"Where is Miss Grey?" he demanded.

"She had to go out. She had an appointment."

An appointment? What the devil did a governess need with an appointment, unless she was ill? In that case a physician would be summoned to the house. Possibilities ran through his brain. She was looking for a different position. She was a Catholic and had gone to confession. She was being fitted by a corset maker with new undergarments especially for him. None of these ideas, conceived in reverse order of desirability, seemed likely.

"Where did she go?"

"She didn't tell us," Laura said.

Someone else was missing. "Where is Fenella?"

"I don't know," Laura said, all innocence. Maria merely shrugged.

"Fenella!" he shouted.

Nurse Bride, who was sleeping in the corner,

twitched but didn't wake up; of the new nursery maid there was no sign. "Where is . . ." Damnation, he had no idea of her name. "Where is the nursery maid?"

"Susan?" Maria said. "She was here a minute ago."

Julian went out into the passage, trying to stay calm. It was probably nothing, merely Fenella playing her old tricks. But the girl should not have been allowed to go out alone. "Fenella! Susan!" he roared.

The maid, a sensible-looking woman who didn't look as though she'd suffer nonsense, emerged from a closet carrying a pile of clothes. Eyes widening at the unaccustomed sight of the master of the house, she bobbed a curtsey while her burden teetered.

"Where is Miss Fenella?"

"She told me she was going with Miss Grey, Your Grace."

"And did Miss Grey tell you she was taking Miss Fenella?"

"I didn't think to ask, sir."

He returned to the schoolroom, where the exchange would have been perfectly audible. Laura dipped her pen into the ink pot and began to write with exaggerated attention. Maria appeared engrossed in a book.

"Where is she? Is she with Miss Grey? I want the truth." Silence. "I admire your sisterly loyalty, when you aren't fighting like gamecocks, but this isn't a game. You need to tell me where Fenella went. Do I have to remind you again that the streets of London are not safe for a young woman alone?"

Maria cracked first. "She went to see the horses."

He'd kill Fenella for her disobedience but he was also relieved; she was unlikely to encounter much harm in the mews where some of his own servants lurked.

"My horses?" he said, to make sure.

"At the Royal Stables."

Hell and damnation! "That's all the way to Charing Cross. When did she leave and did she go alone?"

By now Laura seemed frightened, as well she should. "She went out about an hour ago, just after Miss Grey left. She gave Jemmy part of her pin money to show her the way."

Jemmy, the stable lad, was about to have his neck wrung. Julian strode out of the house, swinging his cane. Electing to walk, faster in the traffic-clogged streets, he kept a weather eye out for Fenella, praying she was on her way home safe and sound. The stables, situated in the King's Mews, were open to the public and full of royal servants, who would surely protect a genteel-looking girl. But there were some rough alleys along the route, and the space in front of the stables, one of London's largest open spaces, was usually packed with all sorts of hawkers, loungers, pickpockets, and other riffraff.

As he tore down to Piccadilly toward Leicester Square, it wasn't casual thieves that made him terrified for Fenella's safety. Whoever had been after the Falleron collection a year ago—most likely Sir Richard Radcliffe—had tried to use Julian's affection for Cynthia Windermere to obtain the pictures. Now, by publicly parading his sisters at the theater, he'd offered his enemy a new group of hostages. Radcliffe must have seen them at Drury Lane. Julian also hadn't forgotten the young man he'd spotted hanging around Fortescue House. He could be a spy for Radcliffe, awaiting the opportunity to snatch one of the girls. With cold anger gripping his chest, Julian increased his pace.

And where, in the name of God, was Jane Grey, who had been engaged to look after his sisters?

Reaching Charing Cross, Julian shouldered his way through the throng, ignoring the importunities of a man hawking matches and a girl with a basket of violets. Closer to the arched entrance to the stable yard, the crowd thinned.

"Have you seen a young lady and a boy recently?" he asked a servant in the king's livery who appeared to be on guard duty. "She is thirteen years old. I'm afraid I cannot tell you how she is dressed."

"We don't allow a young person to visit the stables without proper escort or introduction."

An odd answer since Julian hadn't asked if Fenella had applied for entrance. He was about to go ducal on the fellow when it occurred to him that it would be better if news of Fenella's escapade didn't leak out. Instead he reached into his pocket for a coin. "I am the young lady's brother."

"Congratulations, sir. You come from a generous family."

Deducing that Fenella, a young lady of enterprise, had bribed her way into the stables, Julian forked over half a crown. "Had you seen such a pair, would they still be inside?"

"I can't be certain, mind you, but they could have left a few minutes ago. That way." The guard pointed in the direction of Whitehall, not the route home. Damnation! What was the girl up to now?

Back into the crowd he surged. "Blimey, it's the devil 'imself," cried an alarmed costermonger. Others felt the same way and the crowd parted like the Red Sea to reveal Miss Fenella Osbourne being mauled by a very large man. She was giving a good account of herself, wriggling like an eel to escape his meaty grasp on her upper arms while kicking at his ankles. Jemmy the stable boy, who had not been chosen for his size, flailed at the assailant's back with his small fists. The pair of them might as well have been stingless gnats. The giant, protected from identification by a wide-brimmed hat worn low over his forehead and a long coat that disguised his other garments, though not his girth and muscles, was untroubled by the counterattacks, or by passersby, who hesitated to intervene against such a fearsome brute.

Julian had no illusions that his pugilistic skills would match this fellow's strength. He gripped his cane and struck the man smartly at the side of one knee and then the other. He would have aimed higher for a more sensitive spot but Fenella was in the way.

"Jemmy, find the Watch," he ordered the boy, who was momentarily turned to stone by the arrival of his master. "You! Let her go."

Either Julian looked sufficiently menacing or

the man preferred not to fight. Either way, it wasn't necessary to use his weapon in a crowded place. Fenella's attacker threw her at Julian and, in the time it took the latter to regain his balance, dodged behind a pieman's cart, and streaked at impressive speed into one of the dark side streets around the mews. With little chance of catching the miscreant, Julian told the stable lad not to bother with the authorities and turned his wrath on his sister, her bonnet awry and pelisse missing half its buttons, who glared at him as though he was the villain.

"How often have you been told," he asked, speaking low to keep his anger under control, "not to wander around London by yourself."

"I wasn't alone. I was with Jemmy."

"A small boy is no protection, as you just learned. You could have been abducted by that man and subjected to fearful abominations."

From her expression Fenella had no idea what abominations he meant, which was as it should be, but she at least seemed shaken. Then she recovered. "He wasn't a nice man, but most likely all he wanted was my purse and I only have a shilling left."

"Did he demand money?"

"He didn't have time before you arrived."

A minute or two later and he might have been sure that the incident was no more than a robbery. Or he might have lost Fenella. That Radcliffe and his minions had once more threatened someone dear to him was infuriating. His sisters had been a damn nuisance from the start, and now he had to worry about their safety too. Somehow they'd become more than an unwelcome responsibility, a realization that both pleased and alarmed him.

"Why weren't you going straight home?" He glared at her and she responded in kind.

"I promised Jemmy I'd buy him a pie." The stubborn look was Fenella at her plainest and most irritating, but all Julian wanted to do was hold her and convince himself she was truly unharmed. "Miss Grey said I could spend my pocket money however I wished."

"Miss Grey should have watched you better and you should not have taken advantage of her absence."

"I wanted to see the king's horses."

Julian wanted to tear his hair out. "Why in the name of heaven didn't you ask her? Or me? It's an unexceptional outing that could have been arranged without trouble."

"She said she would take me today, then she changed her mind. She had to go out instead."

Miss Jane Grey, desirable or not, was supposed to be in charge of his sisters, and she had better have an explanation for her absence. Taking Fenella by the shoulder, he turned her firmly in the direction of Mayfair. "Let us go home. I will speak to Miss Grey about a suitable punishment."

"In that case it's a good thing I saw the horses today."

He was hard put not to smile at her audacity. Not for the first time, she reminded him of himself.

"Do you know what, Julian?" Fenella said, tucking her hand into his arm. "I'm glad you came to find me. I was a little frightened by that man. Just a little, mind you."

Patting her hand briefly, and contradicting the message of the small caress with a frown, he marched onward in silence, Fenella tripping along beside him. An hour later she had been consigned to the nursery with orders that she was to have only bread and milk for supper. Julian stood by the window in the library, looking out at the square and waiting for Jane Grey.

He had been careless. Long suspecting that the house was being watched, when his sisters joined the household he should have realized they might be endangered. Whom in his household did he trust? Almost every servant in the place was new, although doubtless subjected to Blackett's meticulous examination of both their persons and references. The one employee not subject to his secretary's conscientious checking was the governess.

He already knew that Jane Grey was not who, or at least what, she claimed. Since confirming his memory that the ostrich was found only in Africa, he'd begun to doubt she'd ever set foot on Saint Lucia, let alone spent her whole life there. He also remembered a woman hovering around the house the day his sisters had arrived. It could have been she. He hadn't seen her since Jane arrived in answer to his advertisement. Instead there was that young man, loitering in the square at this very moment, staring at the upper floors. Itching to get his hands on someone with some answers,

Julian was about to go down and confront the fellow when a familiar gray cloak approached. Jane Grey had returned and was speaking to the man. Her accomplice.

Julian felt as though he'd been plunged into icy water. She'd played him for a fool all the time, and a fool he was to have set aside all the inconsistencies in her stories, each one small but adding up to a damning whole. They appeared to be arguing, the partners in crime, and then she gestured him away and he took off. No need for him to be there when the spy who had infiltrated Fortescue House was in residence. Jane crossed the street and disappeared from sight as she descended the steps to the servants' entrance.

Five minutes later the library door opened. He'd be getting answers, very soon.

"You asked for me, Your Grace?"

They hadn't met for three days and she looked pleased to see him. His own spirits took an involuntary leap. Her cheeks were pink from walking outside in cool spring weather, her eyes bright and untroubled, her smile as provocative as ever.

"Sit down, Miss Grey." No more Jane. He pointed at the chair next to his desk and remained standing for an intimidating effect. "May I inquire where you have been all day?"

"I had a matter of business I needed to attend to."

"And what was so urgent that you abandoned your duties without permission?"

Her eyes widened at his harsh tone, obviously surprised at being spoken to thus by an employer who had made it clear he wished to share her bed and didn't much care what else she did. "You were absent, as was Mr. Blackett or I would have asked him. I left the girls with work to complete while I was gone."

"Where were you?"

For the first time she evaded his gaze. "It is my private affair."

"I see. And is it your private affair to let one of your pupils go wandering around London and running into danger?"

"Good God! What happened?" A hand went to her mouth. "Was it Fenella? Is she all right?"

"Fenella is unharmed, no thanks to her governess. I discovered her being assaulted, perhaps abducted, outside the Royal Stables."

"Poor child, she must be terrified. I must go to her."

"Sit down! My sister is in the nursery being punished for her disobedience. Let's talk about your part in this."

"I am so dreadfully sorry. If I had any idea Fenella would pull such a trick I wouldn't have gone out. Tell me what happened. Oh heavens! Abducted? Who would do such a thing?"

If she wasn't genuinely distressed, she was an actress worthy of comparison with the great Mrs. Siddons. Having enough respect for Jane Grey's talents to believe her capable of anything, Julian hardened his resolve. "What do you have to say about the attack on my sister?"

"I? I knew nothing until a minute ago."

"I'm not condoning Fenella's behavior," he said,

watching her carefully. "She was wrong to have gone to the stables on her own. But you broke your promise to take her, so what was a girl of spirit to do? Did you deliberately provoke her?"

Her brow creased, then lightened to an expression of sweet exasperation with an undercurrent of amusement. Despite himself, Julian found her captivating. "The little devil! I'd laugh if what happened wasn't so grave. I suppose she didn't mention to you that during breakfast, before I was called away, I canceled the outing because she slapped Maria? The girls were quarreling, but Fenella went too far." She shook her head. "I love your sisters dearly, Your Grace, and I have a special fondness for Fenella, but there's no question she's a handful." Minute examination of her face and voice didn't reveal an iota of deception. Her feelings were clear as a bell. "I wish you wouldn't tower over me like that. Once again I apologize for my absence and it won't happen again, but I don't understand why you thought I had anything to do with an attack on Fenella."

"Never mind." Julian had no intention of enlightening her about his frustrated suspicions. "Who is the man you were speaking to in the square, just now?" He spoke dispassionately, as though it wasn't important.

"I don't think I should tell you."

"Oh, I think you should."

"I told Maria I wouldn't."

"Maria?"

"Very well. You have a right to know. Mr. Norville, that's his name, met Maria in the park before I was employed here. I discovered they had been meeting and told him that if he wished to see her he must ask my permission, or yours." Her lips twitched. "I take it he never plucked up the courage."

"Apparently not."

"I am not surprised. He's the most dismal young man. Maria seems to have recovered from her infatuation and I think the only reason she ever considered him was out of ennui. The dressmaker and the theater have put poor Mr. Norville quite out of her mind. I hope I have persuaded him to stop haunting Hanover Square and find a different quarry."

"Quarry, eh? Do I take it that Mr. Norville's motives are not of the purest?"

"Maria is a very lovely girl, of course, but I believe the young man found her loveliness enhanced by being sister to a duke. When I told him in no uncertain terms that he could either meet the duke, or go away, he chose the latter course. He seemed frightened at the very idea of you."

"Must be my reputation for eating small children and presumptuous men for dinner."

Her gentle laugh made something go soft inside him. He moved closer so he was standing right in front of her chair, his legs brushing against her skirts. When she tilted her head, he thought he detected affection; then she took his hand in her cool smooth one and squeezed it.

"I know you don't eat children. On the contrary, I believe you love them, though I'm sure you won't own it. As for presumptuous men, I shall ask Fenella for the details of your heroic rescue."

"In this case no heroics were needed. But don't deceive yourself, Jane." She was Jane again. "I am no hero, nor ever have been."

A hero would have made sure that the Marquis de Falleron and his family were safe before making off with a priceless collection of paintings. A hero would not have said, "I promise. I swear on my honor," when he suspected the entire enterprise was fraught with peril with good odds of failure.

"You are a hero to your sisters." Her eyes were bright with admiration. *And to me too,* he fancied she was saying. If only she knew the truth about him.

Simply holding hands with Jane Grey was among the great erotic experiences of his life. But it was more than that. There was a strange lightness about his heart that felt like joy. He lowered his long body to a crouch so that their heads were on a level. Her eyes were liquid brown, her complexion pink and white and flawless, her just-parted lips a scalding temptation. Why had he ever thought she wasn't a beauty? Turning her hand in both of his, he kissed the soft palm. Time hung in the balance.

"I must go." She stood abruptly, almost toppling him over. "I must make sure Fenella is well and the other girls aren't worried. I'll reassure them you won't let anybody harm them."

Julian already missed her touch but he found it encouraging that she was so flustered. "Bread and milk for Fenella's supper!" he called after her.

She turned and sent him that bed-me smile. "You are much too kind, Your Grace. Bread and *water,* I think," she said, and glided out of the room.

Julian wasn't used to uncertainty. He always knew what to think, be it the authenticity of a Leonardo, the beauty of a courtesan, or an opinion of friend, foe, or relation. No one in his life had sent his brain spinning the way Jane did.

Was she an adventuress involved in a complicated plot against him, or was she innocent of all wrongdoing? His heart told him the latter. Yes, she had lied. Yes, she had secrets. Since he had secrets of his own he didn't hold that against her. With only himself to consider, he'd take the risk and declare her not guilty.

But he had to think of his responsibilities. He was about to leave on a journey of some weeks that would take him into considerable danger. Could he leave his sisters in the care of a woman he didn't trust? But if she *was* trustworthy there was no one to whom he'd sooner entrust them. Instinct told him she told the truth when she had claimed to love them. Why couldn't he credit his instincts as he had always done in the past?

He recalled the one time he had gone against the message of his gut: when he'd entered into the scheme that led to the death of the entire Falleron family. The memory made up his mind. He would trust Jane Grey, but he wouldn't leave his family unprotected in case his instinct was wrong. Added to his list of things to do in preparation for his departure was hiring a couple of bodyguards to live at Fortescue House and keep the Misses Osbourne in sight. While he was about it he'd have Miss Jane Grey investigated.

Chapter 11

The day before the duke's departure, he came up to the nursery to say good-bye to the Osbourne girls. Jane was neither surprised nor displeased to be summoned to the library after dinner. She expected Denford to try again to seduce her before leaving for a journey of some weeks. What thrilled and frightened her was how much she wished to be seduced. She wanted him and she might very well never see him again.

They settled in their usual places by the fire, glasses in hand. *Mon Dieu*, she was going to miss this. Miss him.

He seemed to be in a serious mood tonight. Much as she enjoyed his careless mockery, she found him even more attractive when he was contemplative. His beautiful blue eyes, ever startling beneath black brows and fringed with long black eyelashes, regarded her steadily, as though searching for something. Suddenly she hated that everything about her life was a lie.

He set down his drink and caressed the silver

knob of his cane. "As you know," he began finally, "I'll be away for several weeks, I am not sure exactly how long. Blackett has instructions about any emergencies that may arise, but I will rely on you to look after my sisters until I return."

"I am their governess," she said, a little uneasily.

"I want you to know how much I admire what you have done for them. You are far more than a teacher."

"I am very fond of them."

"I won't say that you are like a mother because you are too young. But an older sister, perhaps."

It was how she regarded them, a bittersweet feeling, but not one she would have missed.

Denford began pacing about the room, swinging his ebony cane.

"It's a weight off my mind to know that you are here," he said, coming to rest in front of her chair. "If anything happens to me. I want to know that they are in good hands until their mother returns. I have made legal and financial provision for their guardianship, but they need a woman. They need you."

"Surely nothing will happen to you."

"Given the poor luck of male Fortescues, I'd be foolish to assume that."

Ironic that he raised the subject of Fortescue men and their mortality. The day of Fenella's incident at the Royal Stables, she had been in the City hearing from Mr. Russell that Charles Fortescue had lately returned to England. Russell had several promising leads as to his whereabouts and expected early success in locating their quarry, if

Jane would cover certain expenses. She had dispersed the required sums, reducing her funds to a perilously low level. At any time she might be called upon to abandon her charges and set off for some unknown destination to murder their brother's heir.

"Since you possess the devil's luck," she said, "I expect you'll continue to avoid suffering the family misfortune."

"Let me be serious. I don't believe in an ill-defined Fortescue curse, but my journey is a dangerous one. I must cross the sea to Belgium to conclude an affair from long ago. France may have made peace with Great Britain, but their subjects in Belgium have been in revolt for years. There are also certain parties who seem interested in stopping me from retrieving my property. I have enemies."

Her eyes grew round. "Fenella! Do you think the attack on her was aimed at you? I couldn't understand why you thought she was being abducted, not merely robbed."

"You're very clever, Jane. I don't know for certain that was what happened, but I have reason to believe it possible." He looked at her with pure steel in his eyes that promised ill for anyone who crossed him. "There is no advantage to be gained from my enemies troubling my sisters while I am gone," he said deliberately. "I have gone to fetch the items they want, so they had much better come after me."

She had no idea why he was speaking to her

thus, as though delivering a message. "Who are these enemies of yours?"

"I'm not certain, though I have an idea. I do know that they are without conscience about using what they perceive to be people I care about against me. I trust they realize there is nothing more to be gained from that ploy, so I will not be astonished if they pursue me abroad."

"Please be careful."

He shrugged his black shoulders and smiled his twisted smile. "Chances are I will continue to plague the world." He leaned down and tilted up her chin with one long finger. "If I don't return, will you be sorry?"

"Of course I will." She lowered her eyelids, afraid to reveal how much. "You must come back, for your sisters' sake," she said briskly. "After you took tea with them this afternoon they could talk of nothing else but how much they will miss you, and how they look forward to the summer at Denford Castle. Admit it, Your Grace. You are fond of them, whatever you may have said to me when I first arrived."

"If I have learned to tolerate my sisters it is because you improved them." He stopped, considering his remark. "No, that's not entirely true. You've made Maria less irritatingly pious and Fenella less defiant, but I see for myself that we have benefited equally from my mother's good qualities and suffered from her neglect."

"There is nothing more important than having a family."

"So you have told me before. You may be bringing me around to your way of thinking, or perhaps the prospect of parting has made me maudlin. I should be sorry to lose that exceedingly annoying smile with which Fenella drives her sisters to the brink of madness. I suppose you taught her that."

She smiled mysteriously. "I don't know what you are talking about."

"Damn it, Jane Grey. I shall miss you."

I'll miss you too.

"Will you kiss me good-bye?"

It might be forever. She was tempted to promise to remain until he returned, even if word came of Charles Fortescue's whereabouts. After she had concluded her revenge she had plans to escape, to disappear and live under a new identity far away from England or France. But it was entirely possible she would be caught and hanged. If so, it was better for Denford and his sisters if she wasn't living under his roof when she murdered his cousin and heir.

"What are you thinking?" he asked.

Taking his hand she rose to her feet. "I think a kiss at parting is proper," she said, and walked into his arms.

This time there was no feigned reluctance on her part, no teasing game on his, nothing except pure mutual desire. She clung to him, encircling his waist and pulling him fiercely against her yearning body. She wanted his hands on her bare flesh, not protected by the layers of cloth on her back. As their mouths joined she closed her eyes and let herself believe that no one in the world existed except Denford and her and there lay a lifetime of kisses before them. She wished she really was a governess, and nothing else.

She'd made a life for herself as Jane Grey and had sometimes been tempted to forget that she had ever been Jeanne de Falleron, never more than now. But guilt pricked her conscience and the dead chided her for indifference. If she did not avenge her family, no one would.

She permitted herself a few minutes of happiness as he deepened the kiss, gathering her in, silently exhorting her to surrender. Perhaps she should. What was she waiting for? The reality that they would soon part forever invoked a convulsive sob.

Immediately he withdrew, relaxing his embrace and looking at her with concern. "Don't cry, Jane." His thumb wiped a tear from her cheek. "Over the years I've proved quite hard to kill. I'll come back to you."

She backed out of his arms and turned away. "I should go."

"Sit with me awhile."

And because she was weak, she let him guide her to the divan and serve her another glass of brandy. She perched on the edge with the poker-backed posture her mother had insisted on since she was old enough to sit up. He lounged beside her, a great black cat sprawled with effortless grace against gold brocade.

"There is no point trying to look prim. It doesn't suit you."

She might look prim but she didn't feel it. Her

face reflected the iron control she exercised over her emotions and her discretion, lest she pour out the truth and then hurl herself into his arms, begging him to take her. Never seeing Denford again was well nigh unbearable.

"Let's talk about you," he said. "How did you become Jane Grey?"

Had he somehow penetrated her disguise? Of course not. He spoke figuratively and he was smiling at her with lazy affection and not an ounce of suspicion. Over the weeks at Fortescue House she had learned a good deal about Denford, perhaps more than he revealed to most people. In this final meeting, Jane wished she *could* talk about herself.

"I'll tell you a story," she said.

"About you?"

"No. It's about a young woman and a war."

A friend of Henri's had recounted the tale at dinner one night and it had affected her deeply. She couldn't describe her own life but she could give him tantalizing hints about part of it.

"This woman, let us call her the contessa, was living on her estate when the enemy arrived. She fled the château to hide in the farm buildings, but some of the soldiers pursued her. She knew what would happen for she had seen what they did to the other women of her household. Alas, she tripped on her gown and was surrounded by the brutes. She had resigned herself to her fate when the army of her own country arrived. An officer swooped down like a great eagle with a sword, killed one of her attackers, and drove off the others. Her savior swept her into his arms and in her terror and relief she fainted."

Jane stopped to sip her brandy. It was hard to speak of the next bit because, although it wasn't what happened to her, it brought back the memory she preferred never to think about. She had been awake when Mathieu took her to his bed the first time.

"When she regained consciousness she was lying on the straw in the barn. The battle had moved on and all was quiet. Shortly afterward the officer called at the château and asked the contessa to marry him. Even though she was filled with gratitude and he was eligible, a baron with a good estate, she asked for a chance to get to know him before she accepted. But he was importunate, pressing for an early marriage before he was recalled to his military duties. Despite his pleas, she refused to agree to an engagement. After he left she found herself with child."

Denford, who had been looking at her lazily as he listened, raised his black brows. "I didn't expect that."

"Neither did she. Since she had always lived chastely, she realized it must have happened after the baron rescued her and left her unconscious. The father of her child might be a common soldier, or even one of her own servants."

"Did she not suspect the baron?" Denford asked.

"Not for a moment. He had saved her and she knew him to be a man of honor. As a lady of honor, she could not accept his proposal and expect him to acknowledge her bastard as his own. At the same time, she needed to be married, or she would be disgraced, an outcast from her family and society. She placed an advertisement in the newspaper, asking the father of her child to come forward. Imagine her surprise when the baron appeared at the appointed time."

"Imagine," Denford said.

"You didn't believe him honorable?"

"I have few illusions about what men will do, even so-called gentlemen. Did the contessa wed him?"

"She was reluctant at first but finally she agreed for the sake of their child. They had a son and in the end their marriage was a happy one."

The duke frowned. "I don't understand why a lady could ever forgive her deceiver. He wasn't just a seducer, he raped her when she was vulnerable and in his care."

"Women must forgive much if they are to survive. What choice did she have?" Unable to maintain the measured tone in which she recounted the tale, her voice fell to a whisper. "Besides, he had saved her life. She was in his debt."

Julian watched Jane gaze into her brandy as though it held the secrets of the universe. It was a good story she had told, one he would have enjoyed had he read it in a novel. Yet he didn't believe it entirely invented. She was telling him something about herself, but what? Which part?

Removing her glass, he set it aside and covered

her hands with one of his. "Look at me, Jane." She didn't move a muscle. "Is that what happened to you?" A tiny shake of denial that he didn't believe. Taking her by the chin and making her look at him, he was appalled by the dull hopelessness in her eyes. "Were you violated like that? Did you have a child?"

"Not like that." He could hardly hear her. "And there was no child."

"Will you tell me? I would be honored by your confidence," he said, despite the inherent irony of speaking of honor at present. He had precious little honor himself, and apparently Jane had been the victim of a man or men who had none.

Though her eyes glistened with tears, it was better than the dead look. "I can't tell you everything, but a little. He did not force me, but he had saved my life and he made it clear that he would not continue to do so if I didn't surrender to him. So you see, I gave in willingly."

"How old were you?"

"Fifteen."

A massive rage gripped Julian's chest. As far as he was concerned it was rape, and he'd like to find Jane's violator and give him what he deserved. "Where is he now?" Not on the island of Saint Lucia, he'd be willing to bet.

"He is dead."

"Painfully, I hope."

"He was a soldier and killed in battle so I expect it wasn't pleasant."

"But he was never punished for his crime?"

"I lived with him as his mistress for three years. I'm sorry that I am not a proper person to live with your sisters." She smiled gallantly. "You were right about that, you see."

"I find you eminently proper. I am not going to blame you for what happened when you were little more than a child. I only wonder that you could bear to live with him, to lie with him."

She shrugged. "He was kind to me, mostly, and I was fed and clothed and not dead. Like the contessa, I made the best of things. Do you think it is impossible to forgive a wrongdoing?"

He shook his head. "There are some sins so dreadful that they can never be forgiven." He should know. He had committed them himself. "Let me comfort you, Jane. You have nothing to fear from me." He leaned back against the cushions, scene of feverish imaginings involving Jane Grey, and pulled her down so her head rested on his chest. One arm encircled her waist, while the other stroked her hair. "I will never let anything happen to you." A stupid thing to say.

She made no effort to escape his embrace but settled into it, laying her palm flat over the heart that was racing fit to burst from his ribs. He'd nurtured a hope that tonight would end with Jane in his arms, but not like this. How could he seduce a woman who had been so abominably used? He concentrated on the simple delight of holding her, inhaling her scent, letting her hair tickle his nose, sensing the rise and fall of her breath as she pressed against him. "I will come back," he murmured. Returning to England alive mattered because he had three sisters who relied on him and their governess whom he wanted to protect, even if her abuser was dead.

Fifteen. Maria's age. It was also the age of the oldest Falleron girl who had gone to the guillotine through his carelessness. He preferred not to think about that now.

"Was it after this brute's death that you became a governess?" he asked.

"I don't want to talk about it and I don't like to think about it."

He knew just what she meant. "What would you like to talk about?"

"I think I would like you to make love to me."

"Look at me, Jane." She raised her head from his chest and he found her as unreadable as ever, not ablaze with passion as he had so long anticipated. "Why?"

"Because I desire you. Did you not think so?"

"I hoped. I also feared you far too sensible to succumb without a long, hard siege."

"There's no time for the siege, with you leaving tomorrow. And now you know that I am not as I should be."

"Don't say that. Never say that." The self-disgust in her voice twisted his heart. "You are exactly as you should be: clever, kind, witty, and beautiful. Even had you not surrendered your virginity by force, it wouldn't matter to me. It would be deeply hypocritical for me, or for most men, to condemn your so-called lack of virtue."

"Few women would agree with you, not respectable ones."

"Try not to care about them." He kissed her lightly and briefly, refusing the invitation of her clinging lips. "Honored as I am by your request . . . What am I saying? *Honored* is a namby-pamby word. I am enraptured by your request."

"So? Why do we wait?"

"You are a member of my household, Jane. One of my dependents. It doesn't sit well with me that you should feel any obligation. Not after what happened to you before."

She rested her arms on his chest. The glow in her mahogany eyes made him dizzy. "I feel no obligation. Remember, you gave me the key."

"I am ashamed you had to ask for it."

"Your Grace, I never felt in danger from you, except from my own desires."

"Julian." He stroked her hair. "My name is Julian."

"Julian." His name on her lips, and her smile, made his heart thud. "Kiss me, Julian. Make me forget."

She had turned the tables and seduced him.

"Come here," he said, and pulled her over so that she was on top of him, lying between his splayed legs. Jane was such a graceful creature, almost ethereal in her movements, that it was a pleasurable surprise to find her substantial in his arms. No fairy creature of light and air, but a woman of bone and flesh that he would finally explore. Through her sensible cloth gown he felt curvaceous hips and a firm, plump bottom. He couldn't wait to see her naked.

But first he kissed her. A lot. She was sweet and spicy and completely responsive and their two previous kisses hadn't been nearly enough. He intended that this evening should last a long time, even if the rocking of her body stimulated him to a perilous degree of arousal.

"Let's take this slowly," he murmured. She might not have had a lover for a long time and, if that villainous ravisher was her only one, she would need a good deal of coaxing to be pleased, an effort he would not spare. He relished the challenge.

For a while they lay still, not even kissing, as he continued to caress her back and let his raging desire abate a little. It was Jane who made the next advance, burrowing under his coat and working loose the buttons of his waistcoat. Her fingers were warm, first through linen and then on the skin of his stomach. She'd tugged the shirt loose from his breeches. He squeezed his eyes shut and shuddered. "You'll kill me, Jane." Without a word she continued the blissful torture until he could take it no more. He rolled her over and pinned her hands above her head. "My turn."

Despite his fantasy of raising her skirts and taking her fully clothed, he wanted more than a quick tumble, at least this time. From the front, her sensible gown was an impregnable fortress, so he kissed her some more, then flipped her. "Buttons," he said in response to her protest, half laugh and half squawk. "If you must wear clothing that fastens behind, expect to find yourself prone. Now she was definitely laughing and he wasn't paying enough attention because halfway through the job she pushed him off and reversed their positions again, ripping off his neckcloth. So with mirth and panting they eventually found themselves kneeling opposite each other on the divan, naked but for her stockings and his unbuttoned breeches barely clinging to his hips.

He drank in the sight of her. "You are beautiful," he breathed, reaching out to touch the little plump breasts tipped with dusky, brownish nipples. "Perfectly soft."

"You too," she said, mimicking his movements and caressing his chest.

"Soft?"

"Not there," she said, eyeing his rampant cock with a wicked little grin that gave him ideas about her mouth. Her experiences hadn't damaged her beyond the ability to joke in bed, but he needed to go slowly. Any confluence of his cock and her mouth would have to be initiated by her. He hated, hated, that her dastardly soldier might have forced her to perform a deed that disgusted her.

"I'm afraid I'm a hairy man, black Irishman that I am."

"I like it." She fingered the dark thatch over his chest. "And I love your hair." In the struggle to undress, his queue had come loose. She wound the inky tresses around her slender white hands and brought them to her lips. He was her captive and she was his, manacled by locks of hair. There and then he was grateful he'd resisted every impulse to cut them.

Her hair remained up, though rumpled like an unruly schoolboy's. But she was nothing like a schoolboy, nothing at all. His fingers explored her small, firm breasts, down over the gentle curve of her belly, to her lower curls, dipping into wet heat. His tension eased a notch. She was aroused. Gently he disentangled himself. "Let's lie down."

He let his breeches drop to the floor and joined her. Stretched out on their sides, they lay face to face, continuing their mutual exploration of any part of the body within reach. Finally he settled on one elbow, nuzzling her lips with quick kisses and compliments while his other hand explored the wet cradle of her quim, stroking her clitoris until he felt her tension begin to mount.

"Come," she said through heightened breathing. "I want you now." She grasped his cock imperiously and gave it a sharp tug. She knew what she was doing.

"I surrender," he said, and let her pull him down on top and guide him in.

Surely nothing in his thirty years on earth had felt as extraordinary as she: hot, tender, magnificent. Moving as evenly and deliberately as he could manage, he kept an iron control on his roiling sac, which urged him to pound away and release as soon as possible. He would see to Jane's pleasure if the effort killed him. And he wanted their union to last, forever if possible. If the rest of his life should be spent entwined with Jane Grey he had no objection.

"Why did you stop, Julian?" she moaned. "Don't stop."

"I'm collecting myself," he said tightly. "I don't want to finish before you."

"Don't worry about me."

Julian added the words *selfish oaf* to the list of epithets attached to her ravisher. "I most certainly will." He withdrew altogether and started to pleasure her with his hand while sucking hard on her taut nipple. She arched into him, rolling her hips to match his rhythm, and uttering tiny, muted cries. "Shout if you want to," he said, raising his head to witness her expression as she reached her orgasm. "No one will hear you."

But she came quietly, just a little diminuendo rippling from her throat. He caught it with a kiss and held her tight as her shudders faded.

"Thank you," she whispered, and flung her arms about his neck, kissing him desperately, sucking on his tongue as though she'd devour him. *"Incroyable,* Your Grace. *Magnifique."*

"Et toi aussi." He had no objection to a little French in bed. *"La plus belle dame de ma connaissance."*

She jerked her head and blinked.

"What?"

"Your turn now," she said.

"If you will take your pleasure again, first."

She had powerful legs that gripped his waist when he entered her again. The muscles of his arms strained so that he could see her face as he worked. Her eyes were closed, her mouth ajar, and he wished she would look at him and he could read her thoughts. Yet he could tell from her breath and the grip of her passage on his cock that she was close to fulfillment again. He longed to increase his speed and attempt to finish at close to the same time. The feeling of intimacy would be incredible, but he dared not try. He was approaching a state of total mindlessness and he might be too far gone to pull out. Instead he let her go over the edge alone, allowed himself a few hard thrusts, and withdrew. Panting, he snatched up his shirt and spent into the linen folds.

Jane lolled on her back, then, seemingly suddenly aware that every inch of her was open to his gaze, pulled a silk pillow over her sex. "Why? Why did you leave?"

"I don't want to get you with child."

She pursed her lips together with a puzzled frown. "I understand that. But surely you could have remained with me a little longer." Her cheeks colored delicately, which he found delightful given their nakedness and recent activity. "It would be more normal, surely, to rejoice in my arms."

"That safeguard against pregnancy doesn't always work. I don't want to risk leaving you with a child when I may not come back to you." With the tale of the contessa fresh in his mind, he wasn't going to risk abandoning Jane alone in the world in such a condition.

She sat up, still clutching her pillow, and stroked his cheek. "You are a good man, Julian."

He kissed her again. "Not so good that I don't look forward to a repetition on my return, with a better method of preventing conception."

The pillow forgotten, she hurled her arms around him and buried her face in his neck, gulping back a sob. Alarmed and touched, he rubbed her back and tried to comfort her. "I'm coming back, Jane," he said. "I promise."

She hiccupped. "I will never see you again." Apparently the act of love had disordered her emotions. He found her disquiet flattering and understandable; he felt the sorrow of their parting too. But instead of desperation, he was filled with a new determination.

"I won't let anything, either my enemies or passing bandits, stop me from returning to you. When I make up my mind to something, I get it. Expect to meet me again in this library within a month."

She sniffed hard, an endearingly mundane action. "I am foolish," she said. "Will you kiss me good-bye again?"

"I will take any excuse to kiss you, but this is not good-bye."

The kiss turned into several. Each time she tried to turn one into a spoken farewell, he gathered her close and silenced the words with his lips. When he withdrew, knowing he must let her go, she clung to him, as loath to part as he. Finally it was he who brought the evening to a close, afraid that the housemaid would discover them naked when she came in at dawn to light the fire.

"I must let you go," he said reluctantly. "This is

only *au revoir*." He found her shift, pulled it over her head, and took a last quick kiss. "Within a month. The usual time and place."

Julian watched Jane leave the room, half dressed and hoping no servants had strayed from their beds. He sat tailor-style on the divan wearing nothing but his breeches and thought about her. His Jane.

He was confident that she was not in league with his enemies. He could now tell when she told the truth because he knew when she was lying. That was when she told him just about anything about her past. But she hadn't lied about the monster who had violated her, though he didn't have the whole story. Julian would bet heavily on the man being French. When she spoke of his orgasm she'd used the word *rejoice*, an odd choice in English but a direct translation of the French term.

Though he had acquitted her of villainy, he was glad he had hired a Bow Street Runner to investigate Jane Grey. He was ragingly curious to know everything about her and couldn't wait to return to her arms.

Both confident in his return and more fearful than he had ever been that somehow he might not make it back, he sat at his desk and wrote two more notes. One to Blackett, desiring a substantial sum be handed over to Jane Grey when the governess left her employment. And one to Jane herself.

Chapter 12

Jane sat at the writing desk in the duchess's chamber, tracing the marquetry of the piece with her fingertips and making a conscious effort not to open the drawer containing the key. It would be so easy to let her unfastened garments fall to the floor and to walk naked into Denford's rooms, his bed, and his arms.

He could be hers one last time if she would but use the key.

She'd enjoyed sleeping with Henri, who prided himself on his prowess in bed. But Henri had been a selfish man and now she had confirmed that he was a selfish lover. He pretended to want her pleasure but his own came first. In Henri's bed her first duty was to like what he liked and to pay for his attentions with fulsome praise. Her enjoyment bolstered his belief in his own superiority.

Denford, however. Denford was superb.

She feared what she would do if she returned to him tonight. She wanted to confess the truth in a torrent of words while he held her, as he had this evening when she told him about Mathieu. He'd make her feel secure and loved and he would absolve her from the task she dreaded more, the nearer it approached.

She shook her head at the illogic of the thought. Denford was a Fortescue. He had no right to release her from the obligation of revenge against a man who was his own cousin. And even if he did, Denford didn't believe in forgiveness. In the end neither did she.

There was no forgiveness for her, and none for Mr. Fortescue.

She scraped back her chair to get away from the lure of the key and looked instead at the bottom drawer of the wardrobe. She envisioned the blade sliding into a man's flesh, closed her eyes tight and felt the cutting of sinew and bone, smelled the coppery blood spurting over her hand, heard a cry of agony followed by the hiss of expiring breath.

Or she could be wrong about how terrifying it would be. Perhaps it was quiet and quick and easy, dealing a mortal wound. She wished it was over and Charles Fortescue was dead.

As for Denford, there was no future there. She could never reclaim her own life and go back to being Jeanne de Falleron. In order to survive she'd surrendered her virtue and consorted with the enemy. She was nothing but a governess with a dubious past. Dukes did not marry governesses.

Jane woke early from a restless sleep. Against her judgment, she dressed and descended to indulge herself with one last glimpse of the duke before he left. Too late. Instead, on the breakfast table was a note addressed to her, and a sheet of foolscap folded in half.

My dear Jane,

I want you to have this. If I don't return, I won't need this reminder of you. If I do, I will have you in all your delectable flesh. I am a better man for having known you. Do not fear for your future. Blackett knows what to do. But tonight I feel lucky. I think my good fortune started when you answered my advertisement.

Denford

With no idea why the portrait meant so much to her, he had given her the Fragonard. The pure lines of the drawing were blurred by her gathering tears.

She wouldn't keep it, of course. When she departed she'd leave it behind for him because she would not be there in the flesh. She smiled a little. He had found her delectable and thought himself lucky to know her. She held his note to her breast. Though he didn't use the word, it was surely a love letter.

While there was no future for her as Denford's mistress, or anything else, she could do one thing for him. In the time remaining to her at Fortescue House she would be the best governess possible.

She looked over the Osbourne girls as they gathered around the schoolroom table, practicing their penmanship. Their toilettes had improved with their new clothes but their posture was too relaxed for good *ton*. The Marquise de Falleron would have shuddered to see Fenella with one elbow on the table and Laura kicking the legs of her chair.

"Why do we have to copy out verses?" Fenella groused. "It's so dull. Besides, I know how to write."

"A lady writes with an elegant hand. Yours, Fenella, is more like something a chicken would scratch in the dirt."

"You don't write the way we do."

"I learned the French style of handwriting."

Laura looked cunning. "Tell us a story about Saint Lucia."

"You can't distract me that way, *chérie*. Look at your eldest sister. You should emulate her."

Maria added a flourish to the end of a perfectly even line of graceful script and smirked, but Jane was in no mood to put up with nonsense.

"Smug superiority is unbecoming in a lady, Maria," Jane said. "True *politesse* demands that you make others feel appreciated and at ease in your company."

"Why are you talking so much about what a lady does, Miss Grey?" Laura asked.

"Because I have neglected your deportment lessons. As soon as you have finished your morning studies in writing and arithmetic, we shall begin exercises in posture and good manners so that you will be worthy to be presented to the highest society, which is no doubt what your brother will arrange for you."

"What kind of lessons?" Maria looked eager.

"You must learn to behave with elegance at all times, both in your movements and your behavior with others. We shall begin this afternoon with walking, standing, and sitting."

"That's stupid. I can do all those things, just as I can write," Fenella said. "I hate these stupid verses. I wish Isaac Watts was dead."

"Your wish has probably come true since this book is dated 1715." Jane had to admit that the volume of *Divine and Moral Songs for Children* she'd found in the schoolroom was quite depressing.

"Listen to this." Fenella read what she had been copying.

Have you not heard what dreadful plagues
Are threaten'd by the Lord,
To him that breaks his father's law,
Or mocks his mother's word?

"I think that sentiment is very proper," Maria said.

"And in the absence of your parents you must obey your governess," Jane added.

"And is this what will happen if I do not?"

What heavy guilt upon him lies!
How cursed is his name!
The ravens shall pick out his eyes,
And eagles eat the same.

Fenella's reading was so bloodcurdling that Laura shrieked and Jane succumbed to mirth. "I agree that Mr. Watts overstates the consequences of disobedience. I have a different idea. You will practice both your handwriting and the polite arts by writing letters."

Even Maria approved this plan. Mr. Watts's book was closed with a slam, fresh paper selected and pens trimmed anew.

"Can we write to Julian?" Laura asked.

"That would be most proper."

"What shall I say?"

"The rules for writing a good letter are similar to those for conversation." Jane held up her hand and enumerated the things her mother had laid down, checking them off on her fingers. "If you tell stories, make sure they aren't too long. Avoid arguments and the expression of strong opinions that your correspondent may disagree with. Always search for the witty turn of phrase, the *mot juste,* so that your writing amuses as well as informs. Think about what will interest the recipient, not what you want to write about. Above all, do not speak, or write, too much about yourself. People, especially gentlemen, prefer to hear and talk about themselves."

"That isn't fair," Fenella said. "Why are gentlemen allowed to talk about themselves if we are not?"

"It is the way of the world," Jane said firmly, not wanting to get into an argument about justice. Yet last night Denford had wanted to talk about Jane. The memory of the sweetness and sympathy with which he had listened to her caught at her heart. "I think your brother would like to hear what you are doing. Within reason, of course."

The two elder girls scratched away at their papers

right away while the youngest flicked her quill over her nose and stared at the window. "Do you not have an idea of what to write, Laura?" Jane asked.

"I'm searching for the *mot juste*. Don't you think my French is getting better?"

"If you can't think of anything to say, perhaps writing *in* French will inspire you."

Laura stopped daydreaming and dipped her pen into the ink pot.

Maria finished first. "Will you check my spelling and grammar, please?"

Since she rarely made an error in either area, Jane deduced that Maria was proud of her epistolary skill.

Dear brother,

I trust this finds you well and that your business is successful and not tedious. The weather today is uncommonly fine for April though it rained yesterday and will no doubt do so tomorrow. It is to be expected and I look forward to the day when April showers bring forth May flowers. I am sure that you do too. The Reverend Mr. Walters preached a fine sermon last Sunday on the virtues of patience. Not much has occurred since you left so I will keep this letter short. I look forward to your return so that you may regale us with tales of your travels.

Ever your affectionate and respectful sister,
Maria Osbourne

"Very nice," Jane said. "Very elegantly written." And very dull. Denford would undoubtedly prefer Fenella's ink-spattered effort.

Dear Julian,

Since you only left this morning and we saw you yesterday, I have nothing new to report. Instead I will tell you a story about something that happened last year. Farmer O'Riley, who was our neighbor in Ireland, let his pigs escape through a hole in their sty. Four piglets got into the garden and began to eat our early peas. Mother sent Maria and me out armed with stout sticks to fight them off. We chased them to the duck pond when their mama, a large sow who frightened everyone in the county including Mr. O'Riley and his pigman, appeared to protect her young. Maria was right on the edge of the pond when Mama Duck quacked loudly because she was concerned about her babies. Maria made a sound very like a duck, only louder and then . . . Oh dear. Miss Grey says if we tell stories they must be short or the reader will find them tedious so I will stop now.

Miss Grey also says we must write about our correspondent, not ourselves. I do not know enough about you to write much. You are tall and thin and wear your hair long, but you know that. If you answer this letter you can be a gentleman and tell me more about yourself. I would enjoy reading it so apparently I am not a gentleman.

Yours etc.
Fenella Osbourne

P.S. Why do letters end "yours etc."? Why am I yours and what else does the etc. imply about me?

Jane laughed. "You are a cruel young girl. Your poor brother will be dying to hear how the story ends."

"What story?" Maria asked.

"Never mind. Have you finished, Laura?"

"Mine is the best. I will read it aloud." The child rose and took up a dramatic stance.

" 'Dear Julian, I hope you are well. When are you coming home? I have a question about you. Will you let me have a puppy? Your loving sister, Laura Osbourne.' "

She handed the sheet of paper to Jane. "When will Julian receive the letters?"

Checking that the handwriting was even and the spelling correct, Jane imagined Denford's enjoyment of these utterly characteristic missives. Rashly, she told the girls that she would post them, but he'd left no address. Since they couldn't be sent to him in Belgium, they would have to await his return. She would leave them on his desk, along with her own farewell.

Spring stretched into early summer, marked by the succession of flowering trees and shrubs in Hyde Park. On their frequent outdoor excursions, Jane and the Osbournes were always accompanied by the two footmen newly hired before Denford's departure. He'd said nothing specific but Jane knew they weren't ordinary servants and she was glad. She herself stuck to her charges like a burr, resolved that no harm would come to them as long as she remained with them. When it came to lesson time, she drilled them mercilessly so that she would leave behind pattern cards of refinement.

Among the innovations Jane introduced for the betterment of the Osbournes' education was for them to take their meals downstairs in the small dining room. Not only were the surroundings more conducive to elegant behavior than the spartan schoolroom, it was also convenient for the servants carrying dishes from the kitchen. Once Blackett managed to hire a reliable cook for Fortescue House, the food had improved. Now Jane became happily accustomed to eating her food hot.

"Do you think Julian will write to us today?" Laura asked the same question every morning at breakfast. By the time Jane realized that her lie about posting the letters was a foolish one, it was too late to retract. Quite a little pile of neatly written missives had accumulated in her room.

"He must have been gone a month," Oliver Bream remarked. The artist almost always joined them for breakfast, whether there was a drawing lesson or not, and quite often for dinner too.

"Five weeks and two days," Fenella said.

Jane almost contradicted her. It had been five weeks and *three* days. Desperately missing Denford was made worse by the fact that she was still in his house and he might walk in at any moment. Or she might hear the terrible news that he was dead.

She was supposed to be long gone. As the weeks had passed with no word from the lawyer, she'd let Charles Fortescue fade from the foreground of her mind and concentrated on life as a governess. They were doing well, the girls, growing into graceful, confident young women. She was proud of them and proud of herself. And now . . .

"Is that a letter?" Fenella asked eagerly when the butler came in bearing a silver salver. All three girls, even Maria, looked as though they'd like to rise as one and snatch it. Despite her anxiety, Jane was gratified to see that her training in deportment held. The Misses Osbourne remained demurely in their seats. Oliver continued to eat as though nothing was happening.

"For you, miss." The butler offered the tray to Jane. It took every ounce of strength not to let her hand tremble as she accepted the folded sheet with the heavy red seal.

"Miss Grey never receives letters," Maria said.

Fenella's voice was thick with envy. "For you? Julian has written to you?"

"Hush, Fenella. The letter is not from His Grace. Have you all finished breakfast? It is time for your drawing lesson."

She needed to be alone when she read Mr. Russell's news, alone to prepare herself and make plans.

Mr. Russell's man had finally traced Fortescue to a village in Lincolnshire where, it turned out, he had a wife. The wife was but a yeoman's daughter, a misalliance for even the distant cousin of a duke, let alone the heir to one. Apparently he had kept his marriage a secret from his family but it hadn't meant much to him either since he'd spent little time under her roof. Russell implied that he might have been forced into the ceremony by an angry father, perhaps because she was with child. The couple had a son, now ten years old.

Jane lowered the letter to her lap. In all these years, it had never occurred to her that Mr. Fortescue had a family of his own, one that would suffer from his death. They would be innocent victims of her revenge.

Or perhaps better off without such a worthless husband and father.

She read on, skimming Russell's rather lengthy description of the ends to which he and his man had gone to discover this household. Jane expected that a large bill would be the result. Impatiently she turned over the page, looking for the exact address where she would find her enemy and stared, unable to believe her eyes.

Charles Fortescue had suffered from a wasting disease. He had returned to his native land to die. Jane didn't have to kill him because he was already dead.

The servants removed the breakfast things and cleaned the room without disturbing her stunned reverie. The goal of almost half a lifetime being wiped out left her numb. A whispered thought that she was free fought against her nagging conscience and gradually took hold.

Free. Free to live and love and forget the past.

Free to await Denford's return with unreserved anticipation.

The house smoldered, about to burst into a terrifying conflagration that consumed everything and everybody. Jane watched, helpless, unable to move, her feet anchored to the ground by invisible bonds. A man stood in front of her, also surveying the fire. She shouted at him to stop the flames but however loudly she cried no sound emerged. The building exploded into an inferno and the man turned around. She tried to see who he was but she couldn't focus on his features before he faded away, leaving her entirely alone.

Shivering with cold she awoke in the duchess's magnificent bed, devastated by soul-crushing loneliness.

She had suffered nightmares for years, especially in her early days as Mathieu's mistress. She would scream as horrors invaded her dreams, all the worse for being imagined and not actually witnessed. Mathieu would cuff her carelessly, tell her she was lucky to be alive and to go back to sleep. They hadn't been so frequent when Henri was her bedmate. Often months would pass without disturbance, until close to the end.

Not all her dreams were vivid and memorable but the man in front of the burning building was a constant. The first occurrence had been soon after Mathieu informed her that the Falleron family had gone under the guillotine. The vision returned periodically, always the same, and always leaving her shivering with grief. She had come to believe that the man in the dream was Mr. Fortescue.

There were a number of reasons why she had refused Henri's offer to settle down to a peaceful bourgeois existence, but the return of this vision had capped her determination. She knew then that she would never be at peace until she expiated her guilt for living while her family died, and her penance was to commit murder. Her family cried out for vengeance.

And now, when she thought she had been relieved of her ghastly obligation, she suffered the renewed night terror.

When the dream returned the second night, she knew what she had to do. She must continue her search for Mr. Fortescue.

But what if Charles Fortescue *had* been the man, supposing the dreams never went away? What if she had to spend the rest of her life waking up to a solitude so profound it could drive her mad?

Intolerable. She wanted to be happy, had always wanted it, and wanted it even more now that she had tasted it in Julian's arms.

Julian. She forced herself to reconsider the possibility that he was Mr. Fortescue. After all this time, her recollection of the man she'd seen in Paris could be mistaken; or he might not have been Fortescue but someone else; or Julian had been unusually mature for twenty. She made herself entertain the possibility that all her previous assumptions had been wrong, that she might be a fool to believe that, for all his shell of world-weary amorality, Julian was at heart a man of honor.

The Duke of Denford was no saint, that was

certain. She was sure he could be selfish, callous, and ruthless. But she also knew him capable of generosity and kindness. Above all, she did not think him a deceiver. She found it impossible to believe that the man she knew would have deliberately lied and cheated her father.

Perhaps Mr. Fortescue was an even more distant relation than Charles. A man who would betray an entire family for gain would think nothing of lying about his relationship with a duke. She must cast her net wider for Fortescue men and Denford Castle was the place to look, home of archives and family trees. She lay in the dark, afraid to sleep, contemplating another terror: that the duke would not return from Belgium and she wouldn't ever get to the castle.

She didn't know which would be worse: to live without revenge or to live without Julian.

On the third night she borrowed a good splash of Nurse Bride's whiskey and went to bed blissfully drowsy, taking back every harsh thought about the old woman's habits. Her dream was a pleasant one and she emerged from sleep with a sense of warmth and well-being. Hugging herself under the soft linen sheets, she didn't at first wonder what had roused her until she heard faint thumps through the open door of the boudoir. Straining her ears, she heard a soft imprecation in unmistakable tones.

Joy flooded Jane's being; her heart beat a merry

tattoo and a hallelujah rang in her ears. Without stopping to think, she leaped out of bed and reached in the dark for her writing desk and the key she kept in its drawer. She jabbed clumsily at the tiny light of the keyhole, and by the time she had it unlocked and the door swung open, the duke was there.

For a moment she was struck motionless by the sight of him, clad only in black breeches, white shirt, and a look of joy such as she had never seen on him before. Her lips opened to speak but she was breathless and nothing emerged. Then she pulled her nightgown over her head and tossed it aside.

"Here's a welcome," he said. "Many times in the past miserable weeks I've dreamed about a greeting like this but never dared hope for it."

Her foolish tongue wouldn't function so she dispensed with the formalities and hurled herself at him, clinging to him with all four limbs. He teetered a little but stayed upright, managing to lurch back the dozen yards to his bed where he fell backward, sinking into the mattress with her straddled over him.

"Good evening, Miss Grey," he said. "I like the way you curtsey."

She wanted to eat him alive, consume him, so great her relief that he had returned to her safe and sound. She still couldn't speak but decided it didn't matter for her mouth was in full working order when it came to other activities.

After a long, blistering kiss, she sat back on her

knees and watched him smile in the way he had only for her: lazy and carefree and filled with sensual promise.

"I thought I'd never see you again," she said.

"I told you I was hard to kill. I've come back to you weary but in one piece."

She leaned forward with her hands on his shoulders, to bury her face in his neck and inhale his heat and scent. A muted wince jolted her back upright. "What?" She clutched the opening of his shirt and ripped the garment to expose his chest, then pulled the sleeve off his shoulder and discovered a bandage around his upper arm. "*Mon Dieu*, you are hurt."

"A scratch, that is all."

"You told me you were in one piece. Who did this?" she demanded. "Who dared wound you?"

"You are very fierce, my sweet Jane. Would you avenge me? There is no need," he continued before she could answer. "A little contretemps with the French occupying authorities, that is all. The gentleman who has been taking care of my property for me was also, it turns out, a leader of the Flemish revolt against the French. They seemed to think me guilty by association but I escaped with no great harm done."

She folded her arms as sternly as was possible when naked and kneeling over a man with a torn shirt. "It is not right for a gentleman in your position to be running around and getting into fights with the authorities."

"Are you instructing me about the proper habits of dukes again, dear governess?"

No, the proper habits of those she loved. Her heart leaped and she averted her eyes from the twisted smile that she now understood was a cloak for tender feelings. She couldn't afford to be in love. "I have an affection for you, Your Grace, as I do for your sisters. I do not like to see any of you in peril. I can assure you nothing happened to them in your absence."

"I know. I spoke to one of the footmen before I came up to bed."

"They never let the girls never leave the house alone, and neither did I."

"I had every confidence in you," he said. Foolish man. It was only pure chance that she was still here. But while she must guard her heart against him, she could still enjoy him. She brushed her naked sex against his breeches. Having hardened her heart, she would harden him too.

"That's a wicked smile," he said.

She increased the pressure.

"I am flattered by your attention," he said, laughing," but I think I should warn you that I may be too tired to rise to the occasion."

She licked her lips. "Leave that to me."

"Sweet words." He gasped as she worked her way down his body, licking and nibbling while her fingers saw to the buttons of his breeches. Almost at once he began to stiffen under her hand but she knew something that would get him hard faster.

His head fell back with a strangled groan of bliss when she took him between her lips and all the way in, as far as she could manage. Wonderful to have him back and under her command, doing exactly what she wished to do to him with every confidence he would enjoy it, no matter what she chose. Gentle hands guided her head until she found the rhythm that made him thick and hard, filling her mouth with his particular taste and texture. Her power to arouse him sent her blood coursing and primed her own desire. She clenched her inner muscles in concert with her mouth and wondered if she could reach fulfillment this way.

Before she could test the theory he lifted her head and pulled her up the length of his body.

"But . . ."

Her objection was silenced with a kiss.

"I wanted . . ."

"I think you'll find," he said, breathing hard, "that I can indeed now rise to the occasion."

"I think you already have."

His penis nudged her inner thigh insistently and it took little adjustment to move her aching core over his straining sex and lower herself, reveling as he glided in and filled and stretched her until she was moaning and panting as much as he.

She rode him in a rhythmic counterpoint of cries and murmurs and mindless words of passion. *We were made to be together* and *I want this forever* were the foolish, incoherent notions that gripped her mind as ecstasy seized her body. And when it was over she collapsed on his chest, and his arms came around her and she knew that at least for a while she had found a home in Julian's embrace.

She remained awake for a long time. He had

fallen into the deep sleep of the weary and she learned that he was a messy bedmate, stretched out on his front. His head rested on one bent elbow while the other arm weighed on her, as did one heavy leg. He did not snore.

It enchanted her to know these things about him and to feel his long, thick hair tickle her neck. There was more she wished to know. Did he like to wake up in the night—unlikely when this tired—and make love? Or was he a morning lover? Or both? Was he tetchy on waking, or lively and cheery? No, not cheery. That was not an adjective she would ever apply to Denford. If he woke in a good mood he would smile lopsidedly and make a sardonic observation about the aggravations of the coming day, which he would proceed to meet with complete competence and a cynical commentary. She would laugh at him and when they met that night, at the usual time and place, he would relate what happened and admit, only when pressed, that it wasn't really so very trying.

She wanted to learn everything she didn't know about Julian and—she smiled into the dark room—do many wicked things with him. They were to spend the summer at Denford Castle. Warm months in the English countryside beckoned where she would surrender to joy. Surely the ghosts of her past wouldn't begrudge her one summer of happiness?

Chapter 13

After over a month's absence, Julian found himself deluged with business, including tasks arising from the unexpected news that his heir had died. First on his list was to send someone to make sure that Charles Fortescue's widow and child were well provided for; if necessary he'd bring them to live at Denford Castle. Unwillingly, he was beginning to accept that his position came with responsibilities, including seeing to the succession. Not suffering from undue modesty about his intellectual abilities, the challenge of learning how to oversee the business of a dukedom surprised him. If he didn't sire a son of his own, he must do something about training Charles's.

He still found most of the work tedious, which was why he was desperate enough to receive a caller he would, under normal circumstances, have shown the door.

The Countess of Ashfield sailed into the library in a swish of petticoats, very much à la mode despite her advanced years and repellent aspect.

He hadn't seen her for a year or two and never had much to do with her. She used to occasionally harangue his old friend Caro Townsend, now Duchess of Castleton, and he'd heard plenty of complaints from Cynthia Windermere, who was terrified of the old witch. The social dragoness, related to half the *ton*, had always made it clear Julian Fortescue was beneath contempt. He wondered what she wanted with the Duke of Denford.

"Lady Ashfield!" He pretended not to notice the lavender-gloved hand he was supposed to kiss, making her settle for a stiff bow. Unabashed, she plunked herself in the chair next to the fire, where she didn't look one hundredth as good as Jane. "To what do I owe the pleasure of your condescension?"

"I come to offer my condolences on the loss of your poor cousin Charles."

"Thank you. I am surprised you were acquainted with him. He wasn't received in your kind of circles. Rather like me."

Trying to embarrass Lady Ashfield was a fruitless endeavor. "I daresay I met him somewhere over the years, but that really isn't the point. Once he became the heir to Denford he was a person of significance."

"And I became Denford and the last time I looked I was still alive and by no means in my dotage."

"Don't be frivolous, Denford. Of course you are not and that is why I have decided to take you under my wing for the greater good of the Fortescues."

"Why do you care about the Fortescues?"

"Heavens above. I am related to the family in half a dozen ways."

"I had no idea we were cousins. You should have told me years ago. I'd have been sure to send you greetings on your birthday."

"I don't know that *we* are connected," she said with a sniff. "The marriages between my connections and the Fortescues are recent and with less obscure members of the family. But since you are Denford, I consider it my duty to help you."

"I wasn't under the impression I needed help. I've managed to reach the age of thirty in good health and fortune without the slightest assistance from you."

"Of course you need me, Denford. Here we are, halfway through the Season, and I haven't seen you at a single event. I am prepared to smooth your entrée into the best circles where you now belong, by reason of your title."

"Thank you but I am quite content in my existing circles. Let me show you to your carriage."

The lady remained planted in her seat. "Don't be obtuse. How are you going to find a suitable bride?"

"Am I looking for a bride?"

"I certainly hope so. You need an heir."

"I was under the impression I had one."

"I was shocked, shocked to learn that Charles Fortescue had married the daughter of a butcher. Is her son to pollute the corridors of Denford Castle?"

Moderately amused for a while, Denford was

getting tired of this. "I don't see how the boy, whose grandfather is a farmer not a butcher, not that it matters, can be worse than me." He shouldn't let her under his skin, but ten minutes in her company brought back every sneer against his native land he'd ever suffered.

"Your mother may have been Irish but I'm told she came from quite a decent family. Think of your sisters. If they are introduced by someone of impeccable connections, unfortunate aspects of their birth will be quite forgotten and they'll be almost as good as Fortescues."

"They will be obliged, I am sure, ma'am." He almost smiled thinking about what Fenella would have to say about Lady Ashfield. He toyed with the notion of ringing for the schoolroom party to come down and make their curtseys to the old harridan so he could find out. "I have no intention of presenting them. My mother will see to the matter. And absolutely no desire to attend a lot of routs and breakfasts and balls. I am too busy."

"Of course you are, and that is where I can be helpful. I have the perfect bride for you and can arrange a meeting without you having to go to much trouble."

At the moment there was no room in his thoughts for any woman but Jane and he was a long way from being tired of that affair. He imagined Lady Ashfield's face if he told her he'd rather marry a governess, and one with a very shady background.

His unwelcome guest droned on. "Her mother

is my second cousin and I am Henrietta's godmother. She's an excellent girl, quite pretty enough and no nonsense about her. I know how to make a good match so I wouldn't inflict you with a ninny. Best of all, she knows all about pictures because of her father."

Julian barely heard her until she reached the last item. "Who did you say this girl was?"

"Cazalet's daughter. I daresay you're acquainted with him."

Julian had been wondering how best to lure Cazalet, advisor to King George on art purchases, down to Sussex. Lady Ashfield was about to achieve her ambition to be helpful.

"May I offer you a glass of madeira or sherry? Or do you prefer tea in the afternoon?"

For the first time since she arrived, Lady Ashfield smiled, an alarming sight involving a display of large teeth. "I knew you'd come around to my way of thinking. Sherry will do very well and don't be miserly when you pour. We have your future to toast and much to talk about."

Taking his time serving the drinks and repressing the horrible notion of the dragon countess in her cups, Julian adjusted the plan he'd been forming since depositing the Falleron pictures at Denford Castle.

"I'd be interested in meeting Miss Cazalet," he said. "With no obligation on either side, of course."

"Naturally."

"I'm planning to spend the summer at Denford with my sisters. Why don't you bring the Cazalets for a couple of weeks? We'll make a party of it."

He was careful not to commit himself to anything more than entertaining the Cazalets at his country house, yet the idea of marriage had entered his mind. Much as it pained him to give Lady Ashfield any credit, if Henrietta Cazalet was everything advertised she would be an ideal partner for him.

He had to think of his sisters. Since he wouldn't give a groat for the chances of Captain and Mrs. Lowell turning up in London anytime soon, he faced the fact that Maria couldn't stay in the schoolroom forever. His current cozy arrangement by which the efficient and delectable Jane oversaw the nursery by day and shared his bed at night would not continue to suit everyone's needs. His, yes. But not Maria's. As her governess, Jane could not present her at court, and even he, careless of appearances, realized she wouldn't be able to do it as his wife either.

Which was a great pity because while a suitable wife seemed a necessary evil, Jane Grey as a bride stirred his soul.

Same time, same place, same brandy. But his evening meetings with Jane Grey were no longer conducted seated decorously in chairs. Julian lay stretched out on the divan with his head in Jane's lap as she read him the letters the girls had written in his absence.

"And finally there is one more from Maria."

"Can we not bother?"

"She is the only one who follows the rules."

"That's why I don't want to hear it." The rules probably said he shouldn't be lolling around on silk cushions with a governess. And the rules mostly definitely said he shouldn't get under her skirts. He turned over and buried his face in the interesting bit. Now to plan a strategy for getting through to the lode.

"It's charming how much your sisters' letters reflect their characters," she said, stroking his head. His anticipatory growl was cut off when she seized his hair by the queue and turned him to his original position. It wasn't all bad; he loved looking at Jane when she scolded him. "They put a great deal of effort into trying to please you—"

"Not Fenella."

"Especially Fenella."

"She certainly amused me the most."

"You must listen to Maria's last letter."

"Will I be rewarded?"

"I expect you will."

He might feign indifference while Jane read out Maria's effusions on the subject of tulips in Hyde Park, but he was touched that his sisters had bothered to write, several times each and sometimes at length. He would have enjoyed receiving the letters while he wandered in disguise around obscure Belgian villages, dodging the French authorities and searching for Jan, who had gone into hiding. It had been a tedious and lonely few weeks. Once he located Jan, things became less dull but much more fatiguing. All the time they managed the transportation of the pictures to the coast, he worried about interference from Radcliffe's agents in addition to the French. In the end it was a French bullet that winged him.

He doubted Radcliffe had given up; he was saving his "irons in the fire" for when the Falleron pictures had been conveniently returned to England. What his next move would be, Julian couldn't guess. He continued to keep a watch on his sisters and his eyes and ears open.

"You have to answer the letters," Jane said. "It is not polite to receive so many and not respond."

"I hate writing letters."

"We all have to do things we do not like."

"Next you will order me to eat up my mutton or sew a sampler."

"If you had written over the years, even if you couldn't visit them, they would not have been strangers to you."

"You're a tyrant, Jane Grey." He shifted a little to put his arms around her waist.

"Why did you not visit your family more often? If you had the time and means to wander all over Europe, you could have gone to Ireland occasionally."

"Because I did not like being beaten by my stepfather."

"As a child, yes, but later? Was he as big as a titan?"

"Your rules may state that a gentleman likes to talk about himself, but I do not. Most likely it's because I'm not a gentleman. Let's talk about something interesting, like that reward you promised me." He drew her down for a kiss. She didn't resist but the caress was perfunctory and over quickly. Her mind was elsewhere.

"What happened to your family, Jane?"

"They died. I have no one. And that," she said, proving that she wasn't the only person in the room who avoided certain subjects, "is why you must answer your sisters' letters."

"I'm not entirely lacking in a sense of family. I've had Blackett invite some of his cousins to the castle for a couple of weeks. I have a few guests coming and I thought I might as well begin a reconciliation with the Fortescue connections. Do you approve?"

"It's not for me to approve or not. They will be useful associations for your sisters. And you have invited some of your own friends?"

Julian considered and rejected explaining the reason for the gathering. He had no real intentions toward Miss Cazalet but, in his experience, mentioning another woman led to tedious arguments and a high likelihood of going to bed unsatisfied. "A few. I hope my neighbors the Windermeres will be back from France in time. You'll like Denford. The castle is splendid and the grounds and gardens possess all sorts of fascinating byways. Once we've disposed of the guests we'll have a glorious summer. We'll send the girls off for long riding lessons while we explore together."

He tried for another, better kiss but still she held him off. "You will write to your sisters?" She was like a terrier when she got hold of a notion.

"One letter for all of them."

"One each."

"I will do it tomorrow. Anything you want from me now?"

"I'll think about it."

"You'll be able to think better lying down."

Thank goodness she made no objection to a rearrangement of their positions, so finally he had her as he had frequently fantasized in this room, sprawled against the cushions, relaxed and ready for him. He stood back for a while admiring the view, but there was something missing. "Do you by any chance possess a hooped petticoat?"

"No. Why?"

"I've always thought it would be amusing to explore a lady's panniers." He knelt and slowly raised her skirts. "I'll just have to manage with what is offered. This is very exciting, rather like opening a portfolio of drawings for the first time, savoring the anticipation of the treasures within."

"Should I be flattered by the comparison?"

"Most certainly. What have we here?" White stockings covered her pretty calves and were secured by garters decorated with embroidered rosebuds. He stroked the smooth limbs—"So far your undergarments are living up to expectations"—and nibbled at the dimples in her knees, drawing a choked laugh and a slight but distinct upward tilt of her pelvis.

Pushing the skirts up further, he discovered creamy thighs and lushly curved hips. They weren't the longest, slenderest legs he had ever seen but they were shapely and, as he had already learned, strong and muscled for a woman, suitable for carrying brave, indomitable Jane through the challenges of her life. He lingered on the thighs, devouring them with eyes and tongue, enjoying and resisting the wild gyrations of her hips. Her heat and scent flooded his senses. Desire gripped him and his cock tightened to the point of pain. No one had ever affected him as profoundly as Jane, no one.

She was clawing at his head, her throat emitting incoherent but demanding sounds as he kissed and caressed her, never touching the place where he wanted to be and she wanted him to be. He breathed into her sex, provoking a gasped "Julian!"

He loved to hear his name on her lips.

"Yes?" he said. "Have you thought about what you want from me?"

"Mon Dieu!" she cried. "You know it!"

He'd made love to Jane a few times now. Each time was better than the last and each time he wanted more. As he came to know the responses of her body and the accompanying sounds, he had become aware that she was holding back in a way he could not define. There was something about her attentions that was too practiced, too selfless, too consciously concerned with his pleasure and not enough with her own. Any man would think him insane to complain about such a woman and it wasn't a complaint. Merely that he wished for . . . more.

"Is this what you want? You can have it if you ask nicely." He parted her sex with his thumbs and gave her a long, languorous lick, planning to pleasure her until she lost her mind and was scrubbed clean of her secrets and mysteries and all thoughts of anything except him and the delight he brought her, and the joy they shared.

He'd barely started when she stiffened and placed a staying hand on his head. "Not that. I want you inside me. Now."

He wasn't a man to refuse an offer of a warm berth from a woman he adored. He also feared that there was nothing at all he would refuse her. If she knew he would be at her mercy.

Chapter 14

"It's grander than Dublin Castle," Maria said.

They were all awestruck by the first glimpse of Denford Castle from the carriage, provoking an unseemly scramble to sit near the window. Jane restored order and allowed them turns in order of age, except for Oliver Bream, who'd seen it before. She was impatient herself. "We'll have all summer to explore, and judging by the size of the place we'll need it."

"Is it the biggest castle in the world?" Laura asked.

"I bet it isn't bigger than Windsor Castle," Fenella said. "Julian isn't as important as the king."

"I think he is."

"They could put you in the Tower of London for saying that. It's treason."

"They wouldn't!" Laura didn't sound entirely certain.

"They would. And chop off your head too!"

"Ow! Fenella pinched me, Miss Grey."

Jane closed her eyes and drove her nails into

her palms. All day cooped up in a small box with the three girls had made her pity everyone who had ever, by choice or duress, become a governess. *Mon Dieu*, no wonder women preferred marriage or polite prostitution. At least husbands and lovers left the house for a good part of the day, and often the night too. She never thought to regret the day she'd left Henri.

She didn't, of course. She was merely irked and disappointed that Denford wasn't there. He was supposed to have made the journey to Sussex with them. Then, at the last minute, some piece of business had come up and he'd remained in London. Instead of the duke, who would not have put up with the bickering for five minutes, they'd been offered the company of Oliver Bream, who'd dozed most of the way from London. He still claimed to be in love with her, but he didn't lose sleep over his infatuation.

To add to the misery in the overcrowded carriage, Oliver's luggage wouldn't all fit onto the outside, so a large portfolio, several rolls of canvas, an easel, and an untidy basket of artist's paraphernalia were crammed in with them. Jane didn't mind his company for the summer at Denford; she did object to traveling with a paintbrush in her ear.

"Change places with me, Maria. It's my turn."

"But I want to see the portcullis."

Letting the words wash over her, Jane contemplated a night in a lonely bed. It was dreadful how much she already missed Denford when she'd awoken in his arms only that morning.

When the carriage passed through an ancient arch, her heart plummeted to her boots. A vast courtyard flanked by a pair of soaring gothic wings with crenellated battlements and, at the far end, a huge circular tower, bore witness to Denford's origin as a *château fort*. She'd never felt inferior to the duke in a worldly sense. She was a Falleron, even if the family had lost its former glory. But compared to the massive power of Denford Castle, her father's pretty Louis XIV–era château was a frivolous thing. Nothing before had driven home the social chasm that now lay between them, no matter what she had once been.

Denford was a duke; she was nothing. Their only future was for her to live as his mistress until he became tired of her, and she retained enough pride to reject that fate. She'd promised herself the summer with him, but that was all.

She went through the motions of reminding the Osbournes to behave like correct young ladies as they left the carriage. The act of performing her duty restored her equanimity. She had always managed to enjoy the good moments, and truly there was nothing so terrible about this one. She'd survived much worse than a visit to an extraordinary castle and estate, even one marred by the absence of its owner.

They were welcomed by the house steward, who led them along ancient stone passages lined with tapestries, old weapons, and suits of armor. Immediately Jane could see that this was a very different household than Fortescue House. If the cleanliness and good repair of all wasn't enough evidence of a large staff, the presence of numerous liveried footmen told its tale. The steward informed them that this part of the castle had been the living quarters of the family for the past century or so. The substantial children's quarters occupied the far end of the wing, on the same floor as the other bedchambers. Jane wasn't placed in the duchess's rooms. In the haphazard London household, no one seemed to think much of her occupying the best bedchamber. The castle staff, she felt certain, would be scandalized. She was allotted a pleasant, perfectly comfortable room the other side of the schoolroom from the children's bedrooms.

Three days later the girls were blissfully happy with a stable full of ponies and kittens; Jane was not. With not a word from Denford, she began to fear he wouldn't come down from London before the arrival of his guests. The Osbournes' riding lessons gave her time to cultivate the acquaintance of Francis Hillthorpe, a retired land steward who now kept the muniment room in order.

"Are there many Fortescues who are not related to the Dukes of Denford?" she asked her informant. "Or perhaps only distantly?"

Mr. Hillthorpe's wrinkled face brightened. "There are a number of branches descended from Richard Le Fort who saved William the Conqueror's life at the Battle of Hastings by protecting him with his shield. That's what the name Fort Escu means—strong shield. The ducal line broke off from the Devon family in the sixteenth century and acquired Denford Castle by marriage to the Lestrange heiress. The castle itself goes back to the early Norman period."

Giving up hope, for the present, of disentangling the various Fortescues, she listened to Hillthorpe's description of the castle's history and found it engaging enough that she accepted his invitation to visit the oldest part of the castle, the round tower known as Maiden's Keep.

"What is that part of the castle used for?" she asked idly as they crossed the courtyard. She'd noticed a good deal of coming and going at the opposite wing, but so far she hadn't seen much beyond the family quarters and gardens.

"The south wing contains the state rooms, which are to be opened for the coming entertainment. The duke has ordered the refurbishing of the Long Gallery, which runs almost the length of the building on the second floor. I've never seen the chamber in use, a shame since the strapwork ceiling is very fine."

"May we look at it now?"

"His Grace has declared it out of bounds for all but the workmen. I believe he is planning a grand unveiling during the party."

"Perhaps he intends to hang his collection of pictures there."

"Very possible. I would like to see the family portraits gathered in one place but I'm afraid His Grace was quite dismissive when I showed him the castle collection." Mr. Hillthorpe shook his head sadly. "He seems more concerned with artistic quality than family history."

They reached the base of the steep hill from which the tower soared over the rest of the castle. "Are you sure you can manage the path?" Jane asked with concern.

"I may pant a little but I don't want to miss the opportunity to show the place to a lady as appreciative as yourself. Not everyone cares for the Fortescues as I do."

"Why is it called the Maiden's Keep?"

"That is a story best told from the summit."

Within the massive stone walls, a staircase wound to a flat roof enclosed by a series of battlements pierced with arrow loops. In the center, a plinth bore a small statue of a woman in medieval dress while a stone bench faced an opening five or six feet wide. Jane looked over the edge. "I didn't expect such a long drop to the river." She stepped back smartly from a barrier that was only waist height. "Has anyone ever fallen from here?"

"I said I'd tell you the origin of the name. The legend goes that Sieur Adam Lestrange, another of King William's knights, fell in love with the daughter of a Saxon chief. When she refused to give herself to one of her country's conquerors, he seized her and imprisoned her in a room at the top of the tower."

"A true gentleman, yes?"

"Those were different times, I suppose. Certainly no Fortescue would ever behave so dishonorably."

"Oh, certainly not," Jane said, refraining from giving her opinion of the universal virtue of Fortescue men. "What happened to her?"

"Rather than submit to her enemy, she threw herself off this roof."

Jane peered over the edge again and shuddered. There was no chance of surviving such a fall. Far below, the river wended its benign way through sunlit meadows where cattle grazed and men in rustic smocks worked at haymaking. But the existence of the great castle was evidence of war, and the plunder and killing and rape that went with it. These battlements must have seen plenty of death apart from that of one unfortunate girl.

"I cannot imagine having the courage to climb up there and jump. If it were me I would have surrendered to the Norman lord."

"I am afraid he did not offer marriage. He had a French wife already. The maiden would have been dishonored had she yielded."

"So she had to die?"

"The greater sin was his, of course. I cannot but admire a lady who chose death over disgrace. Are you well, Miss Grey?"

Jane leaned her back against a solid battlement, the gray-green stone worn smooth by centuries of exposure to the elements. "Just a little queasy. I'm not fond of heights." It wasn't the height that sickened her, but the reminder that most of the world would condemn her for the choice she made in surrendering her virtue to Mathieu Picard.

Two things kept Julian in London. While the bulk of the Falleron collection was safely stowed in the south wing at Denford, a number of the canvases had needed to be restretched. The craftsman who'd done his framing for years expressed some concerns about the condition of a Claude Lorrain. He also wished to consult the duke about the frame of the Raphael, which had been damaged during the journey. Alarmed about any danger to the masterpiece, Julian decided he must stay in town and oversee the work himself.

Just as important was the arrival of the report he had commissioned from Bow Street on Jane Grey.

If that was indeed her name, a fact that appeared increasingly unlikely.

He'd stayed to interview the Bow Street Runner in person, and the man had described the course of his investigation in impressive detail. As Julian sealed the letters he had finally got around to writing to his sisters, whom he was surprised to find he missed, his eyes drifted to the more concise written report, reduced to a few important points.

Before her arrival in London, there was no evidence that Jane Grey had ever existed. It seemed highly likely that she had come from overseas but not, however, from the island of Saint Lucia.

There had never been an English official named Johnson there and almost every story she'd told about the place was false. Since he already knew there were no ostriches, this was no more than

Julian had expected. How disappointing to learn nothing of any substance, not her real name, or where she came from.

France was his best guess. If she was an escaped aristocrat—quite likely given her manners and speech—why had she not joined émigré circles in London? If a woman of the people, why had she come to England in the middle of a war? For a moment he toyed with the notion that she was a spy, and dismissed it out of hand. There was nothing of interest to Napoleon Bonaparte at Fortescue House.

While almost certain that Jane posed no danger to the future of England, his own future was a different matter. Gripped by fear that she would fade away as mysteriously as she'd appeared, he took up his pen and wrote another letter. However much he missed his sisters, it was nothing to how much he ached to lay eyes on their governess.

"We have letters!" Laura cried.

"Our brother has written to each of us. Mine is the longest." This was from Maria.

"That's wonderful," Jane said, and meant it. Finally her nagging had worn him down. "What does he have to say? Does he say when he expects to join us?"

"I'll read mine," Maria said. "Look! It is addressed to Miss Osbourne and sealed with the Denford crest.

"'Dear sister, I trust you are enjoying Sussex.

I have decided that you are old enough to dine with my guests at Denford Castle. I commend you to the care of your excellent governess for the improvement of your conversation and toilette. If you follow Miss Grey's example you will not disgrace yourself.' " She hugged the single sheet to her bosom.

"Is that all he says?" Jane asked. "Nothing about when he arrives?"

"I am to dine downstairs! Will you help me with my gowns, Miss Grey? Can we go now?"

"First let us hear what His Grace has to say to your sisters." And when he was going to see them. "Will you share your letter, Fenella? Does he say when he arrives?"

Fenella smiled mysteriously. "Mine is the best. Here, read it yourself."

Jane tried not to let herself be distracted by Denford's powerful slashes of black ink, neat but distinctive and, unlike their writer, easily read.

Dear Fenella,

Don't go riding alone. It would be a confounded nuisance if you fell off and damaged your horse.

Yours etc.
Denford

"Isn't it a wonderful letter?" Fenella said. Sometimes there was no understanding the girl.

"As Shakespeare says 'Brevity is the soul of wit,' " Jane agreed.

"Mine is even wittier, then," Laura boasted.

"He says, 'Dear Laura. Do whatever Miss Grey tells you. I always do.'"

"I am obliged to His Grace but I can assure you that he obeys only himself."

"We know that," Fenella said. "Julian is so funny."

While he had failed to follow any of the rules of correct correspondence, the duke had managed to make each of his sisters happy and that was what mattered.

These sweet, odd little letters sparked a tender glow in her breast and assuaged any lingering doubts about Julian. A man who could please his sisters so well simply couldn't have willfully caused the death of hers.

"Miss Grey," Maria said. "There's one for you too."

She would have preferred to read it alone, but the girls stared expectantly. Since they would think her very odd if she kissed the letter, or clutched it to her bosom, she broke the seal with all the calm she could muster.

My dear Jane,

I miss you. If I'd known how long my business would take, I wouldn't have let you leave London. Evenings in the library no longer entertain and my best brandy tastes like ashes. I arrive on the sixth with the first of my guests. Ask the house steward if you need anything, for yourself or the girls. Did I mention that I miss you? Don't run away before I get there.

D.

"What does he say?"

"Will you read it to us?"

"Nothing very much," she said. "Your brother doesn't like to write long letters."

Don't run away before I get there. Why did he think she would disappear? He was right, but how could he know it? She was always poised for flight but not yet. Whatever happened, whatever she discovered, even if her family's murderer appeared with the word *guilty* branded on his forehead, she would not leave before she saw Julian again.

Chapter 15

Fenella tore into the schoolroom. "I see Julian's carriage crossing the moat. Can we go down and meet him? Please, Miss Grey?"

It would be more correct to wait for the duke to summon them to his presence, but this particular duke, as he frequently reminded her, didn't care about what was proper. "Very well." Her hand flew to smooth her hair. "No, wait. Let me make sure your appearance is as it should be."

She tweaked Laura's ribbon and told Fenella to straighten her stockings. Maria looked impeccable, as usual, and the other two would do. It was all she could manage to admonish the younger girls for running and not to run faster herself.

"Julian!" Laura shrieked when they reached the foot of the main staircase, which was separated from the hall by an elaborate wooden screen.

Jane grabbed the little girl's skirt. Through the open gothic tracery she saw that he was not alone. "Remember your manners, children. His Grace has brought company."

They made her proud, curtseying like little mademoiselles when presented to the Countess of Ashfield, Lord Cazalet, and Miss Cazalet.

"And this is their governess, Miss Grey," Denford concluded.

Cazalet, a trim, middle-aged man in a blue coat and buff breeches, nodded with the polite indifference her position merited. His daughter produced a friendly smile while looking about her with bright-eyed curiosity. About Jane's age, she had an attractive, intelligent air. She was the sort of young lady Jane would like to have as a friend. Only Lady Ashfield afforded her more than a glance. Jane avoided the old lady's eagle eye and looked at the floor. That one was undoubtedly a Tartar, and unlikely to have missed the significant look Julian had shot her while he made his introductions, or the way Jane found it impossible not to smile back at him. From the moment he'd walked into the hall her heart had threatened to burst from her chest. If only all these people—guests, children, servants—would disappear.

Instead another carriage pulled up at the front door, disgorging three new arrivals. Although she'd only seen them at a distance at the theater, she immediately recognized the lady in the excruciatingly fashionable orange silk spencer and matching bonnet and her much older husband. She hardly had time to wonder why Denford had invited Sir Richard Radcliffe, a man he'd described in brutally unflattering terms, to his house, when their companion sent her into a state of panic.

Quick as lightning, she dodged behind the screen and watched her cousin, Louis de Falleron, presented as Comte Louis de Beauville.

"I hope you can squeeze dear Louis into your little castle," Lady Belinda Radcliffe said to Denford, caressing his arm in a way that made Jane want to hit her. "When he heard where we were going he begged us to take him with us. He adores castles."

This was news to Jane, who remembered Louis as a courtier and Parisian through and through. Her father had vainly tried to interest his heir in the land and country people at the Normandy estate. She'd also like to know why he was representing himself as a scion of an ancient Limousin family with no connection to the Fallerons. His ambiguous appearance confirmed Jane's instinct not to approach him, at least for the present. Since he'd last seen her nine years ago and believed her dead, the odds of his recognizing her were slim. Not that he would notice an inferior. She was safely invisible as long as she did nothing to draw attention to herself.

"Any friend of yours is welcome," Julian said. Through the tracery of the screen Jane saw his most derisive smile. "I'll speak to my steward about a room for him."

"You are gracious, Monsieur le Duc," Louis said.

"I expect you'd like to be placed near your dear friends the Radcliffes. We want you to feel at home. And since you are so interested in castles,

I will ask Mr. Hillthorpe to give you a tour of the place. You must see the Maiden's Keep, Lady Belinda. The view from the top is quite remarkable." Julian glanced at his guest's embroidered satin slippers.

Hah! Julian had her measure and probably Louis's too. She'd like to see that hothouse pair make the steep climb.

"We'll all go together." The lady, keeping her hold on Julian, drew Louis to her other side while her husband looked on complacently. "Are there any bedchambers in the tower? That would be most romantic. If we could stay there, I mean."

Jane ground her teeth.

"Who are those people, Jane?" Oliver's silent arrival behind her made her jump. "I was hoping Cynthia had arrived." He floated out into the hall in his usual abstracted state then stopped short. "Oh my goodness! What a beautiful creature."

Miss Cazalet returned his regard with an alert expression. If Oliver had fallen in love again, he appeared to have picked a lady who might just return his interest. Then he walked straight past the young woman and planted himself in front of Lady Belinda Radcliffe.

"Introduce me, Julian."

Denford disengaged himself from Her Ladyship. "Certainly, Oliver." Jane could hear the amusement in his voice as he performed the formalities.

"I must paint you," Oliver said to Lady Belinda, evincing no interest in either Radcliffe or Louis.

"I'm working on a series of religious pictures. You shall be my Madonna, my Virgin."

"There's a challenge to the imagination," Julian muttered.

"A Madonna in scarlet! I don't think it's been done before."

The lady kindly extended her hand to her new worshipper. "I adore being painted, Mr. Bream. I've sat for Romney and Lawrence and I suppose even they were unknown artists once."

Oliver, oblivious to Lady Belinda's condescension, received support from a new quarter. "Mr. Bream is talented," said Miss Cazalet. "I saw his Rape of Lucrece at the Royal Academy last year."

"No one else did," Oliver said, distracted for a moment from the glories of Lady Belinda's bosom.

"I don't recall the name," Lord Cazalet said. "Did you remark on the work to me at the time, Henrietta?"

"I believe I noticed it when I visited the exhibition with my aunt, Papa. It was ill-hung in a dark corner and deserved better." That would make Oliver happy. Jane had heard his theory that the members of the hanging committee had engaged in a conspiracy to hide his light under a bushel.

Unlike his daughter, Lord Cazalet apparently hadn't much time for a painter whose works were consigned to dark corners. He turned to Denford. "I look forward to seeing those pictures you promised me, Duke. I see that you don't keep them in the hall."

"I don't think you'll be disappointed. The gallery where they are hung has been undergoing repairs and isn't quite ready, but I anticipate an unveiling that will astound all the *cognoscenti.*" He bowed to Radcliffe, whose thin lips stretched without warmth. No love lost there. Louis, on the other hand, expressed enthusiasm for the event, surprising since his lack of appreciation for the family collection had disappointed the late Marquis de Falleron.

Jane scrambled out of the way when the party moved toward the staircase to be shown to their rooms by the house steward. "Keep back girls," she said softly. "Let the guests go first."

None of the guests noticed her but Julian did and dropped back to join her. "Jane," he said in his most caressing tones, the single syllable sending waves of longing through her. "Confound these people. Where can I see you?"

"I shall be in the schoolroom with your sisters, Your Grace. No doubt you will wish for a report on their progress." She raised her voice a little, in case anyone heard them, and to remind him that the children were only a few feet away.

"I wish we could meet at the usual time and place."

"You have guests."

"No need to state the obvious."

"You invited them."

"And so I did. I have my reasons."

"You draw attention to us," she said through clenched teeth.

"Go," he said to the children. "Go . . . somewhere. I need a word with Miss Grey."

"You shouldn't be talking to me when your

guests are waiting for you." For a second she felt alone with Julian in an enchanted circle where they breathed the same air but could not touch. Though out of earshot they were still under observation. With Lady Ashfield and Miss Cazalet regarding them curiously they couldn't even gaze into each other's eyes.

"Dine with us," he said when she looked away.

"Absolutely not. You invited Maria to do so, which is completely proper, but I shall remain in my place with the younger girls."

"That is not your place, Jane." Without moving or touching her with so much as a finger, his whisper sent a tingle all the way down her spine. "Your place is with me."

If only it were so. "You delude yourself."

Mr. Blackett approached and the guests still expected the attention of their host. Maria had obediently followed the house party that she was so enraptured to join, but the younger girls, having circled the hall, reappeared, eager for their brother's company. They'd missed Denford too.

"I'll find a way to see you later," he said quickly. "Where have they put you?"

"Our bedchambers in the nursery quarters are most comfortable, are they not, children?" He needed to be reminded that little pitchers have big ears.

"You could dine with us, Julian," Laura piped up.

"I wish I could."

Lady Belinda Radcliffe might be the love of Oliver Bream's life, but she made a disappointing model. Carrying his sketchbook, he had lured her to his favorite spot among Denford's formal parterres, a walled knot garden, scented with herbs and early summer flowers. The mellow brick wall, covered with espaliered trees, was the perfect background for his scarlet Virgin. He was gripped by the revolutionary idea of making red the color of purity.

"I'm tired, Mr. Perch."

Oliver didn't care if she got his name wrong, but she hadn't given him more than five minutes, ten at the most. He'd barely outlined the smooth white brow, so perfect for the Madonna. "I suppose you could take a short rest."

Dizzied by her smile, he missed the appearance of that Frenchman, Beauville, who was always hanging around and removing her from Oliver's range. "Louis!" she called. She had a voice like rich ochre. "Mr. Pike has been drawing me. So amusing."

"*Ma chère* Belinda. How can a man copy what was created by the gods?"

"All of the great artists," Oliver said, defending his profession.

"*Bien sûr,*" Beauville said. "The great ones can. Will you walk to the river with me?"

"But she's sitting for me," Oliver said.

"He has taken up far too much of your time. I reclaim you."

"I have barely started."

"I am rather tired. Dear Louis, let me lean on your arm."

Speechless, Oliver watched them leave the garden. Where was Jane? he wondered, thinking he should return to his portrait of Delilah. He'd hardly seen her in two days, since the other guests arrived. The Osbourne girls approached, but there was no sign of their governess.

Fenella and Laura ran up to greet him, followed more sedately by Maria, arm in arm with Miss Cazalet. He always remembered her name because she had noticed the masterpiece that had failed to impress anyone at the Royal Academy. Anyone except for this exceptionally perceptive young woman.

"We were looking for you, Oliver," Laura said.

"Are we supposed to have a drawing lesson?" He'd forgotten to wind his watch.

"No, silly," Fenella said. "That's tomorrow. Miss Cazalet wanted to speak to you."

"Why?"

"Ask her. We must go. Miss Grey said we'd have to miss our riding lesson if we were late for geography."

"I'll see you later, Miss Cazalet," Maria said. "I look forward to hearing more about your presentation at court."

While the young ladies made much ado about parting from a lady they would see again in a few hours, a vista through the arch of a box hedge caught Oliver's eye. Perching on a stone bench, he became absorbed in work.

"Ahem. Mr. Bream?"

He looked up and blinked at Miss Cazalet with the sun behind her.

"Do you mind if I watch you draw? I'll be quiet."

"Noise doesn't bother me."

He worked away for a few more minutes until it occurred to him that his composition would be improved by a figure and for once he had a handy model. "Would you let me draw you?"

"I'm flattered. How would you like me?"

He arranged her in a simple pose at the opposite end of his bench. "Do you mind removing your bonnet?"

"Not at all. Who am I?"

"No one in particular."

"A portrait then?"

Oliver scowled. "I hate doing portraits."

"They are the best way for an artist to get noticed," she said "You don't have to do many, just enough to make your reputation and keep your name in the public eye."

Oliver sketched in Miss Cazalet's rather fine profile. "You know a lot about the subject."

"I've grown up among painters and collectors. I find the business of art quite fascinating." Happily, Miss Cazalet had the ability, so important in a model, to speak without moving and upsetting the composition.

"Like Denford?"

"Not buying and selling. I'd like to help artists succeed. I could help you."

"How would you do that?"

"There's a big demand for pictures, not only among the wealthy but also people of the middling kind. I read in the *Morning Post* that Bartolozzi's prints of masterworks have added over one million pounds to the revenue of Great Britain. Artists can do very well nowadays but it's difficult to win the attention of the public because there are too many of you. You need to cultivate those who write about art."

This was a topic on which Oliver could wax eloquent. "Puffery! It is everywhere. Untalented hacks get ignorant fools to praise them in print."

"A necessary evil. I hope you won't be angry with me, but I took the liberty of writing to an editor of my acquaintance reporting that you are staying at Denford Castle for the summer, executing a portrait of the duke's sisters."

"But I am not."

"It doesn't matter. As long as people believe you are patronized by a duke, they will think your work must be good."

"That's dishonest."

"Is your work good? I think so."

"Of course I am good."

"Then there is no dishonesty."

Oliver couldn't put his finger on why that didn't seem quite right. But he couldn't resist Miss Cazalet's enthusiasm for his work. She might be able to help him sell something.

"What are you painting now?" she asked.

"I *was* sketching Lady Belinda in preparation for a canvas." He showed her the meager outline he'd managed. "She is to be the Madonna."

"I'm curious. What made you think of Lady Belinda as the Virgin?"

"She's beautiful," he said reverently.

"So she is, but not in that way. I would think more of a Judith, or Delilah perhaps."

"Jane is my Delilah."

"Miss Grey? I wouldn't have considered her in that light. She seems such a pleasant young woman."

"She's a dangerous temptress. I saw that at once. Secretive too."

"How observant you are. I know this is an intimate question but since I've become your advisor I'd like to know where I stand. Are you in love with her?"

"I was, but not since I saw Lady Belinda."

Miss Cazalet regarded him with a baffled expression and shook her head. "Why? I do not think you and Her Ladyship are well suited. In short, I think she will swallow you whole and spit you out."

Oliver gaped at her. His friends teased him about his inamoratas, but never in such forthright terms. *Oliver's in love again*, they would say, but never asked him why. Why he fell in love so often, and why didn't it last.

"Don't worry," he said. "I like being in love, especially when the lady inspires my painting. It never stops me working."

Miss Cazalet smiled warmly. "I'm glad to hear it. I should hate to see you distracted from the full exploitation of your talents. I would like to hear your plans."

Thrilled to have a willing and receptive audience, he described his religious series and she thoroughly approved his goal of finding subject matter that would appeal to a wide variety of people. "I'm not sure you have chosen the right subjects, however. Samson and Delilah won't do. Their story is too warm for the new rich, or for the patron I have in mind for you. And a Madonna is all very well for the Old Masters but a modern painter might be suspected of popery. How about a nice English scene? St. George and the Dragon perhaps."

"I wouldn't mind trying a dragon, and there's plenty of armor here at Denford." Before his imagination took flight and he tackled the technical challenge of painting metal, he had one more question. "Why do you think I should paint St. George?"

"My father has the ear of the king, you know. What you need is a royal commission."

Oliver stared at this amazing woman, who understood him as no one had in his entire life. "Do you realize," he said, "that while we have been talking I forgot to draw?"

"We can't have that, Mr. Bream," she said. "Get to work."

To their disgust, the Misses Osbourne found their governess only slightly less demanding because of the presence of guests. As the castle became more crowded with every new arrival,

Fenella and Laura would have liked to take up permanent residence behind the hall screen, or in the gardens once the fine weather drew the visitors outside.

Instead Jane kept them hard at work in the schoolroom, as she adhered to her resolution to avoid Louis. Unfortunately it meant avoiding Denford too, since they couldn't visit each other's rooms at night. She kept telling herself it was for the best and almost believed it.

The nursery was not entirely free of visitors. Miss Cazalet had struck up Maria's acquaintance at dinner and came to visit them several times. Jane's first impression that she would like her proved correct. Oliver had always availed himself of the schoolroom, especially between meals. He and Miss Cazalet had become friends and were planning a series of paintings. Miracle, she had managed to persuade him that not all canvases needed to be executed in epic proportions but that smaller works would sell better.

Lord and Lady Windermere arrived late to the party, recently returned from Paris. Their infant son was lodged in the nursery quarters with his nurse. They were amiable and polite to Jane but, like most of their rank, tended to ignore servants. Or if not ignore, at least behave as though their presence was of little account. She didn't mean to eavesdrop when they came into the schoolroom after a visit to their baby; they failed to notice her sitting in the corner, reading Maria's latest essay while the girls went riding.

Lady Windermere knelt on the window seat, set into the thick castle wall. "I had no idea Denford Castle was so overwhelming." An understandable response to the sight of Maiden's Keep, a looming presence that might make the occupants feel protected or threatened, depending on their point of view. "It's so massive and ancient, yet it suits Julian."

Her husband, whose most obvious characteristic was a restrained elegance, agreed. "I would not have expected it since he has always been so dismissive of the place."

"That's because he dared not become attached to a house he didn't feel he really owned. Now that he has come to terms with the Fortescue family he's becoming more ducal by the day. I wouldn't be surprised if soon he refuses to speak to us."

Her Ladyship's observation made Jane smile. She had watched Julian grow into his role as duke, just as he had learned how to be a brother.

The Windermeres sat together in the window embrasure, with every sign of settling in. Jane ought to give a tactful cough, but she wouldn't have stopped them for the world, not when she could listen to them talk about the man who obsessed her thoughts. Even hearing his name was a pleasure to be relished.

"He'll never cut your acquaintance, more's the pity." Lord Windermere laughed softly. "Don't protest, I'm only joking."

"Julian no longer has any feelings for me. But he'll never cease flirting, just to annoy you."

"And I refuse to be annoyed." He kissed his wife's hand, his dark head contrasting with her blond prettiness. A pang of envy pierced Jane's breast. Not at the idea of Denford flirting: Of course he did and she was French enough to expect it. But the sight of so devoted a married couple filled her with hopeless longing for such a loving alliance. "Entertaining guests at his castle," the earl continued, "is the sort of thing a duke should do, but reformed or not, Julian has shown himself true to form in assembling such a strange group. When I asked him why he'd invited the Radcliffes he smiled and told me to expect interesting developments."

"I can't wait. Just as long as I don't have to spend much time in Lady Belinda's company. Fortunately she's quite engrossed by that Frenchman." Lady Windermere laughed. "Poor Oliver. Have you spoken with Sir Richard?"

"Sir Richard and I are on the best of terms. Which is to say I never turn my back on him lest he stick a knife into it."

"And Lady Ashfield! Why did Julian invite *her*? She still terrifies me."

"I suspect it was the only way he could get Cazalet, and we know why he wanted him."

Lady Windermere's voice turned low and confidential so Jane had to strain to hear. "It's my belief that Lady Ashfield is trying to make a match between Julian and Henrietta Cazalet, and she may just succeed. Julian seems quite taken with her."

"Really? You think he is showing her more attention than he would to any guest who is also a pretty girl?"

"Why not? He needs to settle down, for the sake of his sisters if no other reason. Miss Cazalet has been spending a lot of time with Miss Osbourne." Jane froze, seeing the pleasant young woman's entry into their circle in a new light. "I can't help thinking she is cultivating the family," Her Ladyship continued, "and they do share an interest. He'd be hard put to find a suitable bride who knew as much about pictures."

Windermere shook his head. "I don't see it. Julian can't have changed so much that he would tamely agree to a *suitable* match. He's more likely to marry his kitchen maid, just to cock a snoot at the *ton*, not to mention his relations."

"I disagree, Damian. He is different. He has come to care for those girls."

Lady Windermere was right. The duke did care for his sisters, and for once the knowledge stabbed Jane to the heart. Fool that she was, Jane had never thought of Denford taking a bride. He would one day, naturally, but long after she had left. It made perfect sense that he would wed for their sake. As a daughter of aristocracy, Jane approved of such an action. As Jane Grey, the idea sent her heart into the toes of her sensible shoes. An irrational loathing for her stout kid footwear seized her when she'd been born to wear pearl embroidered slippers like Lady Belinda. She hated what she had been forced to become. Hated it. She dipped her quill in the ink pot and corrected an error in

Maria's French with such vehemence that she tore the paper.

"You may be right about what Julian intends, Cynthia, but not why. He has a reason to court Miss Cazalet and it has nothing to do with his sisters, or any other piece of sentimentality. Cazalet would like to net a duke for his daughter and he may make it a condition for using his influence with the king."

"Always the diplomat, my love, and that is not a compliment. I'm afraid you are right about Julian's motives. Yet I believe it will work out well. Henrietta Cazalet is delightful and they share so many interests. I shall do everything I can to promote the match."

"In that case, knowing Julian, you'd do better to leave him alone. Or disparage the lady and he'll offer for her just to be contrary."

To watch Julian court another woman was more than Jane could stand. Was this why she'd barely set eyes on him since his arrival? There were perfectly good explanations, but he could have found a way for them to meet if he wanted it. He was the duke, for goodness' sake, and all-powerful in this house.

"Miss Grey! Are you all right?" Lady Windermere started as Maria's essay floated to the floor, overtaken by Jane's dropped pen. "I hope we haven't been disturbing you."

Jane scrambled to her feet and picked up the quill, which had sprayed ink over Maria's pristine composition. "Not at all, my lady. Just a little headache. I believe I shall rest until the Misses Osbourne return."

The other woman smiled. "They're charming girls and do you much credit. The duke made quite a to-do about finding a governess, begging me to interview the candidates, but I can see he did a splendid job. Shall we go, Damian? I wouldn't want to miss Julian's tour of the grounds. I intend to ask him lots of difficult questions about gardening. Good-bye, Miss Grey. I trust you feel better."

Jane curtseyed and retreated to her room, but she couldn't resist placing her ear to the keyhole.

Windermere's voice drifted through. "Trust Julian to hire such a lovely governess. And they've been sharing a house all these weeks."

"Shame on you, Damian, for suggesting such a thing. I'm sure Miss Grey is entirely respectable."

"But Julian is not."

Chapter 16

It hadn't occurred to Julian that in a castle the size of a small town it would be so difficult to snatch a private hour—or even five minutes—with another denizen. Not that five minutes would be long enough for what he most craved.

He'd tried stealing into Jane's room at dead of night, only to be caught tiptoeing through the schoolroom by Laura, who claimed to be looking for a drink of water. His own room was hopeless: None other than Lady Ashfield had been assigned the rooms adjacent to his, and he feared she had the ears of an owl to accompany her eagle eyes. The last thing he needed was a visit from the nosy old witch when *in flagrante delicto*. Every room in this wing of the castle was occupied by one of the people he'd been stupid enough to invite to his house party.

Even a brief interlude of Jane's stimulating conversation, a quick scolding, a few seconds of her smile, would be better than nothing. He hardly ever saw her. On the rare occasions she emerged from the schoolroom there was never an opportunity when they were both alone. And ever present was his fear that one day she would evaporate like morning dew and he'd have no idea where to find her.

Two days later, desperate for her company, he requested the governess bring the younger girls down after dinner to join their sister for some music. Desperate indeed if he was prepared to listen to the trio's singularly mediocre talents. When the party gathered in the Crimson State Room, so called for the color of its turkey carpet and silk hangings, he listened to Lord Cazalet with half an ear while keeping his eye on the door. Jane, or rather the tantalizing absence of her company, was distracting him from the main reason for this party, persuading Cazalet to recommend his pictures to the king for purchase as the core of a new national gallery.

That evening he'd decided to tempt him with a sample, a good Dutch interior he bought a few years ago and not one of the Falleron pictures.

"I'll admit I am intrigued," Cazalet said. "And impressed too."

"You haven't seen anything yet."

"I commend your strategy for whetting my appetite, if that is what it is. But that's not what I meant. I am impressed by Denford Castle, and I am intrigued by you. You've turned out to be a more worthy duke than I would have expected, given your background and history."

"I am obliged to you."

"Henrietta is impressed too. She says your taste

is impeccable. My daughter has an unerring eye for quality since I taught her myself."

"The quality of dukes?"

Cazalet had no sense of humor. "I was speaking of pictures, of course."

Julian liked Henrietta Cazalet. Everyone did. She was a handsome girl, clever and agreeable, and shared many of his tastes. Lady Ashfield had chosen well for him except for one thing. She was not Jane Grey. He'd been doing his best to pay her attention just short of unmistakable wooing. He didn't want to put himself in a position where he was obliged to offer for her, or risk her father's enmity. Since well-bred young ladies of good reputation were largely outside his experience, he trod carefully.

"Miss Cazalet has excellent taste herself," he said. "What do you think of that portrait of the first duke?"

Cazalet was not to be deflected. "Let me lay down my cards, Denford. I believe you to be a man I could welcome into my family. Naturally, should the pictures be all you say, I would under the circumstances commend you to His Majesty."

That was plain speaking.

He was saved from answering by the approach of the lady herself. "Duke," she said with a bright smile that had nothing wrong with it apart from not belonging to Jane Grey. "Miss Osbourne tells me that she and her sisters have prepared a special appearance this evening. She asked me if I would play the piano for them since their governess is indisposed."

"Unwell? Miss Grey?" He spoke with enough vehemence to draw a curious look from his would-be father-in-law. "My sisters are attached to her," he said in a more measured way. "I do not believe they would put on any kind of performance if she were ill."

"Miss Osbourne says it is only a headache, and I am glad to be of service in her place. I don't know the Mozart piece Miss Grey was to play, but we agreed that Handel's Scipio would do as well."

Julian had heard that Mozart flooding the London house a dozen times; it was the only piece Jane played even moderately well. Skilled musician or not, he'd rather hear her than Henrietta. The fact that she wasn't coming downstairs made the evening an utter waste.

Henrietta took her seat at the instrument and struck a warning chord. The room fell silent, all attention on the double doors at the end. As the notes of Handel's march poured from the pianist's able fingers, Maria and her sisters processed into the room. They looked charming in white silk evening gowns with contrasting sashes, but what amazed was the way they walked, if that was what you'd call it. They entered like stately ships, their limbs not making a ripple in their pristine skirts. The progress across the floor was smooth as silk, as though they were propelled on wheels.

Most of the company looked on with appreciative indulgence but Lord Cazalet's jaw had dropped. A few other guests also seemed astonished, including Windermere, Radcliffe, and Belinda Radcliffe's French lover, Louis de Beauville.

The girls reached the center of the room and halted. Miss Cazalet brought the march to an end and all three of them curtseyed deeply in perfect synchronism.

"The Versailles glide," Cazalet murmured. "I never thought I'd see it again."

"What do you mean?" Julian asked.

"It's the way the ladies of high nobility walked at the Court of Versailles. It is said that Marie-Antoinette learned it from the great ballet master Noverre. How do your sisters come to know it? I did not think your governess was French."

"Miss Grey is English," he said, not believing it for a minute. A Frenchwoman and an aristocrat too, he'd wager his dukedom.

Continuing to glide, though Julian now detected a minuscule wobble breaking the fluency of Fenella's movement, the Osbournes reached him.

"Can we stop now?" Fenella asked. "My knees hurt."

"Hush!" Maria said. "Do not mention your limbs in front of gentlemen."

Noticing that Lord Cazalet was listening, Fenella refrained from further argument. Julian guessed that later he would hear an earful from his opinionated sister. He counted on it.

"How did you learn to glide so beautifully?" Cazalet asked. "It took me back twenty years."

Maria stared. "Miss Grey was preparing us for presentation at court. You said yourself, brother, that I would make my curtsey to the queen."

Yes, but which queen? Miss Grey had slipped

up here, confusing the late Queen of France with Queen Charlotte.

"We've been practicing for weeks," Laura said. "It's very hard. Did we not do it correctly?"

"You did it perfectly," Julian said. "I'm sorry Miss Grey isn't well enough to witness the fruits of her teaching."

Laura tugged his hand and stood on tiptoe to whisper. "She doesn't seem very ill to me. I think she's shy in front of the guests."

She wasn't going to stand it.

After cravenly excusing herself from appearing in the drawing room while the girls made their grand entrance, and lying awake half the night until her head truly did ache, Jane awoke with her pride in full working order.

She was a Falleron, acknowledged or not, and she was not going to be treated this way by her lover, even if he was a duke. If he wanted to marry, that was his right and his duty. In the lost world of the *noblesse* it was not *comme il faut* to keep this fact from his mistress. The mistress should be among the first to know, and then she would know how to comport herself if she encountered the lady with whom she must, henceforth, share her lover.

She didn't expect Denford to marry her; she had deeply disapproved of Windermere's suggestion that he might wed a kitchen maid, even if spoken in jest. But apparently she, Jeanne-Louise de Falleron, had been Jane Grey for too long and absorbed the values of the bourgeois among whom she had spent the last decade. She *would not* share her lover, duke or no duke.

She wrote a stiff little note to him, demanding a private audience. She would tell Denford that it was all over between them and then . . .

And then she didn't know what she would do.

She slumped at the table and stared at her note, high indignation draining away to be replaced by melancholy. Instead of finding Mr. Fortescue, she had entered an *affaire de coeur* with the head of the Fortescue family. With no immediate prospect of love or revenge, her life was in danger of drifting into uncertainty—or perhaps plummeting into a void.

She straightened her back, folded her letter, and set off to find a footman. It took less time than expected. Not ten yards down the passage, a liveried servant greeted her. "A message from His Grace, miss."

Dear Miss Grey,

No visitor to the castle should fail to see the pride of Denford, the Maiden's Keep. I have arranged for a private visit this afternoon. Come to the door at two and you will be admitted. Promptness and correct dress will be appreciated.

Denford

Since proper attire for a tryst with one's lover—Denford's request—was not the same as that for breaking off the affair—her intention—she wore a simple muslin gown, suitable summer attire for a governess.

She climbed the steep hill to the tower, the sun on her back in contrast to the chilled stone of the great fortress looming ahead of her. Absurd to feel that she would never be happy again; she hadn't been happy in years. Yet that wasn't true. She'd been happy as governess to the Osbournes and happy in Denford's arms.

She'd scarcely knocked on the thick oaken door before it creaked open and she was tugged blinking into the gloom. The door slammed behind them.

"I've missed you so much, Jane." He tried to kiss her but she jerked her head aside.

"You've managed well enough for three days. No doubt you have better company."

"Never. You know why I couldn't come to you at night. I've gone to a lot of trouble to send everyone away for the afternoon, and made an excuse about why I cannot accompany them like a good host. I even sent Hillthorpe in my place to tour the cathedral and to prevent him from interrupting us at the keep. He's quite possessive about this place and I wanted to show it to you myself."

"You are too late. Mr. Hillthorpe already brought me here."

He took hold of her hands. "As I would know if we had exchanged more than a few words since my arrival. You're angry with me. Can you accept my groveling apology, on bended knees if necessary?" He was half rueful, half amused. She said nothing. "Please Jane. Did you know there is a bedchamber in the tower?"

"Where the Saxon maiden was supposed to surrender her virtue to your ancestor?"

"Unfair!"

"I take back the implication. Why is there a bed here?"

"I am told that during the long summer, the younger men competed mightily for the privilege of sleeping in the tower. Would you like to see the room?" He stroked her hair, and his low whisper in the gloomy vaulted entryway sent waves of longing through her veins. She broke free and made for the staircase.

"I think not. Let us go to the top. We need to talk and the view is magnificent."

"I don't like the sound of that. It's never a good thing when a lady wishes to talk, especially if she thinks I need the distraction of a fine view."

"You, Your Grace? I was thinking of me."

"I'm glad to hear you still need distraction. I was beginning to fear I had lost my touch."

Unfortunately he hadn't. His touch was as potent as ever and she needed to avoid it until she had said her piece. As she carefully mounted the uneven winding stairs she sensed his warmth two steps behind. Keeping a hand on the rough cold stones of the staircase wall helped her balance and prevented her from drifting into a sensual haze.

Emerging onto the roof, the light was almost blinding, and since she'd left her bonnet behind she risked a red face. She didn't care. Closing her eyes, she tilted her head to the sun's rays. Better the heat of summer than that of her body's reaction to Denford. High above she heard a lark's song.

"Upbraid me for my neglect," he said. "I will take my punishment, for all that it is undeserved. I had affairs to attend to when I would far rather have been with you."

"A gentleman's affairs always come first."

"You would have me neglect my duties? That doesn't sound like my strict governess."

"I understand your duties, Your Grace, and I know that one of them is to marry. I felicitate you. Mademoiselle Cazalet is a very fine young lady. *Très gentille.*" He didn't seem to notice that in her agitation she almost reverted to French. "You should have told me what you intended. I believe I have the right."

"Is that what this is about?" He gave a short crack of laughter. "I should have guessed that nothing can be kept secret in a small village or large castle. I'm sorry you heard this rumor, but I assure you I am not engaged to Miss Cazalet, or anyone else."

"But you will be. And that is why we cannot meet again, alone. I will not be your mistress if you are promised to another." She forced herself to look at him and tender her resignation when all she wanted to do was to fall into his embrace. "It will be better if I leave your service entirely. I shall depart shortly. I'm sure Lady Windermere will help you find a new governess."

He seized her by the shoulders and pulled her

close. "Don't leave me, Jane. How can I do without you?" She had never seen him so serious with an expression that looked like anguish, heard his voice so raw and free of mockery. She averted her face from the power of his eyes, blue as the sky and framed in black lashes. "Who will teach me to be a better brother?" When Denford was teasing she found him delectable; his sincerity was irresistible.

"You will manage," she muttered.

"No," he said, "I will not. I do not think I can manage without you. You have bewitched me like no other woman in all my life."

It was shocking, coming from him. Denford the cynic, the devil-may-care, the scorner of all sentiment, had vanished. His fingers dug into her flesh and she relished the pain that bore witness to the intensity of his feelings. She wanted to tell him that she was his and he could do with her what he wished.

He took a deep breath and relaxed his grip. "Let me try and explain." He led her to the bench, the stone hard and cool through her muslin skirts. "I play a delicate game. I told you of my ambitions to sell a collection of pictures to the king. Cazalet is the key to his acceptance. I must have his recommendation and until he has given it, I have let him believe I may be his son-in-law."

Just as Windermere had surmised. "That's unfair to Miss Cazalet."

"You bullied me into being nice to my sisters. You can't expect me to reform all my wicked ways. Not even Jane Grey can make me a saint."

How could she, when she was hardly a saint

herself? All her sins and lies were intended to culminate in the act of murder. Justifiable, but murder nevertheless. She had never fooled herself that plunging a knife into Mr. Fortescue's flesh was an act that God would forgive. In comparison to hers, Denford's transgressions were peccadilloes.

"I wouldn't want you to be a saint, merely a halfway decent man. And I believe that you are and always were. You like to pretend to be devilish with your black garments and your long hair and your twisted smile but you don't deceive me. You were never as black as you pretend. There is a soft heart underneath that alarming shell."

He retreated into flippancy. "If so, let it be our secret or my reputation for ruthlessness will be quite ruined."

"Not if you break Miss Cazalet's heart." Or another heart in greater danger.

"She doesn't give a damn about me. I can tell if a woman cares, and she does not. If Henrietta Cazalet accepted my proposal, which I have no intention of making, it would only be to please her father and Lady Ashfield."

"Impossible. Why would she turn you down?"

"How delightful that you can't believe a woman wouldn't want me."

She'd given too much away. "You are a duke," she said with a shrug. "Anyone would want to marry a duke."

Shifting along the seat until they touched, side to side, he placed one large hand over the two clasped in her lap. His breath tickled her ear, and his low voice reverberated in her head. "You give a damn about me, Jane Grey. You care for me. Can you deny it?"

She couldn't, *mort et damnation*! Of course she cared for Denford. But it was far worse than that. She had fallen in love with him. The knowledge, long denied, swelled her heart with joy and twisted her gut with misery. She tore herself away, ran across the circular enclosure, and leaning her head against a stone battlement, covered her face with her hands.

"Go away," she whispered when he followed her.

"Deny it," he said with his breath and lips on her ear, his fingers branding her waist. She was bursting with love, ready to explode if she had to keep it in. "Deny it," he repeated. "Tell me you don't care for me."

With her heart a lump in her throat, she could barely speak. "I cannot."

He seized her roughly and turned her so that she was in his arms, holding her fast against his chest. "I cannot deny it either. I care for you. So very much."

Then he captured her mouth in a wet, hot, all-consuming kiss that made her forget every other thing in the world and in her life, past or future. The universe narrowed to Denford and her and the tiny space they occupied under a bright blue sky. There was nothing gentle or sweet about the fever that possessed them. His afternoon stubble burned her chin; she clawed his back in her desperate hunger; he gripped her bottom to lift her against his erection; her hands lowered to his waist, fruitlessly seeking his buttons; she felt the silken summer air on her thighs as he lifted her skirts. Somehow they managed to set aside enough of their garments so that he could push her against the wall, lift one of her legs, and guide himself inside her with a relentless drive.

She cried out, again and again, in chorus with the soaring lark, mindless with bliss such as she'd never experienced. It wasn't gentle or pretty but raw and true, and as she screamed her fulfillment to the skies, she knew that she could never leave this man.

Julian had her in his arms. They'd stumbled laughing, drained of strength, tipsy with joy, down the short, perilous flight of stairs to the only furnished room in the Maiden's Keep to lie naked and entwined in the narrow bed.

"I've never felt better in my life. It must be the nearly two weeks without you that made that so extraordinary."

"We should make a practice of extended abstinence then."

"I'd rather not."

"Is this the longest you have ever gone without?"

"No, Madame Curiosity, it is not. I'm not such a diehard rake. What about you? Was there anyone else after your dastardly solider?"

"I had one other lover."

"I hope he was better than the first."

"I chose him myself and that was an improvement."

Julian was both glad and jealous, an entirely foreign sentiment. He didn't wish that Jane's past had been completely miserable, but it was all he could do not to ask her if he was the better lover. He wouldn't do it, wouldn't put her in the position of having to tell a lie to flatter him. Or tell the truth and make him wretched. Yet he didn't think he was mistaken in finding something new in Jane's response to their lovemaking.

"There was something different between us today. I felt you lose yourself more than in the past. Of course I was fairly lost myself." He averted his head, suddenly unsure that he was right, and turned it into a jest. "Perhaps it was the effect of the open air. Shall we always do it outside? It might be uncomfortable in dead of winter."

"Julian?" She pressed his cheek, forcing him to look at her again. "It *was* different. I never felt anything like that with Henri, and assuredly not with Mathieu. I never felt like this before and I have never given myself with such"—she stopped to think—"lack of thought or worry."

So both her lovers had been French, no surprise. "The act of love should always be without worry, and without thought except for the pleasure of the participants."

"Should one worry about pleasing the other?"

As they talked he had been idly stroking her breasts, ribs, and stomach, relishing the texture of her skin and the pliant flesh beneath. "I can't speak to that in universal terms, but I promise that you need never have the least concern about pleasing me. Whatever you do, or don't do, makes me happy so you should do what pleases you." His cock stirred again at even remote memories of her past attentions and he wanted to strangle those so-called lovers for making her doubt herself. He didn't want any details about them, but he wished she would tell him the truth about herself.

She relaxed catlike into his touch until she fairly hummed with pleasure, but their caresses were for intimacy, not for passion. "Where did you spend your childhood?" he asked, and felt her body tense for a moment.

"In Saint Lucia."

"I wasn't sure if you had lived there all your life before coming to England."

"All of it, yes," she said after a brief pause.

She wasn't going to tell him and he didn't want to hear more of her lies. He wanted her to trust him. If she confessed the truth, perhaps he would respond in kind. They say that confession is good for the soul. Jane, who thought him a good man, might convince him to forgive himself for the past. He tried to imagine what she would say about the Fallerons and what he should do.

He opened his mouth to tell the story, then stopped. Why spoil this sublime moment? He would tell her, but later, after his grand unveiling.

Besides, he didn't have to ask for advice, only absolution. Jane would tell him what he already knew: that he had no right to the marquis's art collection. Since the family had all died he could not return their property. But he need not profit from it either. If the king would agree to build a national gallery for the nation, he would donate the paintings. Given his fortune, it was scarcely a sacrifice.

"I have a big event planned for tomorrow night," he said.

"Yes?" Deft fingers sent streaks of lazy pleasure through his body.

"The Long Gallery in the south wing has been unused for decades. Hillthorpe tells me it was built for the ladies of the house to take indoor exercise during bad weather. I don't know if it stopped raining in this part of Sussex, or if the Fortescue ladies became infected with laziness. I decided it would make a splendid gallery. It has windows all down one side facing north, perfect for the display of pictures. I ordered it freshly painted and my collection has been hung. Tomorrow night I shall unveil it to the world."

"That's wonderful. I hope Lord Cazalet will be impressed and do as you wish."

"Will you be there, Jane? I think you have been avoiding the company."

"I had the headache last night."

He didn't believe her. "Now that you know there's no reason to fear meeting Miss Cazalet, please accompany the children after dinner. I would like you to see my collection and I want you to share it with me, be it triumph or disaster."

There was always the possibility of disaster if Sir Richard Radcliffe decided to make trouble. Julian had invited him to Denford because, whatever Radcliffe had in mind, he'd rather have the wily baronet under his roof where he could see him. He and Windermere also hoped that Radcliffe would be tricked into exposing his part in the troubled history of the Falleron property, whether it was the original betrayal back in France, or the more recent attempt to wrest the pictures from Julian. It was a risky strategy that might end in Julian looking the greater villain, not Radcliffe. Julian had too much unwilling respect for the man to think he'd let the pictures go to the king without an attempt to interfere.

"I will be there," Jane said. "I am curious to see these great masterpieces you are so mysterious about."

"I believe you will bring me luck. I will astonish the world, and Britain will have the basis of a national gallery of art worthy of a great nation."

His decision solved all his problems. The collection was too fine and the offer too generous for Cazalet to quibble when Julian broke the news that he wasn't going to offer for Henrietta. Rolling over, he gathered Jane close and kissed her hard.

The woman he loved was in his arms, and in a dizzying revelation he realized that she was also the only bride he wanted. Astonishingly, he *wanted* a bride. With growing exhilaration the idea of a lifetime with Jane took hold of his head and heart. A lifetime of joy and perhaps, finally, peace of mind.

Tomorrow night he would make his confession and beg her to tell him her history. In a strange way, if he could make Jane, or whatever French name she'd been born with, happy, it might be a small payment against the debt he owed the Falleron family and could never discharge.

Chapter 17

Jane fingered the fine silk of her best evening gown, touched the delicate beads scattered on the overdress. Closing her eyes, she envisioned the blue gleam in Julian's when he saw her dressed as a duchess or a mistress should be. As much as she wanted to look beautiful for him, she didn't forget that Louis was still here. Not daring to present herself in her true guise, she must remain an inconspicuous mouse of a governess, observing the proceedings from a quiet corner in an old blue dress.

Reluctantly she folded the rose gown and put it away. No handsome armoire for her at Denford, only a simple washstand and a corner cupboard. The garments she couldn't wear lived on the bottom shelf, piled on top of her knife.

The blade was a constant reproach to her, a reminder of her failure. Tonight she hated it, railed at the fate that had kept her alive but wouldn't let her be happy. A voice at the edge of consciousness told her that she could forget finding Mr. Fortescue, who was very likely dead anyway, and throw away the weapon. She could be happy. She could go down this evening and participate with an open heart in the excitement of Denford's coming revelation.

It reminded her of the occasions at home when Papa had bought a new work for the collection. He had made a little ceremony of it, leading family and guests to the lovely gallery at the Hôtel Falleron. Champagne would be served as they gathered around the latest acquisition, propped on an easel and draped with a velvet cloth. Then Papa would unveil it with a flourish and they would exclaim at its beauty and argue where it should be hung and toast it, even the littlest child permitted a sip of celebratory wine.

When they left home it had been over a year since he'd bought anything new. In those uncertain times French families were selling their masterpieces, not buying new ones. The last unveiling had been of a Claude Lorrain landscape, supposedly a scene from the life of Aeneas but really an excuse to look at temples and trees, blue skies and the blue, blue sea. It made her feel happy; almost all the pictures did. Papa and his father before him had always bought works that were pleasing to the senses, be it a handsome young man by Titian or the lush Veronese Venus.

Perhaps the echo of past joy made her consider the unthinkable: to tell Julian everything and ask him to help her. He might have a way to prove that Charles Fortescue, safely dead, was the betrayer. If not, no one was in a better position than the Duke of Denford to identify a Fortescue. Julian was a fair man; he wouldn't protect a villain simply because he was a relation. Quite the contrary, she thought with a dark laugh. While not sure he'd go so far as to condone murder, the notion of sharing the truth with him tempted her. She'd borne the burden of avenging her family for years, and alone. She didn't know if Julian would assist her or thwart her, or even absolve her from her task. But she would no longer be alone.

The whole party was agog in the Crimson State Room, promised a surprise. The Osbourne girls chatted excitedly with Lady Windermere and Miss Cazalet, allowing Jane to melt into a quiet corner and avoid Louis. Not that anyone took the least notice of the governess.

Oliver joined that group and exchanged a few words with Miss Cazalet. Jane liked the way the young woman treated Oliver, speaking of his work with respect. Much to Jane's surprise he hadn't fallen in love with her, remaining infatuated with Lady Belinda, who never gave him the time of day.

Lady Belinda, in a scarlet gown that clashed with the drawing room curtains but displayed her considerable assets, smiled at Louis. But her cousin must have had something else on his mind tonight. He kept half an eye on the entrance and exchanged frequent glances with Sir Richard

Radcliffe who did not, apparently, object to the Frenchman's obvious relationship with his wife. Remembering what Denford had said at the theater about Radcliffe acting as his wife's pander, she had to wonder what the trio was up to.

Lord Windermere, for some reason, was watching the Radcliffes. Lady Ashfield held court over a group of other guests, including Lord Cazalet, who also looked eager. He knew what was coming, and Jane hoped for Julian's sake that he would be suitably impressed by the riches to be revealed. Like him, she could hardly to wait to see what Julian had collected over the years.

The double doors opened and Julian stood on the threshold, dressed in embroidered satin and velvet, all black like a king in mourning, brandishing his cane. The room fell silent. "Ladies and gentlemen," he said, looking around the great room, pausing for a moment when he spotted Jane, half hidden by a fire screen. She shook her head imperceptibly, and thankfully the foolish man's gaze moved on. "Please follow me to the Long Gallery, newly decorated and containing a collection of masterpieces of which you will rarely have seen the like."

The buzz of speculation grew loud as they followed him upstairs. Jane brought up the rear, not leaving her seat until everyone else had left the room. By the time she reached the gallery the buzz had swelled to a roar and she heard words like *magnificent* and *extraordinary* tossed around. A footman bearing a tray of glasses offered her champagne and she accepted, despite her status. She would raise her glass to Julian's success.

The gallery was surprisingly narrow, with an ancient arched ceiling embellished with the plastered strapwork Mr. Hillthorpe had promised. With windows down one side, the pictures were hung on the other, and such was the crush of guests who lined up to walk the length of the room and see each piece that it took a while before Jane saw the first picture: a Dutch scene of a skating party, a delightful canvas though not by a first-rate painter.

"I congratulate you, Denford." That was Cazalet's voice halfway down the room, and she heard Julian's deep tones that she would know anywhere, though she couldn't make out his response.

The people in front of her moved on and she was able to leave the skaters behind. She almost fainted at the sight of a picture she had once known as well as her own face: Fragonard again, an exquisite small oil showing a group of musicians in a garden.

Her immediate thought was that her father's collection had been seized and dispersed by the revolutionary authorities, some of the pictures had made their way to England, and Denford had bought one. But next came the Titian of the handsome young man with the white ruffled collar, and the Venus, and a Boucher, and the Claude Lorrain. Like a sleepwalker she passed from picture to picture, oblivious to those around her. They weren't all her family's pictures but most of the best ones were. With dread in her stomach she caught up with an excited trio of ladies gathered around the famous Raphael. How many hours had she spent gazing at the lovely Madonna with the faraway look in her eyes, and the fat, naked baby, standing on his mother's lap with his hand on her breast?

They were almost all here, the cream of her father's art collection. The blinders she'd worn for too long fell away.

"Jane? Miss Grey?" Julian touched her arm as she passed him but she did not stop, and luckily Cazalet or one of the others spoke to him and she was able to walk the length of the room unimpeded and confirm what she already knew.

The treasure her father had given up to get them out of France was his beloved picture collection. His betrayer, the infamous Mr. Fortescue who had let her family die, was now Duke of Denford. Julian. Her love. The man she had sworn to kill.

Jane sat on a velvet-covered bench between two windows, sick in her stomach, remembering every hint to the identity of Mr. Fortescue that she had ignored, willfully or not. Initially deceived by her recollection of the man she'd seen in Paris and by her certainty that a duke could not have been involved in such chicanery, she'd dismissed him out of hand. Even when she learned that he had been a Mr. Fortescue in Paris that year, she'd let her partiality blind her to the truth.

To think that she had considered renouncing her revenge! And fallen in love with the enemy.

She had betrayed the memory of her parents and sisters and shown herself unworthy of the name of Falleron. She'd often wished she'd fallen under the guillotine with them, but never more than now.

Something was happening. Lord Cazalet called the company to attention. "I wish to tender my sincerest congratulations and thanks to His Grace for the assembly of such a magnificent collection. I shall have no hesitation in recommending to the king that he should acquire it for the nation. As one who can say without boasting that I have seen more than my fair share of masterpieces, I can safely declare that in England today only His Majesty himself can rival the Duke of Denford. And now let us raise our glasses to toast one of the great *cognoscenti*. To Denford."

"To Denford." "To His Grace." "To Julian." She gripped her glass so hard it cracked and cut her palm. The chorus of praise drowned out her cry and the crash of shards on the floor. No one noticed her. Even Julian, whose triumphant smile she could see through a gap in the admiring crowd, had forgotten her, and why would he not? The tender words of such a heartless villain weren't worth the breath they'd taken to utter.

"I look forward to hearing how you managed to lay hands on such works," Cazalet said. "His Majesty is always interested in the provenance of his purchases." Jane put her bleeding hand to her mouth and waited to hear the answer.

"I can help you with that, milord." In her anguish she'd forgotten the presence of the one person alive as familiar with the Hôtel Falleron as she. Louis stepped forward and stood in front of Julian, a handsome little bantam cock challenging a black rooster. "The better part of Denford's collection was stolen from the house of the Marquis de Falleron in Paris."

Denford sneered down at him. "I make no secret of these pictures' history. I bought them from Falleron in 1793."

"Can you prove it?"

"What is it to you, Beauville? Making trouble on behalf of your paymaster Radcliffe? Perhaps he has something to say about why the marquis and his family died."

With a collective gasp, the attention of the company turned to Sir Richard. "I have no idea what Denford is talking about." Radcliffe dripped contempt. "Let us not forget that he is the son of an Irish nobody who conducted a shady trade in pictures until he stumbled into the dukedom by the most fortunate and coincidental deaths of numerous Fortescue men."

A high-pitched snarl of fury came from the other end of the room. Fenella. Jane hadn't given a thought to the sisters who would hear about the perfidy of the brother they had come to love. Their governess, who should attempt to shield the blow, was going to make it worse.

Julian started forward, gripping the knob of his cane, but Lord Windermere held him back. "You will retract that statement, Radcliffe," Windermere said.

"Perhaps," the elder man said with an insolent shrug. "Let us hear from the true owner. Allow me to present the Marquis de Falleron. Louis?"

The crowd threatened to erupt at this new revelation but subsided when Julian raised his hand. "The marquis is dead," he said. "He had only daughters. No one knows better than I."

"You should appreciate better than most the distances a title can travel," Radcliffe said. "Louis's father was first cousin to the late marquis. As such he is heir to the Falleron lands and property. The unfortunate state of affairs in France makes it impossible for him to claim his birthright, but he can, thanks to your diligence in bringing the pictures to England, repossess part of his heritage." His smile was purest malice. "I'm sure he will be very grateful."

Julian towered over Radcliffe, a physically uneven match between the duke in his youthful vigor and the slight older man. "I don't believe you. You've been trying to lay your hands on these pictures for years and this is merely your latest devious attempt. How much did you pay your wife's lover to pretend to be Louis de Falleron? Why did he come here under a different name?"

"If you knew who I was, Monsieur le Duc," Louis said, "you would never have revealed your illegal possession of the pictures. My pictures."

"Show me your proof."

Jane staggered to her feet and walked unnoticed through the circle of onlookers riveted by the unfolding drama. Cradling her injured hand, she pushed her way past Radcliffe and Louis to stand in front of the man who had killed her family. His astonishment turned to concern that softened the steel in his eyes. "You've hurt yourself, Jane. There's blood on your gown."

She put her hands behind her back. She would never let him touch her again. "I wish to attest to his identity. This man is, indeed, the Marquis de Falleron."

"How do you know? Who *are* you?"

"I am Jeanne-Louise Marie-Adorée de Falleron," she said, the names rolling out past a suppressed sob. "I am the eldest daughter of the late Marquis de Falleron."

She turned her back on Julian, not wanting to see his reaction, be it defiance or remorse, and looked at Louis. They faced each other, the last of the Fallerons, and she noticed the faint lines of the dissipation on his handsome face, the discontented mouth, the air of conceit and dissatisfaction. She could have wished for a better ally, but Louis was her family and she cast her lot with him. "It is I, Jeanne. I am alive."

Endless seconds passed while she waited for him to take her hand and embrace her. "This woman is mad. I never saw her before in my life."

"Not for nine years, Louis. I have changed since I was fifteen but not so much, I think. Look at me."

He shook his head. "Jeanne is dead. She went to the guillotine with her sister. I don't know what this woman's motives are, but she is an impostor and no cousin of mine."

"It is true," Julian said hoarsely. "Jeanne and Marie-Thérèse died, as did their parents. I don't know what happened to the youngest girl, Antoinette." He had the audacity to sound sorry.

She spun around on her heels. "It was my two younger sisters who were slaughtered. I escaped." Anger and grief welled up so that she couldn't get out the words that needed to be spoken, the beginning of the ruination of Mr. Fortescue.

The three Osbourne girls rushed forward. "Is it true, Miss Grey? Are you French?"

She looked at each of the young faces that had become so dear to her.

Tears that could no longer be held back blurred her vision and her throat was too choked to answer. She stood in the middle of the gallery at Denford Castle, surrounded by the pictures she'd never thought to see again, and wept.

"Let me take you somewhere quiet." She thought it was Lady Windermere. "You are too upset now. You can talk about it later."

She was right. Jane needed to think, away from the competing forces hammering her emotions. Away from Julian and Louis and the Osbourne girls, she might be able to think clearly. She let herself be led to her room. Lady Windermere bathed her forehead with cool water, bandaged her hand, and helped her undress. A servant delivered a posset to the door.

She had to give the lady marks for discretion. She must have had a hundred questions but treated Jane as though she were an ill child. Perhaps she believed her a lunatic, Jane thought hysterically. Louis certainly did. After all her worries about being recognized, he didn't know her or believe she was his cousin.

"This will help you sleep, Miss Grey. I will tell His Grace that he may speak with you in the morning and get to the bottom of all this."

Jane sipped her drink. "Thank you, my lady. You must wonder—"

"Not now. Go to bed."

The posset undoubtedly contained laudanum. Once she was sure Lady Windermere wasn't coming back, she poured it out of the window and got into bed. Much later, she crept to the door and eased it open, half expecting to learn she'd been put under guard, and found the passage deserted. Either they trusted the drug, or they regarded her as harmless.

Not they but *he*. Denford was the lord of this house. As she left the gallery in Lady Windermere's sheltering arm, she had glanced back. Even through her tears she had recognized unalloyed horror on the duke's face. What ultimately happened to her lay in his hands, unless she acted first.

Chapter 18

Julian sat propped against the pillows in the great bed, the oak-carved and velvet-draped resting place of generations of dukes. Never before had his good fortune seemed more hollow, less deserved. He'd remained thus for so long that the lone candle was almost guttered. What the hell was he going to do? Not about the pictures, or the wild speculation among his guests, or Cazalet and the king, or even about Radcliffe and Louis de Falleron. None of these things mattered compared to Jane.

She emerged from the dark recesses of the room like a ghost, clad only in a white nightgown. He wasn't sure that she was real until she reached the end of the bed and he could see wild hair and dark shadows around eyes swollen with weeping. She was beautiful and frightened him to death.

"Jane," he said. He meant to say more but the words were clogged in his brain. What could make the slightest difference? That he was sorry? No apology could bring back her family, or even begin to make up for lost lives, theirs and hers.

She came at him, crawling on her knees the length of the bed while he remained motionless, his hands flat on the covers on either side. A flash of something caught his eye before she fell on him. She seized his head in both hands, digging her fingers into his skull, and took him in a kiss that utterly confounded him. What he most wished for and least expected was for Jane to want him still.

It was ravishment and punishment, agony and heart-stopping delight as she grasped hanks of his loose hair and thrust her tongue in a dark simulation of lovemaking. He relished the pain in his scalp as much as he adored the taste and texture of her greedy mouth. Since logic had no explanation for her action, he let thought slip away and surrendered to desire, his body aroused by her weight. His heart swelled with love and gratitude, and a pressure between the temples he hadn't felt since childhood told him that he was close to tears.

As soon as he moved his arms to draw her in, she stiffened. "Jane?" he whispered, and ran his hands over flesh, firm and vital beneath cool linen. She pulled away, shoved at his chest, and scrambled backward on her knees. Wetness cooled on his face but he hadn't wept, yet. They were her tears.

As he reached out instinctively to offer comfort, she snarled, snatching something up from the folds of the blankets.

She had brought a knife with her, a long wicked blade.

"Don't," she said. "Don't touch me."

He spread and lowered his palms, making no attempt to protect his bare chest. "Jane. Jeanne, I should say, but you'll always be Jane to me."

"Do you believe me?" she asked. Her fingers clenched the handle of the knife, held at shoulder height and pointed at his heart.

"Of course I believe you. When have you lied to me?"

She tilted her neck in that Jane-like way she had. "All the time. Everything I told you about me was invented."

"I knew that, almost from the beginning, but it's not important. You never lied about anything that really matters." He smiled faintly. "Except for a small sin of omission."

"Small?"

"I'm glad you didn't stride into Fortescue House and announce that you had come to kill me. We would never have known each other. If I die tonight I will be a better and happier man for knowing you."

"I will not be cozened with sweet words."

"I have too much respect for you to try. You will hear no more untruths and evasions from me. I ask only that you accord me the same privilege."

She sniffed fiercely and swiped her eyes with the back of her free hand. "What do you want to know?"

"How did you escape?"

She climbed to the floor and stood just out of reach, her knife still poised. He could have told her she had nothing to fear from him, but she wouldn't believe him. Her eyes, wild and wary, never left his face as she told him a story about switched papers that made no sense to him.

"We bribed the member of the committee for passports for your father, mother, and three daughters," he said. "Your governess was never mentioned to me."

"She had left us a month earlier. I later discovered that my father arranged for her to be carried from Normandy to England by a smuggler, the same man who brought me over. That way she did not need her passport or her identification papers."

If this business with the governess's papers had been part of Smith's plan, Julian had been even more ignorant than he thought. "What happened next?"

"We were ready to leave the next morning when the guards arrived."

"I had already left Paris with the pictures."

"I do not suppose you wished to stay once you had what you had come for." Her voice dripped derision.

"No," he said. He scorned to offer a defense for the indefensible, yet he couldn't help asking, "Did the marquis say who betrayed you?"

"Until the last minute he insisted that you would not. 'Mr. Fortescue is a noble Englishman,' he said. But when the knock came at the door he knew."

"He was right," Julian said hoarsely. "I swore on my honor that your family would be safe but

I lied. Even if I did not inform on you to the committee, I might as well have."

She hardly seemed to hear him. Although she kept her dagger poised, her eyes were distant. "The company of guards marched into our beautiful house. Mathieu Picard was their captain and he asked to see our papers. 'I was told there are three daughters. Who are you?' he asked me. 'I am the governess,' I replied, just as Maman had told me." Her cheeks shone with tears. "I denied them. I denied my family."

"You did what you were supposed to." The truth, but weak, inadequate words against the searing pain of her confession.

"We were marched to La Force, led through the streets with crowds jeering at us as filthy aristos. When we reached the prison, Mathieu grabbed my hand. 'You've done nothing. You are a woman of the people and may come with me.' I couldn't even kiss them good-bye."

The last words were wrenched out through gusty breaths. Tears poured down her face and her body heaved with silent sobs. It was agony not to take her in his arms. Julian didn't doubt that in her distress it would be easy to take away her knife but what was the point? He was the last person who could offer her any comfort.

So he let her grieve and reflected on the supreme irony that when, for the first time in his life, he had fallen in love, it was with a woman who wanted to kill him. But he'd always known he deserved to pay for his sins. If Jane would let him, he'd make what reparation he could. Or he'd allow her to plunge her knife into his heart.

Stifling her tears with huge, inelegant sniffs, she couldn't be less like the elegant and self-possessed Jane Grey that he admired, and he didn't care. He coveted every minute he had with her. There was so much more he wished to know about her, so many more times he wanted to make love to her. If all he had left was ten minutes with a weeping avenger, so be it. But perhaps he could persuade her to prolong their time together.

"Why did you stay with Picard?" he asked, once he judged her composed enough to speak.

She wiped her nose on her sleeve. The storm of grief had subsided and she seemed almost meek. "Mathieu knew who I was. I was too young to be a governess, but he wanted me so he pretended to believe me. What he did was very dangerous and could have cost him his life."

"A man with any decency would have let you go."

"To do what?" she demanded, with a flash of spirit. "I was fifteen years old and the daughter of a marquis. I would never have survived alone. Do you know how I found out he knew? He was kind at first, found me a room and asked nothing of me. The landlady said I could pay my rent by helping around the house. I knew nothing of cleaning or cooking or laundry and she became impatient. She was suspicious too, because she believed I was English and she knew I had worked for the nobility. One day she wanted me to come with her to see the latest executions. Things were becoming more violent, more dangerous in Paris, and I feared she would denounce me if I refused. But Mathieu came that morning and he said he would take me and find me a place with a good view. Instead he took me to his lodging. He told me that my parents were already dead and my sisters were to be killed that day and he knew I wouldn't wish to see it. That was the night I became his mistress."

Julian couldn't bring himself to admit that he had been there. That he'd made himself watch as the two youngest and most innocent victims of his mistake lost their heads. It had been the worst day of his life and haunted his dreams for years.

Instead of making her cry again, recounting this terrible tale boosted her determination. "Call me a *putain* if you wish. I used Mathieu, just as I used Henri after Mathieu died."

"I would never think that of you," he said softly.

She scowled at him. "But always I was waiting and planning and saving money so that I could come to England and find Mr. Fortescue."

"I understand."

"No you do not. You know nothing. Perhaps you didn't mean for us all to die. But you took what you wanted with no thought of the consequences." She knew him too well, this extraordinary woman. In dead of night, in the cocoon of light provided by the sole flickering candle, she looked at him and saw through to his worthless soul.

"It made me angry that you didn't know your good fortune in having sisters who live and breathe with heads attached to their necks. But now I understand why. You always told me you were selfish, and you are."

Her words scourged him and he offered no excuse. She examined him stretched out before her, her eyes running the length of his body from the neck to feet and back again. She changed the way she held the knife so that she would stab upward instead of down, a more powerful grip and more lethal. He forced himself to remain still and closed his eyes. He wouldn't even beg for his life by telling her how much he loved her or asking her to forgive him. He did not deserve the indulgence. His greatest regret was that she would pay for his death and he wouldn't be there to protect her from the consequences of her crime.

Leave as soon as the deed is done, Jane, and run far, far away, he silently urged her as his chest lay bare, a willing sacrifice to her blade. If his death afforded her a measure of satisfaction and future peace of mind, it was worth it.

He felt her touch his hair—for the last time—then a tightness in his scalp. She must have seized a handful, pulling it taut. The first time they'd made love she'd told him she loved his hair. That whole night was a sublime final memory to accompany him to perdition.

Expecting a stab to the chest or a slice across the throat, instead his ears were assaulted by a sawing noise and the pressure eased. His eyes flew open to find her brandishing a long coil of the black hair that hadn't been cut short since the day he was sent down from Oxford. She laid down the lock and took up another. He sat up to give her access to the back. Neither said a word until most of his hair lay like a dark nest on the white sheet, only the final strand clenched in Jane's fist.

"Why?" he rasped.

"I love your sisters and I cannot kill their brother." She held his hair to her cheek and his heart pounded. "And I find I cannot kill the man I thought I loved. I am too weak."

He took a deep breath. "Be strong and live. Marry me. Let me take care of you and atone for my sins."

She laughed without mirth. "Did you know that I was supposed to be a duchess? I was betrothed at birth to Comte Etienne de Fleurigny, heir to a dukedom. Perhaps I am still."

"I'll make you a duchess. I won't ask anything of you, only that you let me make meager reparation for what I did." It was no way to propose marriage but he doubted a man had ever offered his hand with greater fervor.

She cocked her head and pretended to consider his proposal. "I could make you very unhappy, but it would be too easy." She waved his hair at him. "I am Delilah to your Samson and I will find a way to take away your strength and destroy you. I'll enjoy your ruin more if you are alive to feel it."

Now that he knew who she was, it was no surprise that she could curtsey with both grace and insolence when armed and clad only in a nightgown. "Good night, Your Grace. Until we meet again."

The door closed, just as the candle sputtered its last drop of wax. He smiled into the darkness.

Jane/Jeanne had made a big mistake in letting him live. The passivity with which he had offered her his breast on the altar of penitence had vanished. Perhaps she could ruin him, and she was welcome to try. But someone else, maybe Radcliffe, maybe another, was even more to blame than himself. Here and now he appointed himself Jane's avenger. *He* would hunt down and kill whoever betrayed the Fallerons.

And then he would convince her that they belonged together forever. Anything less was unacceptable.

Chapter 19

After a sleepless night, Jane crept down the passage, past Denford's rooms, to the other end of the wing where most of the guests were housed.

Half expecting the room to be empty, its occupant sleeping with Lady Belinda, she saw the shadow of a single body in the bed and heard a gentle snoring. "Louis," she whispered. He stirred. She opened the curtain a crack, drew near to the bed, and shook his shoulder. *"Réveille-toi,* Louis."

"Belinda?" he said drowsily, rolled over and grabbed her.

"Non, non." She beat him off and stepped out of reach. He sat up abruptly, rubbing his eyes. *"Je ne suis pas Milady Belinda. C'est moi, Jeanne, ta cousine,"* she said, hoping that hearing her speak French would jog his memory.

"Mon Dieu! It's the crazy governess." Wide awake now, he crossed his arms over his chest. "Get away from me!"

She stepped three paces back and raised her

arms to show that she was harmless. "I know it is a shock to you," she said, continuing to speak French, "but take a good look at me. Ask me any questions you want."

Apparently accepting that she hadn't come to attack him, he lowered his arms and regarded her sullenly. While her opinion of him, colored by her mother's attitude, wasn't high, he surely couldn't fail to delight in a reunion with a close relation. He was a French nobleman, after all, and a Falleron. As far as she knew they were the sole remnants of a great family.

"If you are Jeanne, explain how you escaped the guillotine." Louis's brown eyes were hard and shrewd and she recalled now that they had never softened when he was apparently charming his young cousins.

She repeated the story she'd told Julian, adding little details about the Fallerons to make her tale convincing. No one but a family member would know about the bichon puppy Mou-Mou, or where the dog's basket lived, or be able to describe the secretary desk with the secret drawer in Maman's private sitting room.

Louis responded to a recitation that threatened her serenity with steely composure. "I find this business with the switched papers incredible. Why would your father make such an arrangement?"

"The question has troubled me all these years. The only explanation is that someone else was supposed to come with us, pretending to be Antoinette."

"Who? Why would he go to such trouble to get another small girl out of Paris?"

"I don't know." Jane rubbed her eyes, gritty from weeping and lack of sleep. "None of it has ever made sense, this bizarre chance that saved my life. But I tell you what I do know. It was the Duke of Denford who betrayed us."

Louis's thick brows knitted. "Now I know that you are mad!"

"No, listen! Denford was only a Mr. Fortescue then, and he was supposed to arrange to get us out of Paris. My father trusted him. The night before, Maman was very worried, but I heard him telling her that Mr. Fortescue would never fail them. In the morning, when the soldiers arrived to arrest us, he said that we had been betrayed by the man he trusted the most." She came closer and took his hand. "You must help me, Louis. Denford must pay for his crimes. We will work together to disgrace him in the eyes of the world. I know things about him. He wants to sell his collection to the King of England. We can let everyone know that the pictures were stolen, that he is a man without honor. We can make his name a scandal. Together we can do this."

For the first time, Jane felt she had given him pause. He stroked his chin and looked at her with greater attention. Soon, she was confident, he would match her features to his recollection of his eldest cousin. "Hand me my dressing gown, please. I am not convinced, mind you. I have some more questions."

"Anything."

He drew the curtains to flood the room with morning light and stared at her hard, without giving any sign of recognition. "What have you been doing since then?"

This was the part she had been dreading. "I lived in Paris as Jane Grey."

"What did you live on?"

She held her chin up and told herself that she had nothing to be ashamed of. "The captain of the guard who arrested us looked after me."

Louis smiled unpleasantly. "So you spent almost nine years as the mistress of a *sans culottes* pig?"

"Three. He was killed in the invasion of Italy."

"And then?"

"I had a new protector, an official of the Directoire and later the Consulat."

"Putain."

The word was such a slap that she put her hand to her cheek. "I had to."

"A true Falleron would never have whored herself to Jacobin peasant scum. She would have died rather. I suppose you are Denford's whore too, but you have turned on him and want me to help you get back at him."

Jane narrowed her eyes. She knew now that it was a mistake to expect Louis to do anything that wasn't in his interest. He'd make no real effort to establish if she was his cousin because he didn't care. "Think, Louis. I can help you bring suit against Denford to win back the pictures. I can testify to his fraud."

"Even if you were Jeanne de Falleron, I wouldn't need you. Radcliffe has legal matters arranged and he's going to pay me a good sum for the collection."

"You would sell them? Our patrimony?" she asked, outraged.

"*My* patrimony. You bear a slight resemblance to Jeanne, but that is all. I believe you met the real Miss Grey somewhere and she told you all about our family and lent you her name."

"No, that is not so! I never saw her again. I don't even know if she is in England. She may be dead."

"Perhaps you are a servant from the Hôtel Falleron who managed to escape to England. Who knows? Truly I don't care. I am the last of the Fallerons, and by pretending to be my cousin you prey on my grief." Louis quivered with self-righteous indignation and crocodile tears.

Jane could have asked what he'd been doing for the last nine years. Not starving apparently. Perhaps he had been living off his good looks and the affections of wealthy women like Lady Belinda. So much for his moral indignation over her survival.

Before she committed the crime of assaulting a French marquis, she left his room, reflecting that one can make plans for years and discover it is all for naught because nothing is the way you expected.

Jane had always imagined that when she discovered the identity of Mr. Fortescue, no one would know who she was and how they were connected. With any luck she'd be able to take him by surprise, use her knife, and get away without anyone suspecting her. She'd known it wasn't perfect and there was a good chance that she would be caught, but she had been prepared to take the risk.

She hadn't expected to make the discovery in the presence of a dozen or two people, and proceed to give them all her real name. She hadn't expected the target of her revenge to be an important man, a duke no less. Without knowing much about English law, she guessed the authorities would regard the murder of a duke with deep displeasure.

She hadn't expected, when she contemplated the insertion of her lethal blade into Mr. Fortescue's black heart, that she would know him well, let alone have made love with him on several occasions.

She hadn't expected to love him.

For a few weeks she hadn't been alone in the world; at Fortescue House she had found a home. Even with Henri her emotions had been disengaged, knowing that her life with him was only an interlude. She hadn't resented him as she had Mathieu, but ultimately she'd been able to leave him without an ounce of regret.

Now she had lost Julian. And while her hopes that Louis would be her family were short-lived, their demolishment left her chilled and truly alone, as she had been in the days after her family's arrest, fruitlessly scrubbing the landlady's steps and waiting in terror for news of her parents and sisters. Alone as she had been in her recurring nightmares.

Her physical solitude was immediately dispelled, for the Osbournes had invaded her bedchamber. The three girls, almost filling the small room, looked wary. In some ways to be rejected by them would be even worse than Louis's rejection. She cared about them.

Smoothing her skirt to take the trembling out of her hands, she essayed a smile. "Good morning, *mes élèves*," she said. "I will join you in the schoolroom shortly. Why are you not eating breakfast?"

The three of them exchanged looks. Apparently Maria had been designated to speak, a measure of how seriously they regarded the moment. Nothing less would keep Fenella quiet.

"Are you really the daughter of a French marquis, Miss Grey?"

"If she is she wouldn't be Miss Grey." Fenella's deferral to her elder hadn't lasted long.

"You may continue to address me thus if you wish, but yes, I am truly Jeanne-Louise de Falleron. You don't have to believe me."

"Of course we believe you," Maria said, "and we think we have the right to know how you came to be our governess."

"I agree. Let us sit down, for it's quite a long story." Maria and Laura perched on either side of her on the bed, with Fenella on the floor at her feet. She was glad she could see only Fenella. The other two looked too much like their brother. She was trying hard not to think about Julian.

Jane was becoming quite good at telling her tale. Omitting all mention of Mr. Fortescue, she couldn't have asked for a more sympathetic audience. After she told them about the final loss of hope, when Marie-Thérèse and Antoinette were dead, they gathered around and embraced her.

"Stop," she begged. "You will make me cry again. I've shed so many tears for them but it doesn't bring them back. One must be brave."

"I would never be brave if someone killed Fenella and Laura," Maria said, at which all three began weeping and Jane had to comfort *them*.

"Listen, *mes chères,* don't be too sad for me. Thank the *bon Dieu* that you are alive and well and have each other and can lead happy lives."

Maria dabbed at her cheeks with a handkerchief. "God saved you for a reason, Miss Grey. We do not know why he does things. We shall pray to thank him for bringing you to us."

She'd never thought of it being God who saved her; rather that he had most cruelly punished her and her innocent sisters, and for that reason she had turned her back on the religion of her upbringing. But if her plight was indeed God's plan, would he want her to seek revenge? Was he not a forgiving God?

That, perhaps, was why she had never prayed again. She did not want to forgive.

"Someone must have known you were escaping and reported you," Fenella said. "I hope they *die.*"

"Why would anyone kill little girls?" Laura asked.

"I don't know. I suppose it's because a revolution is like a war and terrible things happen. Many people besides me have lost everyone."

Laura's hand squeezed hers. "You haven't lost me. I'll be your little sister if you like." Jane gave the child a hug and tried not to dissolve into a puddle of tears.

"What about Monsieur de Beauville?" Fenella said. "Is he really your cousin?"

The question stiffened her backbone. "Unfortunately yes, for all that he denies me."

"Have your looks changed so much?" Maria asked. "I didn't see Julian for a long time but I never forgot him."

"It's my belief that Louis knows me but he prefers not to acknowledge me because of what I did after I became Miss Grey." In her bitterness she didn't consider the new questions she'd opened up.

"Because you went to Saint Lucia?" Laura asked.

She was tempted, very tempted. "No," she said. "I lived in Paris and I had to be friendly with some of the revolutionaries."

"How horrible for you to have to live among such wicked people," Maria said.

"They weren't all wicked but it was difficult sometimes."

"When did you go to Saint Lucia?"

"I'm sorry, Laura. I lied to you. I have never been to Saint Lucia."

Laura's mouth fell open. "You never saw ostriches and crocodiles?"

"Never."

Fenella, as usual, asked the difficult questions. "Why did you go on pretending to be Miss Grey after you came to England? You're safe here."

"Miss Grey was a governess and I needed a position as governess."

"What a coincidence that you ended up at Fortescue House. You must have been very surprised when you saw your family's pictures last night."

"You cannot imagine how much."

"Why didn't you know Julian had bought them from your father?"

Jane squeezed her eyes shut, to deny the question she did not want to answer now.

"Stop badgering her, Fenella," Maria said. "Can't you see she's upset?"

"It's all right," Jane said cravenly. "It's just that I have a headache because I couldn't sleep last night."

"Lie down and rest, then. I will watch my younger sisters." Maria fetched a damp cloth from the washstand, pushed her sisters aside, and dabbed at Jane's forehead. "My mother likes me to do this when she has the headache. Is that better?"

"Much better, thank you."

"Would you like us to fetch you a kitten from the stables?" Laura asked.

"Perhaps another time. I will try to sleep now. You are all very good to me." She blinked against the recurrence of treacherous tears.

Fenella spoke from the window where she was closing the curtains. "That is because we all love you. We don't want you to leave us."

Julian's valet, having cut the hacked hair into a tidy Brutus, was disposing of the trimmings when the Earl of Windermere knocked and entered his room without permission.

"Why the radical new style?" he asked.

"It happened on a whim." Most likely the truth since Jane hadn't come to his room with the intention of giving him a haircut.

Obviously bursting with curiosity, Damian waited until Julian had finished speaking to his servant and dismissed the man. "Cynthia sent me, after you failed to appear at the breakfast table. Neither did Beauville, or Falleron, and Miss Grey hasn't been seen anywhere."

"I suppose everyone else is talking about last night's drama. Sit down while I finish tying my neckcloth."

"Of course they are. Even ladies who haven't seen nine o'clock in decades came down early. Cynthia is the most unpopular woman in Sussex for failing to interrogate Miss Grey about her past. I hope she is sleeping off the effects of the laudanum in Cynthia's posset. Do you believe that she is the Falleron daughter?"

"I do."

"I won't ask you why, for now. If so, I don't imagine her presence in your household is coincidental."

"No. She came to kill me." Julian twitched the folds of black linen to get them just so. He hardly knew himself with short hair. He was shorn of his defenses, inside and out.

Damian raised an elegant brow. "An ambition shared by many over the years, I daresay. Did she make the attempt and fail?"

He turned away from the mirror to face the earl, crossing his legs with an air of ease he was far from feeling. "For now I am more interested in discussing Louis de Falleron, and exactly what he and Radcliffe have planned. Were either or both involved in the initial betrayal of the Fallerons, and of Smith and me, or is their alliance a more recent one?"

In the past, Windermere's efforts to get information about the Falleron affair from his Foreign Office colleagues had hit a stone wall of official silence. "My connection familiar with the Foreign Office's secret affairs always denied that Radcliffe knew anything about the business at the time. He gave me the impression that the failure of the operation, whatever it was, came from within Paris."

"Damn closemouthed government snakes."

"Under the circumstances he might now tell me the truth. With the involvement of Cazalet, and thus His Majesty, the current situation seems likely to erupt in a scandal that his masters will wish to crush."

"I wouldn't be at all surprised." Julian didn't mention that his darling Jane was a rocket that might go off in any direction at any time. "Shall I come with you? I'd like to shake the guts out of them." Julian was on fire to get at the truth. "I have a better idea. Let's go and shake the truth out of Radcliffe now."

Windermere looked tempted but, ever the diplomat, he shook his head. "Better not. We'll be in a stronger negotiating position with some facts.

I can ride to London in a few hours." Damian stood. "One thing I wonder about. If the pictures do not belong to you, and your ownership of them seems, let us say, questionable, can Louis de Falleron claim them?"

"Obviously he will make the attempt. I don't like the man but I am perhaps prejudiced by the company he keeps. Now I know why Radcliffe didn't try to stop me in Belgium. He believes he has control of the collection through their rightful owner."

"But is he the owner?"

"I don't have anything in writing from the late marquis so it will come down to my word against his. Oh Good God, lawyers! I thought I was finished with them." Still, Julian wasn't about to let Radcliffe get his filthy hands on the pictures without a fight. "I may need testimony from someone at the Foreign Office."

"I'll do my best," Damian said, "but diplomats like to maintain discretion at all costs."

"I've been cultivating influence in high places. I may just be able to bring pressure to bear on your closemouthed colleagues." Windermere looked intrigued but Julian shook him off. "I'm going to be closemouthed myself for now because I don't want you to delay getting to London."

The door opened again and Julian's three sisters burst into the room, led by Fenella. "Maria said we should wait but I *can't*. You have to help Miss Grey. That man she says is her cousin has made her cry because—" She broke off and ran over to him. "What happened to your hair?"

"You were just leaving, weren't you, Damian?" Julian said firmly, because clearly Windermere wanted to remain and hear the answer to this question. The Osbournes barely contained their impatience until the door closed behind him.

"What's this about Jane and Falleron?" Julian demanded.

"He was cruel to her," Fenella said. "She says he pretended not to believe she is his cousin because he doesn't approve of her being friendly with some of the revolutionaries. But she only did it to save her life."

Interesting. So that was their game—he had no doubt Radcliffe was behind the denial or at least connived at it. Julian didn't believe for a moment that Louis de Falleron hadn't recognized Jane/Jeanne once he got over his surprise and had a chance to talk to her. He just didn't want a rival claimant.

Julian could now see her close resemblance to the late Marquise de Falleron, whom he had met on several occasions. With no idea about the ins and outs of French inheritance law, the plan he had conceived should thwart Louis. And Radcliffe.

Laura tugged at his sleeve. "Your hair, Julian. Why did you cut it?"

"I did it to please Miss Grey," he said simply.

"You called her Jane before," Fenella said, giving him a knowing look.

"So I did. I wish you girls to help me with a plan I have for making sure that Frenchman doesn't hurt Jane anymore."

As they gathered around to listen, Julian reflected that what he was about to do scuttled any influence he might have developed with Lord Cazalet, and hence the king. Every scheme had its cost, and this one was worth it if he began to make amends to Jane and set him on the path to his redemption and her forgiveness.

Chapter 20

Jane had to leave Denford, both the duke and the castle. She couldn't bring herself to kill the former or remain in the latter. In a practical spirit, she wished she'd received her quarterly wages, which were almost due. She couldn't ask for them because she didn't intend to announce her departure. She would pack up everything she owned, including the knife now hidden under her mattress, and disappear during the dinner hour. At almost midsummer there was plenty of daylight to get her to Chichester, where she could spend the night at an inn while waiting for a coach to take her to a port.

The hardest thing was what to write to the girls. No, not the hardest, but she wouldn't think about not seeing Denford again. She wouldn't think about him at all. She dared not, or she would start to cry and she was finished with tears. He wasn't worth a second's grief.

My dear children, she began. *It is with great sadness that I take leave of you forever. I am sorry that I deceived you. I don't know how to tell the whole truth.* She stopped, thought, and crossed out the last sentence. *I don't wish to lie to you any further . . .*

"Miss Grey!"

Judging by the racket, all three Osbournes were knocking at once. Thankful that she hadn't started packing, she slipped her letter under a blank sheet of paper and bade them enter.

"We've come to—"

"Quiet! You promised me you would behave if I let you come." Maria swept her most beautiful Court of Versailles curtsey. All three girls were in their best gowns, as they had been for the theater. "Mademoiselle de Falleron," she said. "His Grace the duke has asked me to convey an invitation. He would be honored if you would join the party for dinner tonight."

Oh, he was cunning. He knew it would be hard to refuse the children. She curtseyed back. "Thank you, Miss Osbourne. Please convey my respects to His Grace and inform him that it is not *comme il faut* for the governess to dine with the guests."

"But you're not the governess," Fenella said with a smirk. "You are Mademoiselle de Falleron and the daughter of a French marquis."

"We're all coming down to dinner tonight, even Fenella and I." Laura brimmed with excitement. "We've come to help you dress and do your hair."

"I have nothing suitable."

"Julian said you'd say that. He sent these for you to wear. Show her, Laura."

The youngest girl fumbled with the strings of

a silk bag. With a flourish she held up a double string of exquisite matched pearls. "The Denford pearls," she said.

"I cannot accept."

"It's only for tonight," Maria assured her.

Jane wasn't so sure about that. Julian was trying to bribe his way back into her good graces. As though a necklace could make up for all she had lost at his hands.

Fenella, meanwhile, rummaged in her cupboard. "What is this?" She had discovered the rose silk gown. "You do have a real evening gown. I've never seen anything so lovely."

"I should not," Jane said, wavering. Truth to tell, she was not averse to appearing just once in her true colors, in the high circles to which she had been born.

"Why not, mademoiselle," Maria asked. "I don't understand why you won't join the party now that we know who you are?"

Impossible to explain but too tempting not to give in. Tomorrow she would leave, no matter what Denford said, but tonight she would be Jeanne-Louise.

An hour later, her coiffure taking longer than it should due to the disagreements and lack of expertise of her self-appointed lady's maids, she was dressed.

She loved the gown, knowing it flattered her with its tiny bodice and slender skirt. How she loved the whisper of gauze on her shoulders and arms and the swish of the modest train.

"You look beautiful," Maria said, tucking a stray strand of Jane's hair into the white satin ribbon circling her head. "You always do. Now put on the pearls."

She didn't even argue. Peering at her reflection in the small mirror, she admired how the translucent spheres made her skin glow. Not even Maman's pearls had been so fine. She wouldn't keep them, of course, though she wasn't certain she didn't deserve them. They'd buy her a lot in America.

Laura took her hand. "I can't wait to see Julian's face when he sees you."

She wasn't going to examine the implication of that remark. "I'm glad you will be with me because I'm a little frightened. Shall we glide in together?"

"Don't forget to smile," Fenella said. "As you once said, everyone loves a smiling face. A happy person makes others feel happy."

"You really are a dreadful child," she said to the grinning girl. But she couldn't help obeying and her heart lightened by a degree. She wondered what Louis would say to her now. She needn't tell him that Henri had given her the gown. And though she'd often wondered what Julian would think of her dressed like this, she no longer cared.

Her lips formed a false simper to rival Fenella's. Denford's opinion of her appearance meant nothing to her, nothing at all.

Dinner that night observed every form, starting with a procession into the dining room according to order of precedence. Her partner was Sir Richard Radcliffe.

The man whom Denford had described at the theater as "one of the vilest men in England" treated her with smooth courtesy and a lack of curiosity she found astonishing. Like the absent Earl of Windermere, he was, she gathered, some kind of diplomat. After listening to a lengthy description of a visit to Versailles twenty years earlier, she replied rather bluntly that she had been too young to be presented to the king and queen.

"I'm sorry if I bring up painful memories," he said. "I wouldn't like the great civilization of the *ancien régime* to be forgotten. England has never been able to rival the magnificence of the French court. My greatest hope is that one day it will be restored." He dropped his voice. "Let me speak confidentially, mademoiselle. If there is any way that I can serve you, please ask. As a member of His Majesty's government I am not without influence."

Jane's glance followed his to the head of the table. "I don't wish to pry," Radcliffe continued, "but it occurs to me that your situation vis-à-vis Denford and certain property of your family is somewhat ambiguous."

Why should she believe Denford's opinion of this urbane man? If the duke had invited the Radcliffes here for purposes of his own, then she wanted no part of them, except to thwart them. Listening to Lady Belinda, he wore his most cynical half smile.

Denford caught them staring at him and raised his brows. Then he had the audacity to favor Jane with one of his genuine grins that used to send her heart tumbling. She snapped her head away. "Thank you, sir. I'm not sure what you can do but I appreciate the kindness."

The duke had barely said a word to her when she and the Osbourne girls made their gliding entrance, merely bowed and welcomed her with a few formal words. He looked particularly magnificent tonight in a suit of clothes of ebony satin with the coat edged in silver embroidery with touches of blood red and a waistcoat to match. But his hair! Someone had neatened the remnants of her hacking and he now wore it as short as any of the other gentlemen, with a rakish black lock falling over his forehead. Judging by the whispered gossip circulating in the assembly before dinner, the duke's new coiffure challenged the altered status of the governess as a topic of speculation. The loss of those beautiful tresses at her hand aroused a pang of regret.

When the last course had been served and the covers removed, leaving only wineglasses, Julian rose to his feet. Without saying a word, he riveted people's attention so that conversation died away and an expectant silence fell over the company.

"Last night at about this time I showed off a collection of paintings. The best pieces were assembled by one French family and I would like to tell you how they came to hang at Denford Castle."

Murmurs rippled around the table and glances were cast at Louis and her before returning to the compelling figure at the head of the table. Jane's nerves jangled. If Julian was going to publicly justify his ownership of the pictures, she would denounce him.

"My tale begins when I visited Paris with a group of friends in 1789. The Bastille had fallen, but during a temporary lull much of aristocratic life continued, which is how we came to be invited to a rout at the house of the Marquis and Marquise de Falleron."

Jane remembered the occasion, her mother arguing for discretion while Papa was certain that after the king's concessions all would be well. In the event it was the last grand entertainment at the Hôtel Falleron, and she had watched from an upper window as the company entered the courtyard. How strange that she might have glimpsed Julian that night.

"My hosts received me politely but with no special attention. The marquis demonstrated the qualities of noblesse oblige and Madame was elegant and beautiful, like her eldest daughter." He nodded at Jane, who felt wretched tears threaten again. It didn't take much to overset nerves rubbed raw. She swallowed, clenched her fists, and looked away. "I was Julian Fortescue, a sixteen-year-old of no importance and back then I spoke French adequately, but without the fluency required of

Parisian levels of wit. I spent most of that evening gazing in wonder at the Falleron pictures, never guessing at the part they would play in my life.

"I returned to England in spring of '93 without intending to return to France until I was approached by a man named John Smith, claiming to be an agent of the British Foreign Office. He offered the chance of a lifetime for a young man struggling to establish himself as a dealer in pictures. I'd picked up works here and there in Europe, especially France, and I was cultivating a clientele in England, but with no capital sum I couldn't obtain the quality of works my aspirations demanded. Smith and I returned discreetly to Paris that autumn to arrange the escape from France of the Falleron family. We both visited the marquis, but I was the one who gained his trust, through our shared love of art and because of my distant connection to the Duke of Denford."

This Smith must be the man Jane had seen. Had she known there were *two* Englishmen calling on her father, she might have discovered the truth much sooner. Denford would be dead and her heart would not have broken.

"I won't go into the details of the plot. An influential member of the Committee of Public Safety supplied passports in exchange for half the Falleron collection of pictures. Smith and I were responsible for transporting them to northern France, where the division was to take place. However, as I discovered later, the Fallerons never managed to leave their house before their safe conduct was revoked and they were arrested for treason."

Although his face remained impassive, Jane knew that the tale was directed at her. The fact that the British government had been involved, not just a young man picking on the bones of the beleaguered French aristocracy, opened new vistas. Yet on the face of it his story was incredible.

"This *histoire* about dividing the pictures in half is bizarre," she said, raising her voice so that all could hear. "How would you and this official settle on the value of the picture and decide who got which? Were you going to slice the Raphael in two pieces, right down the middle?"

"You are right, mademoiselle. That part of the plan *was* absurd. I never questioned it because I wanted them so much, even half. Even without the Raphael. I understand what it is to be led astray by blind ambition." Ignoring the murmurs around him, he spoke to her directly. "I did not betray your family but neither do I excuse my part in their deaths."

She believed him and she felt herself weakening. Before she had excluded him from suspicion because of his youth, only twenty years old. Now she wanted to excuse him for the same reason. His face as he regarded her was impassive, but she, who knew him so well, could detect the anxious pleading in those astonishing blue eyes. She frowned back, her mind racing this way and that, unable to decide what she thought. Without someone to hate, someone to blame, her life would be empty. For so many years she had held on to her hatred of Mr. Fortescue. For a time, a short time, love had made her want to let go of revenge. How could she live with neither?

So intent had she been on Julian that she forgot Louis's interest in the proceedings. "And so conveniently for you," he said, "you ended up with the entire collection. My cousins lost their lives and you got everything you wanted."

"Believe me, Monsieur le Marquis, I would rather they had lived and I had nothing. As for convenience, we were betrayed too, and I almost lost my life. Smith was killed and I only escaped with the pictures through the fighting skills of one brave Fleming. I have my suspicions about who would benefit." His eyes narrowed. "Sir Richard Radcliffe, a Foreign Office official who could have known about Smith's secret operation, has shown himself uncommonly interested in acquiring the Falleron collection."

This inference caused a sensation in the room. Lady Belinda, seated between Julian and Lord Cazalet, fainted into the arms of the surprised peer. It seemed to Jane that the lady's swoon was more effect than genuine loss of consciousness. Certainly she recovered soon enough and Cazalet regained his aplomb, handing her a glass of wine and retrieving her brooch that had come loose and attached itself to his waistcoat.

"Thank you, dear Lord Cazalet," she said in her huskiest tones. "That piece is a favorite I would be devastated to lose." She pinned the butterfly-shaped ornament on her bosom as she smiled at Louis, then cast Denford a reproachful look, as though the entire scene was intended to upset her and make her mislay her jewelry.

Sir Richard remained calm in the face of Julian's inference and his wife's theatrics. "I've never made a secret of my interest in the acquisition of important pictures, nor of my ability and willingness to pay well for them." He smiled smoothly at Louis, who looked smug. The earlier impulse to trust Sir Richard faded. In this if in nothing else Denford was correct: The man was vile.

Julian continued. "After that disaster I was powerless to find those who betrayed Smith and me as well as the Fallerons. Fortuitously, though, I am no longer an ordinary man. I intend to wield all the influence I can as Duke of Denford to discover the truth."

Jane had to give Radcliffe credit for sangfroid. He merely shrugged, despite having attracted the avid curiosity of the entire company, a vicious frown from the usually equable Lady Windermere, and a stare from Julian that would freeze the wine in his glass.

"Nevertheless I want to make one thing clear. I swore on my honor that the Fallerons would be safe, ignoring my doubts about the plan. I'm not the only one responsible, but I will not deny my share of guilt."

It was what she wanted to hear and what the world would soon know. With a dining room full of guests and a full complement of servants, the news would spread quickly. Yet she was disappointed. She realized the plan she'd proposed to Louis, of exposing Denford to public scorn, would fail. By confessing, Julian had made himself appear more hero than villain. Cazalet didn't look appalled; he was nodding in approbation. She wouldn't wager a sou against the probability that her family's pictures would end up in the possession of the King of England.

She was not going to cry again.

"I believed that the Fallerons were all dead. While I rejoice in learning that the eldest daughter, Jeanne, survived under circumstances that she may reveal herself, if she wishes, I can never repay the debt I owe her for the loss of her family through my carelessness." Julian walked around to her chair. Before she could gather her wits, he had led her from her place to the hearth, visible to everyone at the table. Framed by the arches of a vast stone mantelpiece, he took her hand. Every muscle stiffened and she turned her neck to avoid the impact of his intense gaze.

"I'm sorry, Jane," he said softly, then for all to hear. "The only reparation I can make to Mademoiselle de Falleron is to return her family's pictures to her. They are hers, given freely, to do with as she pleases. I have certain hopes but I make no demands."

Hand over her mouth, Jane organized her scrambled wits at this unexpected offer.

Before she could answer, Louis shot to his feet. "You would turn over my property to a lying adventuress? The collection is mine as the heir to the marquis."

"You forget yourself," Denford said in a voice cold with menace. "You will speak of Mademoiselle de Falleron with respect."

"This woman is not my cousin. I don't know who she is—I suspect a former servant of my family—but I do know her to be a whore. Has she told you about the men, lowborn Jacobins, who had her in their beds? She is no Fall—"

The last word was cut off by Julian's grip around his neck. The duke shook Louis like a rat and might have killed him had Jane not run to tug at the hands choking the flailing Frenchman. A couple of other gentlemen assisted her intervention. Reluctantly Julian stepped back, a dark angel of naked rage.

Jane still didn't know what she wanted, but it wasn't Julian's arrest for killing Louis. "Your Grace," she said. "Will you accompany me to the gallery to see *my* pictures?" The possessive pronoun emerged without forethought.

Breathing heavily, he stared at her. "Really? You'll leave this room with me? Will you come alone, or do you think you need protection?"

"Alone. There are a few things we need to discuss."

"Thank you."

The assembly seemed to know they had not been invited, with three exceptions who waited for them at the door. Fenella had appointed herself their spokeswoman. "We want to see Mademoiselle de Falleron's pictures too."

"You saw them last night," Julian said.

"I wish to speak to His Grace," Jane said. "I leave you in Maria's charge."

"Are you are still our governess?" Fenella said. "Do we have to obey you?"

"You have to obey *me* because I can ruin your life and I will if you don't leave us alone," Julian said, and closed the door in Fenella's outraged face.

Chapter 21

Jane didn't say a word on the way upstairs, and Julian held it a helpful sign that she wasn't attacking him with her bare hands. There was no room to hide her knife in that incredibly gorgeous gown. She was beautiful in the sparkling pink stuff and his family pearls, and he ached to hold her in his arms again.

Small steps.

"Are they really mine?" she asked at the threshold of the gallery. "Do you have the right to give them away? I would think they belonged to Louis now." Her spirits remained subdued but she was still Jane: practical, direct, and altogether enchanting.

"I bought them from your father, paying him in gold, as well as with the passports out of Paris. I choose to give them to you. I hope you won't feel bound to turn the collection over to your loving cousin, but I shall not stop you if that is what you think is right."

"Louis will dispute you and I think Sir Richard

Radcliffe will help him. Lawyers are expensive, yes?"

"Very expensive but I don't fear them. I have more weapons at my disposal than Radcliffe guesses."

"Radcliffe would buy them from me, instead," she said, as ready to defy and challenge him as she had been the day she walked into Fortescue House and he had wanted her on sight.

"You must do as you wish, but don't trust Radcliffe. He tried to steal the pictures from me last year, using Lady Windermere as a hostage. He may also have been involved in the original business. I regard him as a candidate for your betrayer."

Jane sighed. Dark shadows under her eyes emphasized the pallor of her usually glowing complexion. She was a strong woman, amazingly so, but confronting the truth of her tragic past must be straining her endurance. He yearned to offer comfort, and there were a thousand things he would like to do for her. Given the chance, there was nothing he wouldn't give her.

"Do you think I will ever know the whole story?" she asked.

"There are people in the Foreign Office who know more than we do. Windermere has gone to London to see if he can coerce the truth out of someone. He has never been able to break through the wall of Radcliffe's influence, but we hope your reappearance may shake loose at least part of the truth."

"I feel the switching of papers is the key to the truth. If only I knew why I became Jane Grey."

"I don't know how I will stop thinking of you as Jane, now that you have resumed your real name."

"I'm not sure that I can either. Jeanne seems like a different person."

Encouraged by her smile—a faint one but the first sign of light he'd seen since she learned of his perfidy—Julian curled his fists and tested his luck. "Jane," he said softly, stepping forward so she was tantalizingly near to his touch, "I never thought I would ask for pardon for the unforgivable, but I am doing it now. Will you forgive me?"

He had to bend to catch her words. "I don't know."

"That is better than no. Last night I offered to marry you, not perhaps under the best of circumstances. I intend to ask you again."

She met his wretched proposal with her roguish tilt of the head. God, he was pleased to see that again. "To get back the pictures after you have given them to me?"

"I would say that was unworthy except that I know when you're teasing me and that encourages me even more. I shall not, however, ask you now. Just remember that if you decide you can forgive me, I will make you a duchess and pamper you with luxury. I'll make you forget every privation you have had to endure." His throat grew thick and parsimonious with words.

"I would like to be happy, but I dare not try. It's unfair that I am alive. What did I do to deserve it?"

He looked at her bent head and tried to find an argument to contradict her. He'd often felt the same way, never more than when witnessing her sisters' execution. But he had culpability to justify his remorse. "If I thought it would do any good," he said, "I would say that you were an innocent victim. Capricious fortune picked you to survive, and that is no more your fault than the deaths of your family. But I doubt anything I can say will dispel your guilt."

"You do understand." She touched her fingertips to the back of his hand for a fleeting moment. "I wish I didn't feel like this. I fear that I always will until I have avenged my family."

"I wish I could relieve you of the burden."

"You cannot."

"I am optimistic enough to hope that learning the truth will lighten it. Look at me, Jane." He placed his hand over his heart. "We will find out who is responsible for the loss of your family and if he is alive, whether it's Radcliffe or someone else, I promise you he will pay. Together we will make him."

"Together?"

"You are no longer alone."

He waited an age, observing the parade of expressions on the face he loved: a gleam of tears swiftly blinked away; slow relaxation of a pinched mouth; then a deep breath and a smile. Not a deep, heartfelt smile that reached the eyes, but it was a beginning.

"Thank you, Julian. Now," she said briskly, "I

am going to look at my pictures and pretend to be happy."

"May I accompany you?" He offered his arm, and when she accepted he felt the triumph of a boy coaxing a wild bird to take food from his hand. "I looked forward to showing them to you. Ironic that I hadn't the least notion that you already knew them well."

"You gave me a Fragonard. Did you know that my father had a similar pastel of the same model? It's not here, is it?"

"The prints and drawings were not included in the purchase. I don't remember the marquis showing me that."

"It was one of his favorite pieces and he kept it in his private rooms. He said it reminded him of me. I am very glad to have the other one since his is likely lost forever. I thank you for it."

Now was not the time to press her to let him keep the flesh and blood woman. Instead he asked her to talk about the Falleron collection. They walked arm in arm the length of the Long Gallery and she told him the stories behind the paintings as she knew them.

"I've always judged a work of art rigorously, according to quality alone," he said, in response to her story of lighting candles with her sisters in front of the Raphael Madonna on feast days of the Virgin Mary. "I now appreciate how much the viewer's personal feelings and experience enhance the act of observation."

"I shall turn you into a sentimentalist." She cocked her head at him. "Or perhaps not."

They came back to an exquisite painting of musicians in a garden, one of his favorites. "Fragonard, again."

"We always loved this one because the garden reminded us of that at Bel Etang, our château in Normandy. It may not even be there anymore. So many great houses were burned down during the Revolution. I thought Papa was good to his people but it didn't save him and perhaps not his house. When I went to the coast nearby to find passage to England I did not dare ask." She blinked a couple of times. "I can imagine that it is just as lovely as ever and one day I may see it again."

He couldn't restore what she'd lost, only offer compensation. "Do you suppose one could create such a garden in England?" He ventured to kiss her hand while he waited for an answer.

"I do not know," she said. Pleasure and gratitude flooded his chest when she did not withdraw, a first step toward winning her forgiveness and, *please God,* regaining her love.

Chapter 22

Julian wanted the truth and he wanted it now so that he could lay it at Jane's feet and join her in plotting the downfall of the betrayer. He paced around his suite of rooms, avoiding his guests. Jane was the only person he ached to see but he wanted to bring her news. He was sick of waiting for Windermere to return from London, but Damian was navigating the byzantine toils of the Foreign Office, and who knew when he would exit that den of liars in possession of the facts. The more Julian thought about it, the less likely it seemed that anything would come of his journey.

Meanwhile Radcliffe was here and if the baronet hadn't actually betrayed the Fallerons, he'd wager the fox knew who had. Through the window he saw Radcliffe taking his morning exercise among the formal gardens, exuding self-satisfaction and obviously enjoying the amenities of the ducal castle.

His castle. His home. His dukedom.

Julian Fortescue had taken two years to reach

the point of accepting his unexpected, unwished for, and surely undeserved position. He accepted it now and embraced it. He was a duke and he would behave like one, for his own sake, for Damian and Cynthia's, and above all for Jane's. The Duke of Denford would not let Sir Richard Radcliffe get away with his crimes. About to charge downstairs and confront the elegant old scoundrel, he stopped and thought.

"Ask Sir Richard to attend me in the library," he told one of the footmen. The Denford book collection was housed in a vast chamber decorated in the Jacobean era with a heavy coffered ceiling, a massive fireplace, and lots of gloomy portraits of past dukes. The art wasn't to Julian's taste, yet waiting for Radcliffe he sensed the weight of history and the presence, even the approval of his predecessors.

Radcliffe entered, predictably undaunted by his surroundings. "I hadn't been in here before," he said, having a good look round. "Very fine collection, I have no doubt, Denford. If you are considering culling the books—"

"I am not," Julian said coldly.

"Oh well. I'll have to settle for the Falleron pictures once Louis establishes his rights."

"That's not going to happen. But I didn't bring you here to talk about either books or paintings." Radcliffe had reached the hearth, shadowed by the elaborate stone chimneypiece. Julian, years younger and a foot taller, wasn't ashamed to use the advantage of youth and size to physically intimidate the older man. And his superior rank. "You are going to tell me all you know about the death of the Mademoiselle de Falleron's family and the part you played in it."

"Are you renewing your absurd implication that I had something to do with the matter?"

"Absurd? As an official at the Foreign Office you would have known about the affair. I'm tired of playing games and want the truth. Now."

"I'm curious, Denford. If I know anything, which I by no means admit, why should I tell you?"

"Because I am in a position to make your life uncomfortable."

"I doubt it." The man's confidence was impregnable.

"I could whisper a word into the ear of my new friend the Prince of Wales, who was quite delighted by the Bosschaert I gave him recently. I should thank you for that inspiration."

"My felicitations. I didn't know you had the gall."

"You will find I have limitless gall and growing power."

"The Prince of Wales is not the king." Radcliffe sounded slightly less sure of himself.

"But since the recurrence last year of His Majesty's illness, no one wants to displease the prince. Including your superior the foreign secretary, who owes me a favor because of some assistance I was recently able to render him over a by-election."

"Is there more?" Radcliffe asked.

"There will be. But if you're not convinced I

don't have any objection of beating the truth out of you."

The baronet threw in his cards gracefully. "What do you want to know? Probably more than I can tell you." Julian somewhat regretted his capitulation; he would have enjoyed applying just a little force to get at the truth. He still might have to, he thought optimistically.

"Were you conversant with John Smith's plan to remove the Fallerons from Paris at the time?"

"I was not," Radcliffe said. "It is a pity for I would have opposed it. It was ill conceived from the start." Julian couldn't argue with that. Just because Sir Richard was an untrustworthy reptile it didn't mean he wasn't a shrewd politician. "I learned about it later when I was looking through some files and the name Falleron caught my eye."

"Because you knew of him as a collector."

"He beat me to a couple of pictures back in the mid–1780s." Radcliffe had been buying important paintings for decades, including some that Julian had wanted. "The story was odd. Falleron wasn't connected to Louis XVI's regime and was innocuous as far as members of the nobility were concerned. Early in the Terror passports were still obtainable. There was no reason why he shouldn't have offered a hefty sum in the right quarters and got the whole family out of France. Why all this business about the pictures? Their value was far greater than necessary for a simple bribe. Why did he need you, or John Smith?"

"I thought you were going to answer questions, not ask them."

"To get the real story I had to obtain the secret files, which wasn't altogether easy." With some reluctance, Julian decided Radcliffe's tale had the ring of truth. He had never been able to work out a way that the baronet could have betrayed the Fallerons from his office in Westminster. "You can't spread this tale, Denford."

"I make no promises."

Radcliffe raised his hands in surrender. "I don't suppose it matters after all this time. John Smith was part of a British plot to rescue the Dauphin from the Temple prison."

Julian whistled. All unawares, he had been caught up in a conspiracy that was far more dangerous than he knew. The so-called Dauphin, after the execution of his father Louis XVI, was the rightful King of France should the monarchy be restored.

"The eight-year-old boy," Radcliffe continued, "was to be dressed as a girl and taken out of France in the guise of the youngest Falleron daughter while the eldest pretended to be the governess."

The complicated nature of the plot finally made sense. The stakes were enormous and he had been played for a fool. A naïve, overambitious, twenty-year-old fool. He probably wasn't supposed to get away with even his half share of the pictures.

"Who betrayed us?" He wanted the answer badly, mostly for Jane but also for himself. He had blamed himself for so long, yet he had been nothing but an impotent pawn. No man likes to think he has been played.

"I put quite some time and effort into that whole question. The consensus among the people who know this kind of thing"—Julian ground his teeth—"is that John Smith was double-crossed by the official you bribed and the ambush intended from the start, to obtain full possession of the pictures. I do congratulate you, by the way, on your presence of mind in keeping them all in your possession. But a different person betrayed the plot to rescue the Dauphin and thus sent the Fallerons to the guillotine. We never discovered who."

"There must be any number of people involved who could have denounced the conspiracy," Julian said.

"True. It was a rash endeavor with a high probability of failure. There were reports from our spies that the child was being subjected to unnatural abuse and his rescue was thought worthy of any risk."

Radcliffe's dispassionate speech aroused Julian's ire. "Including the risk to a perfectly innocent man and his family?" He thought of the little girls he'd seen executed and Jane forced into virtual prostitution at the age of fifteen. "You and your kind make me sick."

"As a loyal French monarchist, the marquis must have thought it worthwhile," Radcliffe said.

"The marquis was terrified for his family." Julian was cold with rage. "He repeatedly begged me for reassurances that I now know I had no right or reason to give. Quite the opposite, in fact."

"I'm sorry, Denford," Radcliffe said. "But you do understand that I had nothing to do with it. I am guiltless in the whole affair."

The damn weasel wanted to make sure Julian didn't make trouble for him. "I acquit you in *this* matter," he said. "Now if you will excuse me, I have business to attend to."

Radcliffe still needed to pay for his other sins, but they could wait. Jane must hear the news immediately.

Jane went out for an early walk, disturbed only by birdsong and the silent presence of laboring gardeners. All this could be hers: the shaded paths, the intricate parterres, and noble trees. She stood under the veil of a willow by the river and observed the fierce ramparts of the castle, smoothed and mellowed by the morning sun.

Julian had promised her a garden like that of Bel Etang if she married him. There were acres of parkland at Denford, plenty of room for a French garden with broad walks and classical statuary. They would stroll arm in arm discussing every topic under the sun, then they'd retreat to a library, a tower, or even a bedchamber and make love. She could have a busy, satisfying, stimulating life. She could be happy. She only had to forgive him.

That wasn't all. Essentially she had forgiven him, or rather accepted that he was as much a dupe as her father, though with infinitely less dire consequences. He had blamed himself more than he should, as a very young man would, possessed of youth's certainty that he was of supreme importance in the world.

Youth? She was only twenty-four years old herself. For more than a third of her life she'd been gripped by the ambition to do one thing. Could she embrace joy as long as her family's killer was alive?

She had no answer and little optimism that she would ever know. The urbane Sir Richard seemed an improbable Jacobin informant.

Returning to her room, she found a letter on her bed. Her heart quickened, then sank; those were not Julian's bold black words, but addressed, in the unmistakable penmanship taught by French masters, to Mademoiselle Grey. Written in French, it contained an invitation to discuss certain matters with a hint that Louis de Falleron, might, just might, be prepared to acknowledge her as his cousin. It was important that they meet in private so he suggested an assignation that morning in the *très pittoresque et historique* Maiden's Keep.

What did Louis want? Not a tour of an historical monument in her company.

Her impulse to consult Julian startled her, accustomed as she was to facing her own problems and making her own decisions. She hesitated, not solely because she didn't accept that he had a right to be consulted. There was something else, something she'd seen last night that had been nagging at a corner of her brain. Something about Louis.

She let her mind relax as she walked through the courtyard and climbed the hill. By the time she reached the door to the keep she had remembered, and by the top of the winding staircase she was sure of what happened, though not why.

"Bonjour, Jeanne." He called her by her real name, leaning carelessly against the wall with his arms folded, elegant in the latest style of morning clothes from a first-rate London tailor. Now she knew how Louis had been able to live prosperously all these years. He had lured her to the top of a tower famous for the suicide of a woman, and Jane knew she was right.

"You have decided to accept who I am?" she asked, with feigned wonder. "That makes me so happy, Louis. We should love each other since we are the last of the family." He'd made sure they were, the treacherous, lying rat. "What made you finally see the truth?" If this conversation were genuine, on both sides, they would embrace now. Loath to touch him, she hovered out of reach.

"I knew you from the start because I knew Jeanne had escaped. I wouldn't have expected you'd possess the cunning to prostitute yourself and survive all these years, but your father always said you were his cleverest child." He made no pretense of amiability.

"He often wished I had been a boy. It would have given him hope for the future of the family."

"You are showing your claws, *ma cousine."*

Jane walked forward, assessing the now familiar territory of the tower. Louis had taken up position to the south, near where the parapet was lowest, overlooking the river. Keeping her distance and her hands hidden by her full skirts, she veered to the opposite side, where she and Julian had made love against the wall.

"Why don't we skip the *politesse* and talk about why we are here?" she said.

"I came to this party to get the pictures and I am not pleased that Denford decided to hand them over to you. It's a high price to pay for services rendered. He must be infatuated."

"Perhaps he possesses a sense of justice."

"I am Falleron and the heritage is mine, no thanks to your father. What he did ensured the ruin of the family. The pictures are all that remains and I must have them."

"Unleash your lawyers, then. Or should I say Sir Richard's lawyers?" Although it might be wiser to let him think her naïve, she couldn't resist offering a little provocation. "I think he may prefer to deal with me directly. It's sad to see thieves fall out."

A stiffening of his stance was his only reaction. "Your reappearance causes a little difficulty, my dear. While the domain lands would be mine by right, other kinds of property can be inherited by women. Even in the absence of your father's will, judgment could go against me in the English courts. As for France, it appears that the barbarians have drawn up a new code of laws that abolishes primogeniture and gives daughters full rights of inheritance." He sighed and shook his head at her. "I say this with all sorrow. There was no reason why you couldn't have lived perfectly happily for the rest of your life as Jane Grey. But Denford had to interfere. With his support, I know you will easily be able to establish your identity."

"So you decided to acknowledge me after all?"

She walked forward until only half a dozen feet divided them. Louis wore the expression of self-satisfied superiority with which he had always addressed his young cousins. Conceited to the core, he might claim to think her clever but in his eyes she was no match for his superior strength and cunning.

"I tried to save you by refusing to accept you as Jeanne but you insisted on making trouble." Lunging forward, he seized her by the shoulders and swung her around, crashing her against the battlement next to the low opening. "I've written a new *histoire,* little cousin. As I claimed all along, you are an *intrigante* taking advantage of my family tragedy. You are also more than a little deranged. Now, overcome by remorse, and inspired by the sad story of the Maiden's Keep, you have decided to take your life by jumping off this very convenient tower."

As he pressed all his weight against her, one hand groped the base of her throat and squeezed, making her gasp for breath. She tightened her grip on the knife concealed by the folds of her skirt and hoped she hadn't overestimated her ability to fight him off.

"You said I was clever, Louis," she gasped. "Did

you really think I would come unarmed to a deserted high place to meet the man who betrayed my family?"

Julian was on his way to the schoolroom when accosted by three panicked young ladies.

"We were just coming to find you, Julian," Maria said. "We are worried about Miss Grey. She thrust a paper into his hand. "Read this."

"We didn't mean to pry," Laura said. "We went to her room to find her and I was looking at the papers on her desk because she *never* writes letters and this was underneath some blank sheets."

"And it's addressed to us so of course we read it."

My dear children,

It is with great sadness that I take leave of you forever. I am sorry that I deceived you. ~~*I don't know how to tell the whole truth.*~~ *I don't wish to lie to you any further or to your brother. I am not Jeanne de Falleron, neither am I Jane Grey. I killed the real Miss Grey and stole her name and her money. She told me all about the Falleron family and I decided to pretend to be the oldest daughter. But I know Louis de Falleron will expose me and I can no longer live with my guilt. I cannot face His Grace the duke again.* Adieu, mes enfants.

Julian waved the sheet at them. "This is arrant nonsense. Is this even Jane's handwriting?"

"It looks like hers," Fenella said. "She told us she wrote like a French person because that's what they taught on Saint Lucia."

"I'll wager Louis de Falleron writes like a French person too." Julian folded his arms, closed his eyes, and forced himself to calm down. "Where can she be? You girls spread out and ask everyone if they have seen Miss Grey today. Tell them I want every servant on the estate looking for her. If you learn something, find me at once. I will go to Falleron's room."

"Do you think Miss Grey's nasty cousin wrote that letter?" Fenella asked.

"I am sure of it. Every word is a lie. Besides, Jane would never leave without telling me. She hasn't a craven bone in her body. Now run, all of you. We must find her."

Louis de Falleron's room was empty. Julian's blood ran cold when he read the note again.

I can no longer live with my guilt. Suppose the writer of those words meant them literally.

He ran down the stairs to a hall bustling with curious servants bringing reports of places where Jane was not. Then a footman came in and informed His Grace that one of the gardeners had seen the governess climb the hill to the Maiden's Keep.

Sick with worry, Julian gripped his cane. They were supposed to find that letter later and read it as a suicide note.

Chapter 23

Heart pumping with exertion and fear, Julian burst out onto the roof of the Maiden's Keep. As he blinked in the noonday sun, the dark shadow of two forms in close embrace resolved itself into Louis de Falleron with his hands around Jane's neck. She was struggling in her cousin's grasp, trying to plunge her knife into his side.

Grasping his cane, Julian twisted the silver knob and withdrew the slender, tempered steel blade from the shaft.

Then he stopped cold. Writhing in a perverted simulation of lovemaking, Jane and Louis were precariously balanced on the lowest part of the wall overlooking the river far below. One false move and they would both go over the edge.

He advanced silently under cover of guttural cries and grunts from the combatants, too absorbed in their struggle to notice him. He laid down his sword because he dared not risk injuring Jane with it. He was about to snatch Jane's skirts, desperate to hold on to her before she went over the edge, when Falleron succeeded in rolling her onto her back. She croaked feebly and raised her right arm but he removed one hand from her neck and knocked her arm back. The knife went flying into the air and disappeared over the wall.

Julian dived in, grabbing limbs and skirts and pulling hard in the direction of safety. By a miracle the three of them landed on the ground in a mass of indiscriminate kicking and punching. Louis de Falleron managed to extract himself and retreated to the wall, panting heavily. Julian was interested only in Jane. Sitting on the cold stone floor, he cradled her between his bent knees, caressing her bruised neck, dizzy with relief to feel her pulse race and hear her labored breath.

"You're alive," he murmured. "You're all right. You haven't left me." And other nonsense, hopelessly inadequate to express the depth of his gladness that he had been on time.

"Louis." She gulped. "He did it." Only with painful effort did the words emerge from her throat.

"I've said it before and now it's proven: The woman is insane." Falleron had recovered his equanimity. "She lured me up here with a ridiculous story about selling me my own paintings. I agreed to see her because I felt sorry for the poor, mad creature. She attacked me with a knife and I was forced to defend myself."

Jane gurgled with rage and tried to spit at her cousin. "He attacked," she rasped.

"Why would I wish to kill her?"

Julian looked over her head. "Why indeed, Falleron? Why would you wish to kill your cousin, the sole survivor of your family tragedy?"

"She is not my cousin," he ground out.

Jane struggled to her feet. "Water."

Keeping his arm around her waist and a wary eye on Louis, Julian led her to a shaded section of the wall where a gutter collected rainwater. She scooped up the water, a meager half inch after a few days of dry weather, and swallowed it.

Shaking off Julian's support, she faced Louis with clenched fists. "You betrayed us to the Committee of Public Safety. It is your fault they all died."

Even with his clothes in disarray from the struggle, the Frenchman maintained his arrogance. "What new madness is this?" he asked with a curl of his lips.

"I have proof." Jane's voice grew stronger. "The morning of the arrest, my father was distraught. I heard him tell Maman that her jewelry was lost. Later, when the guard demanded entry, he said that the man he trusted most had betrayed them. Since I believed it was Mr. Fortescue who denounced us, I assumed he had taken the jewelry. When I first learned that the price of our escape was the pictures, I forgot about the jewels. Last night Lady Belinda Radcliffe dropped her brooch, but even then I did not see the truth. I had other things on my mind." Her glance flickered to Julian, then settled on Louis again. "Something about milady's brooch preyed on my mind. It is a butterfly with diamond wings."

"Such pins are common."

"The body of this one is unusual, striped with jet and yellow diamonds like a wasp. Maman rarely wore it because she thought it ugly. I think if we ask Lady Belinda she will say you gave it to her."

"That proves nothing, not even that my cousin's wife owned such a thing. This woman invented the story."

She turned to Julian. "Do you think it would be possible to discover if a French émigré such as Louis had been selling a magnificent collection of jewelry, piece by piece, over a number of years?"

He smiled at her, his clever love. "I imagine that an ingenious investigator would be able to trace such transactions, if he had a good description of the pieces. I know the very man for the job."

"What of it?" Louis said. "Perhaps your father entrusted the jewels to me for safekeeping."

"Do you know, Falleron?" Julian said. "I think you have issues with consistency. Rather bold of you to claim that Mademoiselle Jeanne is insane when your stories resemble the inventions of a raving lunatic."

"But *why*?" Jane burst out. "Why did Louis betray us and why am I Miss Grey?"

"*Exactement*," Louis said. "At last the madwoman makes sense. There is no reason."

"Dear Louis could answer both those questions," Julian replied, "but I doubt he will, so I shall make the attempt. You became Miss Grey so that the former Dauphin and rightful King Louis XVII could leave the country dressed as your youngest sister, Antoinette. I will hazard a guess that your father confided in Louis, who thought, understandably I am afraid, that it was a foolhardy attempt, likely to end with the arrest of anyone who knew about the plan, himself included, followed by the mass condemnation of the entire family."

Jane's mouth fell open. "Of course!" she said. "Of course Papa would try to save the Dauphin and of course Louis would not, the dirty pig. So he stole the jewels and gave us up instead to save his skin."

Julian nodded. "He does appear to have got out of France without trouble, along with a fortune in jewelry if your supposition is correct."

"*Mon Dieu*, what a fairy tale you have all concocted. There is nothing you can prove against me. Nothing."

Jane glared at Louis in frustration. "We can prove it, can we not, Julian? Louis won't get away with this. He admitted he knew I had escaped. He knew about the Jane Grey plan. If he was innocent he could not have known that, could he?"

"Of course we will," he said, taking her hand. But he feared he offered her false hope. Without the open cooperation of the Foreign Office, which wasn't likely to be offered, proof would indeed be hard. He was certain to the depths of his soul that Falleron was the villain Jane claimed; he would always believe her against anyone.

But what of others? The tale was a fantastical one and Louis could be convincing in his protestations. It would come down to her word against his. If they couldn't bring Louis to justice, what would Jane do? He was terrified she would kill Louis and he wouldn't be able to protect her from the legal consequences of the crime.

"I am a duke," he said. He was being damnably ducal this morning. "I have power and influence. I will ruin you, Falleron. I will bring you low. I will grind you into the mud as a poisonous insect deserves."

"How?" Jane asked.

That was Jane, always challenging him. Louis, on the other hand seemed convinced. Too convinced. Carelessly Julian had left his unsheathed sword stick leaning against the wall. The blade glinted in the sun and caught his eye just as Louis snatched it up. "I'll kill you first, Denford, and your *putain*," he shouted, and recoiled in preparation for his lunge forward, the blade aimed at Julian's heart.

"No!" He had taken his eye off Jane and now she charged in full tilt, ramming her body into Louis and knocking him sideways against the low part of the wall. "You will not kill him, you will not. You have killed too many of the people I love."

Taken by surprise, Louis hovered on the narrow parapet until Jane lifted his thighs and sent him over the edge. His cry faded during the long fall, leaving them silent and stunned under the June sun with the song of a lark high in the blue sky.

Julian stood beside Jane, who stared down at the riverbank where the body of her cousin was little more than a speck. He took her hand and waited.

"I did it," she said. "I killed the man who betrayed my family." Her eyes were dazed, her voice distant as though not fully comprehending what had occurred. She started to shake and he put an arm around her, silently offering support, comfort, or congratulations. Whatever she needed. And his heart soared at the words she used. She had included him among those she loved.

"That's not why I did it," she continued, her voice filled with wonder. "In the end, after all this time, I killed Louis because I couldn't let him kill you."

"No one has killed anyone." Windermere's voice came from the entrance to the tower.

Julian and Jane turned around. "When did you arrive, Damian?"

"I drove in and found the place in turmoil and your sisters full of a story about Mademoiselle de Falleron and her cousin. I didn't wait to sort it out because I thought you might need my help."

"You would have been useful five minutes earlier. As it was we attended to matters."

"The unfortunate accident, you mean. I witnessed the whole thing. The Marquis de Falleron finally realized that he had maligned his cousin. When he heard the terrible tale of his family's arrest, he was overcome with grief and tumbled off the tower. You know, Denford, it's extremely irresponsible of your predecessors to allow this dangerously low wall. I expect you to do something about it to prevent future tragedies."

"I quite agree, Windermere. We can't risk the children taking a tumble." He tightened his hold on the woman next to him and hoped that some of those children would be theirs.

Chapter 24

While Julian and Lord Windermere saw to the retrieval of Louis's body, Jane retreated to her room, drained of all emotion. The realization of Louis's guilt and the fulfillment of her revenge should have caused her to exult, but all she felt was a strange void inside her. She closed her mind to any thought of Denford, of whether Julian could fill the emptiness in her heart or leave her in solitude forever. Since she wasn't sure which alternative frightened her more, she lay on her bed and stared at the ceiling, refusing to contemplate the future.

There were three people in the house who wouldn't leave her alone. Tenacious as a pack of endearing terriers, the Osbourne girls invaded her privacy again. Given the choice between being interrogated by her former pupils and joining the ladies of the house party for a luncheon, she chose the latter.

A distraction from the subject of the Falleron family was provided by the arrival of Oliver

Bream's parents, followed by the surprising announcement of Miss Cazalet's betrothal to Bream.

Lord Cazalet appeared to be making the best of things since he had failed to win a duke for his daughter. "My future son-in-law is a painter of great talent, as my daughter recognized. I can say nothing official, but I believe there may be a royal commission in his future."

The happy couple stood beside them, Henrietta looking triumphant and Oliver dazed as though he couldn't believe his good fortune. Jane wondered if he were really in love for the last time; she'd been too wrapped in her own concerns to notice the transfer of his fickle affections from Lady Belinda. Yet there was something in the way he looked at his betrothed that gave her hope. She also had a feeling Henrietta was strong-minded enough to see off any new candidates for Oliver's admiration.

Oliver's father spoke next and Jane learned that he was a gentleman and a titled one too. "I never thought," Sir Walter Bream said, "that my youngest son would make anything of himself as a painter. Seemed a foolish occupation for a gentleman. But when we read in the newspaper that he was staying at the castle painting the duke's sisters, Lady Bream and I decided to make the fifteen-mile journey to call on him. I'm proud of the boy."

Standing in the cluster of ladies surrounding the engaged couple, Jane looked up to find Denford's dark presence framed in the doorway. Her heart shifted with excitement and fear. Across the width of the large saloon his eyes found her, conveying a message that sent her into a panic. When Lord Cazalet approached him she escaped through the door at the other end of the room.

Jane managed to dodge him for a couple of hours until, with a sense of inevitability, she saw the shorn head over the wall and waited for Julian to stride into the knot garden where she had been hiding.

"Why have you been avoiding me?"

She couldn't admit that faced with the prospect of happiness, she was terrified. Terrified that none of it was true and she would wake up one morning in Mathieu's bed. Or terrified that it would be Julian's bed but she would be just as unhappy.

"I've been busy," she said. "I've been making the acquaintance of your not-quite-Fortescue cousins. They are quite *aimable*."

"I'm glad to hear it since I doubt we'll be able to prevent them visiting Denford regularly now that I've raised the portcullis to them."

"And then," she continued, ignoring that *we*, "I was talking to Miss Cazalet. I always knew she was the most delightful young woman, very intelligent. She would have been a perfect wife for you if she hadn't preferred Oliver. Did you know Oliver's father was a baronet? It's a kind of chevalier that we don't have in France."

His forefinger to her lips cut off her babbling. "Hush, Jane. May I sit with you? We don't have to talk but I am sorely in need of your company."

"I'd rather walk." It was safer to keep moving.

The path along the river was lovely in the June late afternoon, the warm air a silken caress. With a parasol borrowed from Miss Cazalet, Jane went hatless. Perhaps the soft breeze riffling through her hair cooled her overheated brain, or maybe it was the idyllic pastoral scene. The edge of panic that had gripped her heart since they descended from the tower that morning loosened its hold. True to his promise, Julian said not a word, merely keeping pace, hands behind his back. His dark figure at her side became a comfort, familiar and beloved, instead of a threat to her peace. He was right; she had been avoiding him, and after twenty minutes of silent communion she couldn't even be sure why.

"C'est incroyable, this affair of Oliver and Henrietta," she said, picking up where they had stopped. "And Lord Cazalet has given his consent."

"A bit of luck the Breams arriving this morning or he might have had an apoplexy. I knew Oliver was from a good family but that is all. He never talks much about himself. His art, yes."

"And his ideas about art. And his stomach."

"Miss Cazalet will be the making of him."

"That is her intention."

She told him about Henrietta's plans for Oliver's future. He told her the Radcliffes had ordered their carriage without saying good-bye to their host while he was busy with the coroner, reporting Louis de Falleron's "accident." The man had swallowed Lord Windermere's account without demur and the inquest should be only a formality.

It was like being back in the library at the London house, trading news of their day's activities. Though today she avoided mention of his sisters. All they could talk about was how much they wanted her to marry Julian. Neither did she report that everyone else in the castle assumed they would wed, though not with the same enthusiasm. Lady Ashfield was barely civil.

A pang of longing for those evenings assaulted her. From today's perspective they seemed like simple times when an enjoyable flirtation hadn't interfered with her life's goal. Now her heart was in knots and her brain made of cotton wool. They'd almost reached the farthest end of the river walk when the discourse turned personal.

"You're very beautiful today, Jane. You always are, but it's a pleasure to see you in such fine gowns as you wore last night, and now. I don't miss your governess attire."

She countered the caress of his voice with a remark perversely designed to wound. "Henri liked his mistress to be well dressed. It flattered his importance, you understand."

"It would be unreasonable to be upset because your clothes were the gift of another man. He is the other side of the English Channel and I am here. I would like to give you gowns and much more besides, but not because it flatters my importance."

"Your importance is such, Monsieur le Duc, that it needs no flattery."

"As always, you like pretending to misunderstand me. Last night I said I wanted to marry you and shower you with luxury, and I do. But not from a sense of debt. Any sense of obligation is a tiny drop of water in the vast ocean of my love." He stopped abruptly and took her hands in his. His blue eyes dazzled her, with their beauty and with their heat. "I adore you. I never knew what love was, but I recognize the joyful weight in my heart and the abject terror that you will leave me. Damnation, this is hard to talk about."

He was doing very well, judging by the eddies of sensation in her chest. Joy and terror afflicted her too, but her terror wasn't the same. She still didn't know if she was more frightened to live with him or without him.

"Will you marry me, Jane? Will you stay with me forever as my wife and my love?"

"It is not correct for a duke to marry such as I am," she said.

"I'm not offering as a duke, but as a man. Your blood is almost certainly more noble than mine, and if you insist on having this argument I'll remind you that you are the daughter of a marquis."

"But I have not lived as one. *Ma mère* would say it shocked the conventions for a duke to wed a woman of *mauvaise réputation.*"

"Goodness, you've become dreadfully French. You must always do as you please, but I'd just as soon you went back to being an English governess from an exotic island. While I am sure your mother was an admirable woman in every way, could you bring yourself to ignore her precepts in this one small matter?" He brought her hands to his lips, one after the other. "That was a smile, just a little one. I made you smile."

She snatched her hands away and schooled her mouth back to stern sobriety. "This is serious. We shouldn't be laughing now."

"We should always laugh. No one knows better than you that life is grim, so all the more reason why we must find happiness where we can. Let me count the ways in which your mother would find me wanting as an alliance for her daughter. I am an Irishman who made a living in trade. I tried to seduce the wife of my former best friend. What else, oh yes! In many years I never wrote a single letter to my sisters in Ireland. I could go on, but you know my sins and I don't want to confess to any that somehow escaped your notice."

"I didn't know about seducing the wife."

"Condemned out of my own mouth. I won't say another word but you can ask Lady Windermere."

Julian was far too clever. His foolishness had eaten away at her defenses and she was drowning in love.

"And now I'm going to ask you something and I want you to answer seriously."

"J'écoute."

"If you won't marry me, why? Is it because you don't love me and cannot forgive me for the past?"

She owed him the truth but she would not look at him when she gave it. Turning her back, she took a deep breath. "I'm not even sure there is anything to forgive and I do love you. I loved you almost from the start and I've been lost in love with you for many weeks."

"But? There's a but. I can hear it in your voice."

"I don't have the courage. I am afraid of what the world will say. I am afraid that Sir Richard Radcliffe and Lady Ashfield will tell everyone I am a *putain* and I will disgrace you and your sisters."

"Do you believe yourself a whore?"

She'd thought about that question a lot over the years and had come to be certain of the answer. "No. I am not ashamed to have done what I had to do to live. In the end Louis paid and that is what matters."

"I don't believe it either. I am not without allies and there is a lot I can do to silence the gossip. I can't promise there will never be whispers, but anyone who slanders you will answer to me."

She spun around on her heel. "Fool! Don't you see that's what I fear the most? You will fight a duel and die. It is better to have no one than suffer the pain of losing those you love."

"Jane," he said, his deep tones vibrant with love and understanding. "Have some faith in me. If I've proved anything over the years it is that I am hard to kill."

"I cannot." Her breath shortened and she felt the onset of panic. Backing away, she fended him off with her palms.

"Where's my brave girl who's afraid of nothing?"

She had lost the courage that had borne her upright for so long and she despised her weakness.

"I don't want to be brave anymore," she shouted. "I'm sick of it." She stumbled back a few yards, fighting to suppress her sobs. She'd done nothing but weep for two days, shed so many tears she should be a dried-up husk. "Leave me alone."

Letting the parasol fall, she covered her face with her hands until her breathing returned to normal and she looked back at Julian who waited without a word.

Behind him the river flowed peacefully and his black figure was stark against the summer greens, his stance eloquent of dejection, unlike the unlimited confidence and arrogance she was used to. Bound up in her own feelings, she'd ignored those of the man she loved. She shied from commitment to a future because she feared losing him. Julian had already pledged his heart and she had made him suffer. She wasn't just a coward but a cruel one.

Stiffening her back as her mother had taught her, she walked toward him in the Versailles glide, her head held high so that she could see his transformation from despair to delight. The sight sent her heart soaring, free at last from the snare of doubt.

"Monsieur le Duc," she said with a deep curtsey, and walked into his arms, embracing happiness with the man she would love forever. With incoherent words of joy he gathered her close and accepted the invitation of her smile.

How long they would have remained kissing in the sunshine, she didn't know. Forever, perhaps, or until they could decently retire to bed. But the terrier pack hunted them down.

"Julian!" Fenella called.

"Miss Grey!" That was Laura. Maria, when Jane reluctantly pulled away so he kept her only in a loose clasp, was blushing deep scarlet and averting her eyes from the shocking sight.

"Are you going to be married?" Fenella went straight to the point.

"I hope so. You are going to accept me, aren't you, my love?" Julian asked.

"You have to," Fenella said. "You were kissing." The other two nodded.

"I suppose I must then," Jane answered.

"Hurrah!" Laura said. "You can stay our governess forever."

"She will be much too busy being my wife to teach you hellions," Julian said firmly. "I shall engage a new teacher for you, a strict one. Miss Grey was far too indulgent."

"Quite right," Jane said. "Your brother had no idea of the qualifications of a good governess, otherwise he would never have engaged me."

"I knew," Julian said, pulling her closer. "The moment I set eyes on you I knew you were perfect."

Epilogue

Eight years later, 1810
Lady Ashfield to her daughter

The talk of the town this week is the opening of the Denford Picture Gallery, built by the duke and duchess to house the collection of the duchess's unfortunate family and presented to the nation. No one would miss the event since the dear duchess is London's most popular hostess. I hear the patronesses of Almack's are beside themselves with anxiety lest she turn down the offer to join their ranks. If Jane Denford snubs them, others will surely follow.

One couple certainly will not attend. My dear, I must tell you that Lady Belinda Radcliffe was discovered in what I discreetly call a submissive position with Lord Yarmouth in a closet at Lady Beaufetheringstone's ball. Sir Richard is quite disgraced and has been dismissed from all his offices for reasons that are not entirely clear. My infor-

mants tell me (and they are usually right) that Denford and Windermere have something to do with the matter.

I have told you often that one should never give anyone the cold shoulder because one doesn't know how fortunes will change. That a pair of rogues like Julian Fortescue and Marcus Lithgow should now be Duke of Denford and Earl of Camber, respectively, is enough to make me believe in democracy. That Caro Townsend is the highly respectable Duchess of Castleton is enough to make me believe in miracles. And the fact that I have to be polite to that nouveau riche merchant's niece Cynthia Windermere just because she is dear friends with Jane Denford is enough to make me grind my teeth.

Julian stood in the airy marble hall designed by John Soane for the display of sculpture, his duchess at his side, welcoming every notable artist and collector in London, as well as the cream of the *ton*, to the Denford Picture Gallery. Soon after their marriage Jane had announced her intention of giving her family collection to the British nation, a move that helped everyone to forget any shadow over her name. Julian had no doubt, however, that she was admired and influential because of her beauty, intelligence, and wit, the same qualities that made him grateful every day and kept him enthralled eight years after they met.

He watched her charm Cazalet and Bridges, both trying to hide their chagrin that they were not the heroes of the day. Among other advantages of having a wife everyone adored was being allowed to retain his sardonic pose. He'd grown his hair again and still dressed in black to intimidate the unsuspecting. Only Jane knew that his heart was as soft as their infant son's cheek. Perhaps his sisters knew too. And his two young daughters had him wound around their tiny fingers.

"Mr. Soane consulted the duke at every stage," Jane said, laying a hand on his arm and tilting her head at him. She was too modest; they'd worked with the architect together. "We hope to set a new standard for the display of paintings. You must tell me what you think of the ceiling lights in the Raphael Gallery."

Next to greet them were a group of their oldest and closest friends: the Windermeres; Marcus and Anne Lithgow, now Lord and Lady Camber; and Caro, the irrepressible Duchess of Castleton, with her adoring, staid husband.

A little way off Mrs. Oliver Bream was surrounded by half a dozen wealthy self-made men, none of whom bought so much as a print without Mrs. Bream's say-so. Julian was damn glad he no longer had to make his living selling pictures: Bridges constantly complained about Henrietta Bream scotching sales to her collectors. Every now and then she would kindly allow one of them to pay a breathtaking price for her husband's latest canvas. Oliver, in attire matching his prosperity but his hair still a bushy mop, gave Henrietta's group a wide berth and joined his friends.

"Caro! Castleton!" Oliver kissed the duchess on both cheeks but had no need to greet Anne and Cynthia, having joined the rest of his friends for breakfast that morning at Windermere House. No longer a starving artist, he sometimes dropped in at mealtimes out of habit. He looked around warily. "You haven't brought your children, have you?" Oliver constantly complained about the group portrait Caro had made him paint of her little imps.

"They're at Hanover Square with the other children," Caro said. "I thought you could go over later and do a first sketch for a conversation piece: the next generation of the Townsend set."

Oliver blanched. "How many is that? You each have two or three, at least."

"I have five," Anne Camber said.

"Don't forget the dogs. We all have dogs."

"You are joking, aren't you, Caro?"

"Perhaps." Caro smiled evilly. Years of practice meant she knew just how to drive Oliver mad.

"I see my father-in-law beckoning," Oliver said hastily and scampered off, leaving the rest of them in gales of laughter.

"My dear Anne," Marcus said. "Last time I counted we had only three. Do you have an extra couple of children hidden away somewhere?"

"I couldn't resist."

Caro giggled. "Lady Ashfield always said Marcus would destroy Anne's morals, and look at her: inventing offspring out of whole cloth. I, on the other hand, have become sadly virtuous." She turned to Castleton, a duke whose dry exterior disguised his sense of humor. Julian liked him enormously. "When was the last time I did anything irresponsible, Thomas?" she asked with a provocative smile.

Red tinged the ridge of Castleton's cheekbones. "This morning . . . you suggested we all go to Vauxhall Gardens and drink too much champagne."

"And so we shall. It looks to be a fine night for getting lost in the paths off the Dark Walk. And yet what could be more respectable than erring with one's own husband?"

Jane, who had been following the nonsense with an amused smile, took Julian's hand. "I'm sorry, Caro, to be a *bourgeoise,* but I don't permit Julian to be lost with anyone but me."

Caro sighed. "I am the same. What a dull pair of duchesses we are. Such is the penalty of marital bliss."

Author's Note

Despite numerous efforts to establish a public art collection in Britain, the National Gallery in London wasn't founded until 1824, coincidentally on the site of the Royal Stables, which make an appearance in this book. Julian's efforts to sell his collection were inspired by the attempts of dealers Noel Desenfans and Francis Bourgeois to sell a readymade collection, first to the King of Poland and later to George III. Bourgeois ended up donating the pictures to Dulwich College and commissioned the architect John Soane to build a state-of-the-art gallery to house them. The result was the Dulwich Picture Gallery, opened in 1817, England's oldest public art gallery.

Attempts to rescue the young Dauphin have often been depicted in novels, most notably *Eldorado*, Baroness Orczy's sequel to *The Scarlet Pimpernel*. The young prince died in prison in 1795.

Some readers may recognize the story Jane tells Julian about the contessa, adapted from *The Marquise of O* by Heinrich von Kleist. Kleist's novella was published in 1808 so Jane could not have read it. I choose to imagine that the story was a true one and somehow made the rounds in early nineteenth-century Paris.

For their help and advice with this book I thank Kathy Greer, Jill Tuennerman, Susan Hanewald, Leslie Carroll, Lauren Willig, Megan Mulry, Chelsey Emmelhainz and the team at Avon Books, Meredith Bernstein, and the many friends and relatives, e-mailers and tweeters, who kept me somewhat sane as I brought the Wild Quartet series to a close.

The Duke of Dark Desires concludes the stories of Caro and her friends. Earlier books are *The Importance of Being Wicked* (Caro Townsend and Thomas, Duke of Castleton), *The Ruin of a Rogue* (Anne Brotherton and Marcus Lithgow), and *Lady Windermere's Lover* (Damian and Cynthia Windermere). In addition, there is a prequel novella, *The Second Seduction of a Lady.*

As I say good-bye to these characters, I'd like to thank my readers, whether they've been with me for the whole journey or joined me late for Julian and Jane's story. Without you there would be no reason to write.

Best wishes,
Miranda

Give in to your Impulses!

These unforgettable stories only take a second to buy and give you hours of reading pleasure!

Go to ***www.AvonImpulse.com*** and see what we have to offer.

Available wherever e-books are sold.

IMP 0811